Elizabeth Williams Champney

Witch Winnie

Elizabeth Williams Champney

Witch Winnie

ISBN/EAN: 9783743407893

Manufactured in Europe, USA, Canada, Australia, Japa

Cover: Foto ©Andreas Hilbeck / pixelio.de

Manufactured and distributed by brebook publishing software (www.brebook.com)

Elizabeth Williams Champney

Witch Winnie

WITCH WINNIE

The Story of a "King's Daughter"

BY

ELIZABETH W. CHAMPNEY

OLIPHANT ANDERSON & FERRIER
EDINBURGH
AND 24 OLD BAILEY LONDON
1890

PRINTED BY

MORRISON AND GIBB, EDINBURGH

FOR

OLIPHANT ANDERSON & FERRIER

EDINBURGH AND LONDON

MY LITTLE WITCH MARIE.

WHERE she's been the sunshine lingers,
  She's my witch and she's my mouse ;
She has helpful, fairy fingers,
  Busy keeper of the house.

She is tricksy and she's elfish ;
  Sure no plague could e'er be worse ;
She is thoughtful and unselfish,
  She's my gentle angel-nurse.

All their jokes the brownies lend her,
  She's a merry, mischief thing ;
But her heart is very tender—
  She's a Daughter of the King.

Yes, there's something nice about her,
  And I'll love her till my death ;
No, I could not do without her—
  I'm her ma, Elizabeth.

CONTENTS.

INTRODUCTION.

IT is but just to explain that, while all of the characters introduced in this little story are purely imaginary, the founding of the Home of the Elder Brother was suggested by the work of some real children, younger than Madame's pupils, who gave a little fair, and, helped by charitable people, instituted a lovely charity, the Messiah Home for Little Children, at 4 Rutherford Place, New York City. This Home still opens its doors to the children of working-women, and is helped by different circles of King's Daughters, some of whom have adopted children to clothe. It is a beautiful work, founded by children for children, and it is hoped that others all over the land will join in it, and that the work may broaden until no such dens as Rickett's Court will remain in our fair city or country.

E. W. C.

WITCH WINNIE.

CHAPTER I.

WE never had any until Witch Winnie came to room in our corner.

We had the reputation of being the best behaved set at Madame's, a little bit self-conscious too, and proud of our propriety. Perhaps this was the reason that we were nicknamed the " Amen Corner," though the girls pretended it was because the initials of our names, spelled downward. like an acrostic—

*A*delaide Armstrong,
*M*illy Roseveldt,
*E*mma Jane Anton,
*N*ellie Smith—

formed the word *amen*. But certainly the name would not have clung to us as it did if the other girls had not recognized its fitness in our forming a sanctimonious little clique who echoed Madame's sentiments, and were real Pharisees in minding the rules about study-hours, and whispering, and having our lights out in time, and the other lesser matters of the law which the girls in the "Hornets' Nest," Witch Winnie's set, disregarded with impunity.

And verily we had our reward, for Madame trusted us, and gave us the best set of rooms in the great stone corner tower, overlooking the park, quite away from the espial of the corridor teacher. They had been intended for an infirmary, but as no one was ever sick at Madame's, she grew tired of keeping them unoccupied, and assigned them to us.

Sometimes the other girls annoyed us by making calls in study-hours, and we virtuously displayed a placard on our door bearing the inscription, "Particularly Engaged."

It caught Witch Winnie's eye, as she strolled along the hall, and she scribbled beneath it,

> " The girls of the Amen Corner
>   Would have us all to know
>   That they're *engaged*, each one engaged—
>   Particularly so."*

We hardly knew whether to be amused or vexed at this sally of Witch Winnie's. We acknowledged that it was bright, but we deplored her wildness, and had no idea how much we should love her in time to come. After all, our reputation as model pupils had a very slender foundation. It rested chiefly on Emma Jane's preternatural conscientiousness. The night that the cadet band serenaded our school, some of the pupils, presumably the girls in the " Hornets' Nest," threw out bouquets to the performers. Rumor said that when Madame heard of this she was greatly shocked.

" I don't see how she can punish them for it," said Adelaide ; " there's nothing in the rules about not giving flowers to young men. Still, it was a dreadful thing to do, and Madame is ingenious enough to twist the rules some way, so as to 'make the pun-

---

*This incident is borrowed from an actual occurrence.

ishment fit the crime.' I am glad the Amen Corner is guiltless."

Then we marched into chapel on tiptoe with excitement to see Madame wreak vengeance on the wrong-doers. Witch Winnie sat behind me, and turning, I saw that she looked pale, but resolute.

Madame rose in awful dignity, her wiry curls, which Milly said reminded her of spiral bed-springs, bristled ominously.

" Young ladies," she exclaimed, in a sharp tone of command, "you may all rise." We rose.

"If you turn to the printed rules of this institution," she continued, "you will find under Section VII. the following paragraph —' Pupils are not allowed to disfigure the lawn by *throwing from the windows* any bits of paper, hair, apple-parings, peanut shells, or waste material *of any kind.* Scrap-baskets are provided for the reception of such matter, and any pupil throwing *anything from her window upon the school grounds* will be regarded as having committed a misdemeanor.' "

An impressive silence followed, in which Witch Winnie gave a sigh of relief, and whispered to Cynthia Vaughn, " We're all right; we didn't disfigure her precious lawn. The bouquets never touched the ground. I lowered them, with a string, in my scrap-basket (just where she says we ought to have put them), and the drum-major took them out and distributed them to the other boys."

"Young ladies," Madame continued, in tones of triumph, "those of you who have not broken this rule within the past week may sit down."

We all sat down—all but Emma Jane Anton, who remained in conspicuous discomfort. Adelaide pulled her by the basque, "Sit down!" she whispered; "Madame doesn't mean you."

Emma Jane stood like a martyr while Madame regarded her through her lorgnette with astonishment depicted on every feature.

"If you committed this infringement of the rules at any time other than last evening you may sit down."

Emma Jane remained standing.

"Then," said Madame, drawing herself up frigidly, "Miss Anton, you may explain: what was it you threw out?"

"Madame," replied Emma Jane, "the window was open—we were listening to the music—and a bat flew in; and, Madame, he

would not stay in the waste-paper basket
and so, Madame, I threw him out."

Every one laughed; discipline was forgotten for the moment, until Madame rapped
smartly on the desk and called for order.
She complimented Emma Jane highly on
her conscientiousness, but she looked provoked with her all the same, while Witch
Winnie, who was stuffing her handkerchief
into her mouth, nearly went into convulsions.

After the sketch which I have endeavored
to give of Witch Winnie, and the position
which she occupied at Madame's, I trust that
we, as self-respecting pupils, will not be too
severely blamed when I confess that we received, with great disfavor, Madame's announcement that Winnie was henceforth to
room in the Amen Corner.

The bedrooms at Madame's boarding-
school were clustered in little groups around
study-parlors, five girls forming a family.
For a long time there had been only four in
our set. Emma Jane Anton, who preferred
to room alone, had the little single bedroom ;
Adelaide and Milly were chums ; while I,
Nellie Smith, familiarly nicknamed Tib, had
luxuriated so long in the large corner chamber that I had almost forgotten that Madame

told me, at the outset, that I must hold myself in readiness to receive a room-mate at any time.

Adelaide Armstrong was the daughter of a railroad magnate. She had been brought up in the West, but, though she had traveled much, and had seen a great deal of society, her education had not been entirely neglected. She had studied a great deal in a desultory way, and contested the head of the class with Emma Jane Anton, who was a "regular dig," and had prepared for college in the Boston public schools.

It was really surprising how Adelaide had picked up so much. She had studied Latin with a priest in New Mexico, and had profited by two years at a lonely post on the confines of Canada, where her father had been interested in the fur trade, to become proficient in French. Strikingly handsome, a brunette with brilliant complexion and Andalusian eyes, energetic and spirited, she was popular both with her instructors and her classmates.

Milly Roseveldt was her exact contrast—a milky-complexioned little blonde, shy and sweet; she was also a trifle dull. Adelaide translated her Latin, and worked out her prob-

2

lems, and I wrote her compositions, while
Milly rewarded us with largesses of love and
confectionery, for she was the most generous as well as the most affectionate of girls.
Her father, a wealthy New York banker,
placed large sums of money at her disposal,
and Milly deluged her friends with gifts of
flowers and bonbons. It seemed very natural to me that Adelaide and Milly should be
sworn friends; but my admittance into the
sacred circle was a mystery to me, and to a
number of aspiring girls who asserted that I
was nobody in particular, and who envied
me my place in my friends' affection. My
presence in the school itself was almost as
great a wonder. My father was a Long
Island farmer. We opened our house to
city boarders during the summer, and one
season Miss Sartoris, the teacher in Art at
Madame's, boarded with us. I had taken
drawing lessons at the Academy, and Miss
Sartoris took me out sketching with her. I
worked like a beaver, and was never so
happy in my life. I delighted Miss Sartoris,
who wakened mother's ambition by telling
her that I was the most talented pupil she
had ever had. More than this: we three in-
duced good, easy-going, generous father to

let me go back to the city with Miss Sartoris
as a pupil at Madame's. My wardrobe was
meagre, but not countrified, for I possessed a
natural sense of color and a quick faculty
for imitation. I had seen plenty of city
people at Scup Haven, and my few dresses,
I fancied, would pass muster anywhere. I
was a fair scholar, and took the lead in the
studio. I was not brilliant and stylish like
Adelaide, or rich and pretty like Milly, but
they liked me, and I liked myself the better
for the consciousness that there must be
something nice about me which attracted
them. I believe now that it was an absence
of self-consciousness and selfishness on my
part, and my hearty admiration and devotion to them. Adelaide called me, playfully,
"the great American Appreciator."

It was just before the theatricals given by
our literary society that an incident occurred
which showed me how much they really
thought of me. We three were arranging
the stage ; I was touching up the scenery,
and Milly holding the tacks for Adelaide,
who was looping the drapery, when we overheard the conversation of a group of girls
on the other side of the curtain.

Cynthia Vaughn was the first to speak.

"I think Adelaide Armstrong is perfectly splendid!"

"So do I," said another; and there was a chorus of confused voices exclaiming, "So stylish!" "Perfectly elegant!" "The handsomest girl in school!"

Adelaide left her work and placed her hand on the curtain, but Milly threw her arms impulsively around her. "Let us hear what they will say," she whispered; "when they are through we can pull the cord, and all bow thanks."

By this time other voices were chanting Milly's praises, and Adelaide turned reluctantly away, remarking, "Well, if you enjoy that sort of thing, you are welcome to it. I should not be surprised, by the way they are loading it on, if they knew we were here."

They did not know it, for at that instant Cynthia Vaughn spoke up again, "I don't see what they find to admire in that pokey Lib Smith."

"I should think Milly would be ashamed to be seen with her," said another; " her dresses always remind me of a chicken with its head through a hole in a salt-bag."

Adelaide sprang forward with flashing eyes to confront the speaker, but this time it was I who held her back. "Let them say their say," I whispered, hoarsely, while Milly cowered, trembling. "I believe her mother makes her dresses at home," said Witch Winnie; "and, as she can't have Tib to try them on, she fits them on her grandfather."

There was a hearty laugh at this sally, and another added: "I don't see how Adelaide can endure her, she is so stingy. Have you noticed that the girls place a fresh bouquet at her plate every morning? and I never could find out that she ever gave either of them so much as a single flower."

Adelaide nearly writhed herself from my grasp, but I held her tightly. "Milly," she gasped, "are you a coward, to stand there and hear our friend reviled so? Can't you stop them?"

The blood surged into Milly's pale cheeks, and she sprang before the curtain. "Girls," she cried, "how can you talk so? Nellie Smith is our dearest friend. She is not one bit stingy; she gives us more than we have ever given her. Because she does not parade her presents on the breakfast-table is no reason that she has not given me lots and lots of things, and no girl can consider herself my friend who talks so about our darling Tib."

Here Milly broke down in tears, and Witch Winnie exclaimed, "Good for you, Milly Roseveldt; I didn't know you had so much spunk!" But at this point we all fled to the Amen Corner, and bolted the door, refusing to admit Witch Winnie, who impulsively shouted her apologies through the keyhole.

"Oh, Milly!" I cried, "what made you tell a lie for me? I never gave you a thing." And I might have added, "How could I, when my allowance for spending-money is hardly sufficient to keep me in slate-pencils?"

But Milly stopped my mouth with kisses, and pointed to sundry original works of art with which I had decorated her apartment, and declared, besides, that helping her on that last horrid composition was a greater gift than all the roses in Le Moult's greenhouse.

So we of the Amen Corner disliked Witch Winnie and loved each other, all but Emma Jane Anton. We could not be said to exactly love her; we tolerated her in our midst, in spite of her uncongenial nature, because we took pride in her eminent respectability, and in the higher average of reputation for creditable scholarship and exemplary behavior which she gave to our corner. But love her! We might as well have tried to love an iceberg.

Witch Winnie arrived on Adelaide's birthday, and was a most unwelcome birthday present. Emma Jane Anton had obtained permission for us to celebrate the occasion by sitting up an hour later that evening. Milly had ordered a form of ice-cream and a birthday-cake from Mazetti's, and we had invited in a half-dozen friends to share the treat. As a damper on this beautiful fête, Madame had called us into her private study that afternoon, and had told us that she had decided to assign Witch Winnie as my room-mate. She did not scruple to tell us her reasons for doing so. Winnie (according to Madame) was the head-centre of a wild set of "ne'er-do-weels" who roomed in the top of the house, "a perfect hornets' nest under the eaves," Madame said. Madame felt that if the queen hornet was taken away, the rest would be more amenable to discipline, and that Winnie, placed among such proper and well-behaved girls as we were, would herself feel our beneficial influence.

"I think," said Madame, "that if you knew Winnie's history you would understand her better. Her parents were both very talented and highly imaginative people. Her father is a playwright of reputation, who married a very lovely young actress who had sustained the leading part in several of his plays. They were tenderly attached to each other. Mrs. De Witt had great dramatic talent ; she made it the study of her life to realize his conceptions, and succeeded to his perfect satisfaction. She said that she so lived in her part that frequently she forgot her own personality, while Mr. De Witt was always cudgeling his brains to invent new plots, situations, and characters for his wife. Mrs. De Witt died when Winnie was but three years of age. The child has lived with different relatives, and has been spoiled and neglected by turns, but never quite understood. I have studied her carefully, and think I see in her a combination of both parents. She has her father's highly organized imaginative nature, but instead of constructing plots for plays, it develops itself in plots for scrapes. She delights in dramatic situations, and is a natural and unconscious actress. Her father hopes that she may never adopt the stage as her profession, for it was that life of mental and physical strain which killed Winnie's mother. Something remarkable in organization or in action the girl will certainly be, and as she takes her color, like a chameleon, from her surroundings, or, rather, her cue from the other actors, I have great hopes for your influence over her."

Madame's confidences made little impression upon our prejudice. We listened in silence, and, returning to our rooms, held an indignation meeting, in which Emma Jane led. Adelaide, who ought to have sympathized with the neglected orphan, for she had lost her own mother when a little girl, and who did find in this fact a bond of fellow-feeling later on, now ignored all her claim for pity, and chose to feel that we were all grossly insulted. Milly pitied me the enforced companionship, several of us were in tears, and in the midst of it all Witch Winnie appeared. The clatter of voices sank to sudden silence, and the new - comer, looking from face to face, instantly understood the situation.

"If you feel half as badly as I do, girls," she said, with a merry laugh, " I'm sorry for you; I wouldn't intrude on you in this way

if I could help it. Madame tells me you are
to have a spread to-night, and have invited
your particular friends. It's too bad she
wouldn't let me put off moving till to-morrow
morning. I'll tell you what I'll do—I'll sit
in the recitation-room and cram for examination until the party is over Of course you
don't want me, a perfect stranger to your
friends ; it isn't to be supposed you would."

Emma Jane Anton looked relieved. "We
provided for a limited number," she explained ; " if we had known that we were to have
the honor of your company—"

But Adelaide interrupted her instantly.
" Sit in that dismal recitation-room while I
am having my birthday party ! Indeed you
shall do nothing of the sort !" while Milly
came gallantly to the rescue, assuring her
that she had ordered more ice-cream than
they could possibly consume, and I did the
best I could to make Winnie believe that
she was welcome.

The girls appeared *en masse* as soon as the
bell struck for the close of evening study-
hour—congratulations were offered to Adelaide, and Winnie was introduced. All made
extravagant efforts to be gay and sociable,
but there was a certain constraint, a forced

quality, in it all, which had for its reason something beyond the fact of an unwelcome addition to the Corner: the refreshments had not arrived. Mazetti had forgotten to send them. There stood the study-table neatly spread with a table-cloth borrowed from the steward's department, and set with saucers, spoons, and plates, all disappointingly empty.

Adelaide tried to carry off the situation as an immense joke. Milly alternated between hope and despair, fancying each noise of wheels the confectioner's cart. The guests showed their disappointment plainly, some confessing that they had slighted the evening prunes and rice in anticipation of this treat. And I heard Cynthia Vaughn whisper that it was a very cheap way to give a party—to pretend that there had been a mistake. At this juncture I suddenly noticed that Witch Winnie had disappeared.

A few moments later a loud knocking, or kicking, for it was evidently bestowed with feet instead of hands, was heard at the door. "Let me in, girls!" cried Witch Winnie's voice—"let me in, quick! before Madame catches me." We opened the door, and Witch Winnie burst in, and sat laughing on the floor; from her dress, which had been gathered up in her hands, and had served as a market-basket, rolled a quantity of paper bags and parcels—lemons, bottles of olives, sugar, mixed pickles, crackers, sardines, macaroons, nuts, raisins, candy, etc., etc.

"Help yourselves, girls," she chuckled. "We'll have the spread, after all." I have been around the corner and bought out Mr. Beeny's little grocery." Then broke in a chorus of voices—

"How did you ever get out of the house?"

"Was Cerberus asleep?" (Cerberus was our nickname for the janitor.)

"How very sweet of you!"

"But how extravagant!"

"O girls! these pickled limes are too lovely for anything.

Adelaide appeared with her ewer. "I'll make the lemonade," she said, and began rolling the lemons with Milly's curling-stick, while Emma Jane Anton manipulated the can-opener with energy and success. Each girl flew to her room for her tooth-mug, and we drank Witch Winnie's health in brimming bumpers of lemonade.

"How did you ever manage it?" Milly asked again.

"I climbed down the fire-escape." Witch Winnie giggled.

"But you had to drop twelve feet onto the sidewalk!"

"What of that? I've done it in the gymnasium from the trapeze many a time."

"But you never came back that way?"

"Hardly. I rang the basement bell, and when Cerberus said he'd tell Madame, I made him a present of three packages of cigarettes and some Limburger cheese, and I am quite certain that he will never say a word."

Witch Winnie's generosity and good-fellowship had won the day. From that moment we took her into our hearts.

The ice-cream which Milly had ordered arrived the next day, but we were all too ill to touch it; we had feasted without restraint on our new chum's bountiful but somewhat heterogeneous repast, and were paying the penalty with rousing headaches, but in our fiercest pangs we were still ready to declare that if there ever was a trump it was Witch Winnie.

CHAPTER II.

ARISTOCRATIC Adelaide was now as deeply attached to "that little witch" Winnie as she had been prejudiced against her, and Winnie, who had hitherto spoken of her new friend as "that stuck-up Armstrong girl," was now her devoted admirer.

Although this state of affairs was perfectly agreeable to the Amen Corner, it was not equally so to the Hornets. They had endured Winnie's removal as a piece of Madame's tyranny, had looked upon their Queen as a martyr, and had taken it for granted that we would make things extremely uncomfortable for her. They perceived, with astonishment, that we welcomed her heartily, and when it dawned upon them by degrees that Winnie was herself happy in the change, that she actually promenaded in the corridor with an arm lovingly twined about the waist of that odious Tib Smith, that the placard "Engaged" appeared as frequently on the outer door of the Amen Corner, and that Winnie's lessons and behavior improved so much that she was actually becoming a favorite with the teachers instead of their special torment —the indignation of the Hornets' Nest knew no bounds.

It showed itself in a practical joke originated by Cynthia, which might have been very amusing had it not been spiced with malice. I have spoken of our literary society and its projected entertainment. We were to have a series of tableaux; among others, Guinevere kneeling before an altar. Milly had been chosen to represent Guinevere on account of her beautiful hair, and because she spent her Saturdays and Sundays at home, and could have any costume arranged for herself. What was our disappointment, one Monday morning, to receive a note from Milly saying that she would not be able to take part in the entertainment, as her mother was going to Washington for a fortnight and had decided that, as Milly looked pale, a little outing would do her good. This note was read to the literary society amid groans from the members. "We can't give up that tableau." "Adelaide, *you* take the part." "Can't; my hair is as black as a crow's wing. Tib's hair is lovely when it is down. It falls to her knees, and it has the sheen of molten gold. Girls, you must see it," and Adelaide proceeded to pull my braids apart; I protesting all the time that it was absurd to have a freckled Guinevere who was as homely as a hedge fence.

"Granted," replied Witch Winnie, "but nobody is going to see your face, child; you pose with your back to the audience, and as none of the girls know what regal hair you have, it will be such fun to have them guess who it is."

All of the other girls joined in persuading me, excepting one of the Hornets, who lifted her voice in favor of Cynthia Vaughn.

"But, girls, what am I to do for a costume?"

"Why didn't Milly think to send hers along?" said Adelaide. "We might write her."

"No, there's no time; she leaves this morning on the 'limited.'"

"If you would like, I'll take the part," Cynthia Vaughn suggested. "I've all that canton flannel ermine, and the ruff made out of the old window curtains, which I wore when I was Queen Elizabeth."

"That ruff would be a frightful anachronism," said Emma Jane Anton.

"And the ermine has served three times already. Thank you, we'll manage somehow," Witch Winnie asserted, confidently.

We retired to the Amen Corner to talk it over. "If worse comes to worst," said Witch Winnie, "I know I can make a magnificent train out of the plush table-cloth in Madame's library."

"But how will you ever get it?"

"Emma Jane must ask her to lend it to us; she'll do anything for Emma Jane."

"Emma Jane declines to act in this emergency," said Miss Anton, firmly.

"You wouldn't be so mean!"

"But I would; Adelaide, please read Milly's letter again; I didn't half hear it."

"I must have dropped it in the Society hall; I will get it after dinner. If she had thought that Tib might be chosen to take

3

her place, she would have done anything for the honor of the Amen Corner."

Here some one tapped at the door, and announced, " A letter for Miss Armstrong."

"It's from Milly! " exclaimed Adelaide, " and it looks as if it had been opened, and pasted up again."

" I thought Madame boasted that she never submitted her young ladies to that sort of espionage," said Witch Winnie.

"Girls, girls !" Adelaide fairly shrieked ; " just listen to this ! Milly writes—

" ' I forgot to say in my last that mamma's maid is putting the finishing touches to my costume, and Gibson will bring it around to-morrow. The dress (purple velvet) is one which mamma wore last summer when she was presented to the Queen. The lace which trims it was made to order from a pattern of her own selection in Brussels. You may keep the crown, for the gems in it are only Rhinestones. Aunt Fanny wore it at a costume ball, and they sparkle like the real thing. Be careful of the lace, for mamma prizes it highly.

'Yours, Milly.

'P. S.—I've coaxed papa to lend you a silver chatelaine, old French repoussé, linked with emeralds, which he keeps in his cabinet of curiosities. It shows finely against the velvet.'"

How we all exclaimed and chattered! "Now what will the Hornets' Nest say to that?"

"Canton flannel ermine indeed!"

"I should like to see them bring on their old mosquito-netting ruff!"

"Real emeralds! A diadem flashing with diamonds!"

"Don't tell them a word about it until Tib dawns on them in all her glory on Wednesday night."

It was hard to keep this resolution, but we did. The Hornets were giggling and whispering among themselves as we marched in to dinner, with all the importance given by the possession of a state secret. The other girls relapsed into silence as we took our seats, and watched us with strange, significant looks.

"I've been looking up the matter in Racinet's work on Costume," remarked Cynthia Vaughn, "and I find you were right, Miss Anton; ruffs did not come in until long after Arthur's reign."

"I would like to consult the book," Emma

Jane replied, "unless you can tell me whether chatelaines were worn at that period."

Here a small Hornet was seized with strangulation, and had to be vigorously thumped upon the back by her friends.

"Oh, I think so," Cynthia replied, sweetly, disregarding her friend's condition. "Wouldn't it be sweet to have Guinevere wear one? Miss Smith is so artistic, I'm sure she could cut one out of gilt paper."

Adelaide scouted the idea. "Whatever we get up for that costume," she said, "I am determined shall be *real*, no *imitation* chatelaines, or anything else."

Cynthia lifted her eyebrows. "Perhaps you will secure one of Queen Victoria's court robes?" she remarked, icily.

It was on Adelaide's lips to reply that we might have a robe which had figured at a court reception of the English Queen, but she felt Witch Winnie's foot upon hers, and replied that in undertaking this tableau the Amen Corner felt confident that they could carry it through creditably, and we therefore begged to be excused from the dress rehearsal that afternoon. We left the dining-room in a body, and the Hornets laughed aloud before we closed the door. "'They

laugh best who laugh last,'" said Witch Winnie. "Won't those girls fairly expire when
they see Tib in her grand rôle!"

Tuesday was a long and weary day for us.
We started at every knock, expecting a summons to the janitor's room to receive a package, but none came. We retired much disappointed; and we held a council of war
before breakfast. The Roseveldts' butler
had evidently proved false to his trust, and
the costume was waiting for us at the family
mansion on Fifth Avenue.

"I will ask Madame at breakfast to excuse
me from my morning lessons to do an important errand," said Witch Winnie; "I will tell
her the entire story, and I know that, rather
than disappoint us all, she will let us go to
the Roseveldts' for the things."

Madame proved to be in good-humor, and
on reading Milly's letter readily gave Winnie and me the desired permission, sending
for a hansom to take us to our destination.
All of the Hornets at the lower end of the
table heard this conversation, and Adelaide
thought that Cynthia Vaughn turned green
with envy. An hour later, as we came down
the front stairs to take our hansom, Cerberus
popped his head from his office to tell us

that a package had just been received for
Miss Adelaide Armstrong. "Come back,
girls!" Adelaide cried excitedly; "here is
the costume. It can be nothing else. My,
what a big bundle!"

We carried it between us in triumph up
the staircase. The Hornets were clustered
on the very top landing; their faces peered
over the balustrade, and as they caught sight
of our procession a peal of derisive laughter
echoed through the hall as they scuttled
away to their nest under the eaves.

"Those Hornets have certainly gone
crazy," Emma Jane remarked, practically.
She was carrying her corner of the package,
and was as interested as the rest of us in the
arrival of the costume. We entered our
study-parlor in suppressed excitement, and
impatiently cut the knots, and tore open the
wrappings, when, behold! another package,
scrupulously tied. This paper removed re-
vealed another, then another, and another,
and the fact slowly dawned upon us that we
had been victimized. "Girls!" exclaimed
Witch Winnie, sitting down on the floor in
despair, "it's a wicked sell of those Hornets:
there is nothing here."

Emma Jane Anton kept on methodically

removing the wrappers and folding them neatly. "Perhaps," suggested Adelaide, "they have merely arranged this hoax to fool us, and the costume is still at the Roseveldts'."

"It's just like that Cynthia Vaughn to do such a thing; we'll go, all the same," Witch Winnie replied, rising hopefully and tying on her veil. At this juncture Emma Jane reached a pasteboard box marked "Violet velvet court dress." Lifting the lid discovered a quantity of trash. An empty sardine-box bore the label "Diamond Crown;" a dilapidated bustle was marked "Brussels point lace;" a mixed-pickle bottle was filled with apple-parings and labeled "Old repoussé châtelaine, reign of Arthur I.; the *real* article; must be returned."

A howl of mingled laughter and dismay rose from our corner. "Cynthia Vaughn wrote that letter which purported to be from Milly. Well, it's a real good practical joke, anyway," said Witch Winnie; "better than I thought the Hornets could get up without my help. Let us show them that we can take a joke, and good-naturedly acknowledge ourselves sold."

"And in the mean time what am I to do

for a costume? You know the tableaux
come off to-night."

"That puts another face on the matter."

'I suppose Cynthia would be only too glad
to take the part even now."

"After all we have said, and your name
printed on the programme—never!" This
from Adelaide.

"I'll tell you what we will do," suggested
Winnie; "the hansom is still waiting at the
door; Tib and I will drive to a costumer's
and hire something. I found the address of
a place on the Bowery the other day and
fortunately saved it. Hold your heads up
high; we will not acknowledge ourselves
defeated yet."

As Witch Winnie and I sped out of the
quiet square and down the great teeming
thoroughfare, the Elevated trains jarring
overhead and the motley crowd surging
about us, a misgiving of conscience swept
over me. What would Madame say? This
was not what we had obtained permission
to do. This was very different from Fifth
Avenue, and not at all a quarter of the city
in which young ladies should be wandering
without chaperons.

We were quite desperate, however, and it

seemed too late to turn back. The hansom stopped before a Hebrew misfit clothing store where dress suits were announced as on hire by the evening. Flaunting placards above told that costumes for the theatrical profession and for fancy balls were to be let in the fourth story. We climbed a dirty staircase, and after knocking by mistake at an intelligence office for *Dienst Mädchen*, a hair-dyeing and complexion-enameling rooms, a chiropodist's, and a clairvoyant's, we found ourselves in a room piled from floor to ceiling with costumes. A fat German, who looked as if he were some second - hand piece of furniture, very much soiled as to his linen, and the worse for wear as to his physical mechanism, admitted us and did the honors of the establishment. I glanced around at the motley objects which filled the wareroom; gaudy spangled dresses, with a sprinkle of saw-dust (suggestive of the arena) clinging to the worn cotton vel-vet, many-ruffled shockingly brief skirts of rose-colored gauze that had spun like so many teetotums behind flaring foot-lights, tinfoil suits of armor that had come in all mud-besplashed from parading the streets at the last grand procession, the faded ban-

ners which flapped above them so jauntily,
drooping wearily now from the rafters,
covered with dust and festooned by the
spiders. A row of dominoes dependent
from a neighboring clothes-line rustled with
an air of mystery, and a heap of masks upon
the floor seemed to leer and wink from their
eyeless windows.

"I am afraid," said Winnie, drawing nearer the door, "that you haven't anything so
nice as I want."

"I haf effery dings, effery dings," replied
the ponderous costumer; "you don't t'ink I
keeps dose fine procade for the costume ball
out here in te tust, ain't it?"

"I wanted something for a school entertainment," Winnie explained.

"So, so; I haf effery dings, I tole you, for
de school. Ya, from dose kindergarten to
dot universities. Dings for little peebles
and dings for big peebles."

"I should like to know what kind of big
people patronize your establishment?"

"Sometimes dose ladies who make de
church fair. I have some angel wing for de
Christmas mystery, de mask for de Muzzer
Goose pantomine. Sometimes dose fine
ladies dey make some peesness mit me.

When de shentlemen step on dose trail or spill coffee on dot tablier, den I buys dot dress, and my designer she make it all new again. I haf one ferry nice designer; she haf many times arrange ze historical costume for dose grand painting what make ze artists."

"Then I think I would like to talk with her," said Winnie.

"Ya, ya, dat vas right. Here, Mrs. Halsey, Mrs. Halsey! Perhaps you petter go in de sewing-room, ain't it?"

He opened the door into a back room where a sweet pale-faced woman sat sewing little bells on a jester's cap.

We were struck from the outset with Mrs. Halsey's refined appearance, and we were not surprised when she showed, by her complete understanding of what we required, that she had read Tennyson and had some idea of historical periods in costume. She drew a purple velvet robe from a great bundle. I exclaimed in disapproval as I noticed a horrid crimson border.

"But this is coming off," said the little woman, using her scissors briskly, "and instead, I will stitch some gold braid appliqué in a lily design. See, how do you like this effect?" and her deft fingers flew, coiling and twisting the gilt braid until a really regal combination was produced.

"Then we will have it open at the side to show a white satin petticoat, also laced with gold, and the sleeves can be puffed and slashed with white satin. I arranged a costume like that for Mary Anderson."

"Is it possible that such a noted and successful actress gets her costumes at a place like this?" asked Witch Winnie.

"Oh, no," replied Mrs. Halsey, with a sigh; "when I made Miss Anderson's dresses I was designer for Madame Céleste's establishment. I should be there now if it were not for Jim."

She was fitting the dress to me, and as this would take several minutes, Winnie asked,

"Who is Jim?"

"Jim is my son; he is twelve years old, and the brightest little fellow, for his age, you ever saw. He leads his classes at the public school, has a record of 100 in mathematics, for all that he has such a poor chance at preparing his lessons."

"How does that happen?" It was I who inquired this time.

"Jim is an ambitious boy; ambitious to

help me as well as to keep a place in his class, and a milkman pays him a dollar a week for driving his cart over to Jersey City to meet the milk train and fill his cans for him every morning."

" That is very nice."

" If it did not break so cruelly into the poor boy's hours for sleep. In order to dress and snatch a bite before he goes down to the stable and harnesses, he has to rise at 3 o'clock. This enables the milkman to sleep until Jim arrives with the milk at 6 o'clock, in time to begin the morning rounds. I make the boy take an hour's sleep after this, but it is not enough."

" He ought to go to bed very early."

" Yes, but the lessons; when are they to be learned? He shouts them out in his sleep. 'If I gain seven hundred dollars from a rise of 2½ per cent. in Pennsylvania Railroad stock, what was my original investment?' He has his father's quickness for figures. Bless his heart! he never had any money to invest in railroad stocks, and by heaven's help he never will."

" I am not so sure about that," said Witch Winnie. " How did it happen that you lost your position at Madame Celeste's on account of Jim?" She had finished the fitting and was removing the pins from her mouth, but Winnie drew on her gloves very slowly; we were both interested.

"Madame kept me for such late hours that I did not reach home until Jim was asleep, and at last she proposed to raise my salary, but said that I must sleep in the establishment, so as to be on hand to open early in the morning. This was after Madame's very successful winter, when she bought a house out of town, and did not find it convenient to come in until late in the day. I told her that I would accept her offer if Jim could be with me; but there was no room for him, and we thought it best to stick together. I get through here at 6 o'clock, and can cook Jim's dinner. But it's hard for the boy. If I could only afford to let him have his entire time for his study—but his dollar a week half pays our rent."

"Wouldn't it have been better for you both if you had remained at Madame Céleste's, and had sent Jim to boarding-school? There are such nice cadet schools up the Hudson."

A faint smile overspread the woman's face. "Madame always insisted that her employees should dress well. I know exactly what it cost me. It would have left just a dollar and a half a week for Jim. Do you know of any boarding-school that would have taken him at those rates?"

Winnie sorrowfully confessed that she did not, and we reluctantly took our leave, Mrs. Halsey promising to finish the costume immediately, and to send it by Jim in ample time for the evening's performances.

Our escapade lay heavily upon my conscience in spite of our success in obtaining the costume, but I felt still more troubled for poor Mrs. Halsey and her overworked boy. "I wonder," I said to Winnie, "if Madame could not make him useful here at the school, and let him work for his board, tend furnace and run errands."

"You could not tell her about him without confessing our lark, and don't you do that for the world!"

"No," I promised, against my will, "of course not, unless you consent ; the secret is half yours, but I really think it would be the best way."

Adelaide was greatly interested in our report. "I am to have my violin dress for the concert made at Madame Céleste's," she said, "and I mean to ask her about this Mrs. Halsey."

Jim came with the package while we were at supper, and Adelaide ran down to the office to receive it. She told us that he was an undersized, stoop-shouldered boy, with a cough which she fancied he had contracted by driving in the early morning mists. He took off his hat like a little gentleman, however, and his finger-nails and teeth were clean. Any clown might wear good clothes, Adelaide insisted, but these little details marked the gentleman. He had at first declined the dime which Adelaide proffered, but accepted it on her insistance that it was only for car-fare and it was raining. He put it away carefully in a little worn purse which contained just one cent, at the same time remarking, "I don't mind the rain, and I can get Ma the quinine the doctor says she ought to be taking."

"That's the boy for me," Witch Winnie remarked; "he's got clear grit, and tenderness for his mother besides."

And Guinevere's gown? It was a beauty. The golden lilies gave it a sumptuous effect, and it fulfilled almost exactly the promises of the forged letter; there was even a *rivière* of fish-scale pearls and glass beads down the side, which really resembled a châtelaine. The Hornets were overcome with amazement—simply dazzled and dazed. According to Adelaide—who always resorted to French to express her superlatives, and, when that language proved inadequate, pieced it out with translations of American slang or coinage of her own—they were "*Completement bouleversées, stupéfiées, mortifiées, et frappée plus haute q'un—q'un—kite!*"

CHAPTER III.

THE PRINCESS.

WHAT'S the dear old lady,
In a green tabby gown
And a great lace cap,
With long lace ruffles hanging down.

There she sits
In a cushioned high-back-
ed seat,
Covered over with crimson
damask,
With a footstool at her
feet.

You see what a handsome room it is,
Full of old carving and gilding ;
The house is, one may be sure,
Of the Elizabethan style of building.

—*Mary Howitt.*

Our interest in Mrs. Halsey and her son
slumbered for a time ; not that we forgot

her, or gave up our determination to do something for Jim whenever the opportunity offered. It was soon to come, but our time and interest were filled with other things. Just now it was a mystery—and what so dear to a girl's imagination?

It was brought up for discussion afresh, because Miss Prillwitz had said to Emma Jane Anton that the diadem which I wore as Guinevere was not a suitable one for a queen, but a rather nondescript arrangement half-way between that of a marquis and an earl.

This assumption of authoritative knowledge in regard to coronets revived an old rumor as to the noble birth of Miss Prillwitz.

No one could tell who first circulated the report that Miss Prillwitz was a princess. It developed little by little, I fancy, but when it began to be whispered we received it without a shadow of doubt. Miss Prillwitz was a prim little woman, who always came to Madame's receptions dressed in the same brocade dress, once gaudy with a great bouquet pattern, but now faded into faint pink and primrose on a background of silvery-green, with the same carefully cleaned gloves and fine old fan of the period of Marie Antoinette. She wore her perfectly white hair à la Pompadour, and further increased her diminutive height by French heels, but in spite of these artificial contrivances she was a tiny woman, though she had dignity enough for a very tall one. Adelaide said she had "the unmistakable air of a *grande dame*," and that she would have suspected her in any disguise. Milly had once spied, half tucked in her belt and dependent from a slender chain, a miniature, set in brilliants, of a handsome young man in uniform, a row of decorations on his breast, crosses and stars hanging from strips of bright ribbon. This was a great discovery, and Milly was sure that the original was no less a personage than Peter the Great. She had thought out a thrilling romance of true love crossed by jealousy and heartbreak, which the rest of the girls accepted as more than probable, until Emma Jane Anton suggested that as Peter the Great died in 1725, it would really make the princess much older than she appeared, to fancy that he was the hero of her girlhood. Emma Jane Anton always had a disagreeable faculty of remembering dates. The other girls were unanimous in the opinion that she knew entirely too much, and each one looked and longed for an opportunity of publicly detecting her in a mistake and correcting her—an opportunity which never came. Milly never made herself offensive by being certain of anything, and was loved and petted accordingly. The myth of a royal lover was a congenial one, and gained credence, though none of us dared to give him a name or date, at least not in the presence of Emma Jane Anton. No one had the temerity to question Adelaide's infallibility in detecting a great lady at first sight. It did not ever occur to Emma Jane Anton to ask how many princesses she had met, and what was the "unmistakable air" of distinction and nobility which announced them like a herald's proclamation. Perhaps this was because Adelaide herself possessed this grand air by nature, and was far more regal in appearance and feeling than many a Guelph or Stuart. Witch Winnie, perhaps because she was the mad-cap of the boarding-school, and was always getting into scrapes herself, snuffed a political plot, and suggested that the princess had been exiled on account of deep-laid machinations against one of the reigning families, a supposition which would account for her living in exile and disguise, and even in comparative

poverty. This explanation, as being the
most ingenious, and affording fascinating
scope for the imagination, was the most
popular one, and was more or less elaborated
according to the individual fancy of the
young lady. Emma Jane Anton was obliged
to admit that she might be a princess, and
that there was no harm in calling her so
amongst ourselves. Madame had let fall
some very singular expressions when she
announced the fact that we were to have
her for our teacher in Botany. Emma Jane
had heard her, and it was she who had
reported the news to the others.

"Girls," she said, "did you ever hear anything so absurd! We are going to recite
our Botany to the princess."

"You don't mean it !"

"Honest! She lives in that funny old
house across the square, that Winnie always
pretends to think is haunted. We are to
parade over there three days in the week.
Madame says it's a great opportunity,
for she is really quite eminent ; writes for
scientific journals, has traveled in all sorts
of foreign countries, and *has moved in court
circles.*"

"I told you so !" exclaimed Adelaide,

triumphantly. "I always said she was a true-blue princess."

"I don't know that you have quite proved it yet," replied Emma Jane Anton, coolly, "but Madame did say that we would have an opportunity of learning much more from her than mere botany—etiquette, I presume—for she went on to hint that she had been brought up in a different school of manners from that of our own day and country, that we would find her peculiar in some ways, and that she trusted to our native courtesy to humor her little foibles, and a hundred more things of the same sort, winding up with that stock expression which she always uses when she has talked a subject to shreds and tatters—'A word to the wise is sufficient.'"

"I wish I had heard her," said Witch Winnie; "I don't consider this subject talked to tatters, by any means. I propose that this Botany class constitute itself a committee of investigation to clear up the mystery in regard to the history of the princess. We are supposed to be devoted to the study of nature, but I consider *human* nature a deal the more interesting. It will almost pay for having to mind one's *p*'s and *q*'s. I wonder what she would say if she caught me sliding down her palace balusters! We'll all have to practice curtseying—one step to the side, then two back. Oh! I'm ever so sorry I knocked over that stand. Was the vase a keepsake or anything? I'll buy you another. No, I can't, for I've spent all my allowance for this month. Well, you may have that *bonbonnière* of mine you liked so much. The vase was a treasure, but no one could be vexed with Witch Winnie, and I forgave her, of course, and would none of the *bonbonnière*.

Our first glimpse at the house in which the princess lived was as appetizing to our imaginations as the little lady herself. It had been built as a church - school, and straggled around the church, shaping itself to the exterior angles of that edifice, and in so doing gained a number of queerly shaped rooms, some long and narrow, and others with irregular corners, but all bright with southern sunshine. The princess rented only the upper floor and the front room in the basement. The rest of the house had been let to other parties, but was now vacant. How strange and lonely it must seem, we thought, to go up and down those

long staircases, and peep into the unin-
habited rooms! Rather eerie at night. "I
wouldn't live that way for the world," shivered Milly. "I should be afraid of robbers."

"Burglars don't usually choose an unoccupied house for their operations," Emma
Jane remarked, sententiously.

Later, when we were better acquainted
with the princess, Milly asked her if she was
never timid. She acknowledged that she
was, but assured us that rats *were one great
comfort.*

"What do you mean?" Milly asked.

"Whenevaire," said the princess (in the
quaint broken English which we always
found so fascinating, English which had only
the foreignness of pronunciation and idiom,
and which Adelaide insisted was rarely so
maltreated as to be really *broken*, but was
only a little dislocated)—"whenevaire I hear
one cautious sawing noise which shall be as
if ze burglaire to file ze lock, I say to myself, 'Ah, ha! Monsieur Rat have invited to
himself some companie in ze pantry of ze
butler.' When zere come one *tappage* on ze
escalier, as zo some one make haste to
depart ze house, I turn myself upon my bed
and make to myself explanation—Rats!

When ze footsteps mysterious steal so softly down ze hall, and make pause justly at my door, then I reach for ze great cane of my fazzer, which I keep at all times by ze canopy of my bed, and I pound on ze floor—boom, boom, Monsieur Rat *scélérat*, and it is thus I make my reassurance."

The princess received us in what had been the basement dining-room, which she called her laboratory. The entire south side was one broad window of small diamond-shaped panes. Forming a sill to this window was a row of low, wide cases for the reception of herbaria, and the room had a peculiar herby smell, a mixture of sweet-fern and faint aromatic herbs.

The cushions which converted the tops of these cases into seats were stuffed with dried beech-leaves.

The princess quoted Latin to us for her preference for the fine springy upholstery which beech-leaves give. *Silva domus, cubilia frondes.* ("The wood a house, the foliage a couch.")

The other furniture in the room was a long table placed in front of the book-case divan, a table covered with piles of MS. books, a press for specimens, two micro-

scopes, and a great blue china bowl containing pussy-willows in water—our specimens
for the day's study. High book-cases, whose
contents could only be guessed at, for the
glass doors were lined with curiously shirred
green silk, were ranged against the wall opposite, and at one end of the room stood a
monumental German stove in white porce-
lain; at the other was Miss Prillwitz's chair, a
high-backed Gothic affair, which had once
served as an episcopal *sedilium*, but had been
removed on the occasion of a new furnishing
of the church.

It formed a stately background for the
little figure. I often found myself making
sketches of her on the sheets of soft paper
between which we pressed our flowers, instead of listening to the lecture. I liked to
imagine how she would look in a great ruff,
not of Cynthia Vaughn's mosquito net, but
of real *point de Venise*.

And yet her talks were very interesting;
she was a true lover of nature, and made us
love her. She regretted that she could not
take us into the deep woods, but she opened
our eyes to the wealth of country suggest-
iveness which we could find in the city. She
introduced us personally to the scanty two

dozen or so of trees in the little park, and
from the intimate acquaintance formed with
each of these, our appetites were whetted
for vast wildernesses of forest primeval

She opened to us the beauty which there
lies in the simple branching of the trees in
their winter nudity, the tracery of the limbs
and twigs cut clearly against a yellow sunset, or picked out with snow; how the elms
gave graceful wine-glass and Greek-vase
outlines; the snakily mottled sycamore un-
dulated its great arms like a boa-constrictor
reaching out for prey; the birch, "the lady
of the woods," displayed her white satin
dress; the gnarled hemlocks wrestled up-
ward, each sharp angle a defiance to the
winter storms with which they had striven
in heroic combat, the bent knees clutching
the rocks, while the aged arms writhed and
tossed in the grasp of the fiends of the air.
She showed us the beautiful parabolic curve
of the willows, a bouquet of rockets; the mili-
tary bearing of a row of Lombardy poplars
standing, in their perfect alignment, like tall
grenadiers drawn up in a hollow square.
Before the first tender blurring of the leaf-
buds we knew our trees, and loved them for
their almost human qualities.

Miss Sartoris had taught me, the preceding summer, to look for the decorative beauty to be found in common roadside weeds, and we had made sketches together of dock, elecampane, tansy, thistles, and milkweed. I had one rich, rare day with her in a swamp, when I ruined a pair of stockings, and made the discovery that a skunk-cabbage was as beautiful in its curves as a calla. I brought these sketches to the princess, and she congratulated me on the possession of my country home with its gold-mines of beauty all around.

"You are one heiress, my dear," she said, " to ze vast wealths which you have only te learn how you s'all enjoy. Only t'ink of ze sousands of poor city people who haf never had ze felicity to see a swamp!"

I grew to appreciate the country, and to feel that I was richer than I had thought.

Milly found a branch of study which was not above the measure of her intellect. She soon mastered the long names, and learned to think, and teachers in other departments noted an improvement. There was need for this, for the Hornets long kept up a tradition that at one of the history examinations Milly had been asked, "What is the Salic

Law ?" and had replied, confidently—"That no woman or *descendant of a woman,* can ever reign in France."

CHAPTER IV.

RS. GROGAN, the baby-farmer of Rickett's Court, could hardly have been described as a court lady, and yet she was a very typical specimen of the women of this locality. But before introducing the reader to the society of Rickett's Court, I must first explain how it was that we came to make its acquaintance.

As the time approached for the concert of which I have spoken, Adelaide was reminded of her determination to have a " violin dress " made by Madame Céleste.   Adelaide played the violin, as we thought, divinely ; she was at least the best performer at Madame's. "The violin is the violet," I said, quoting from "Charles A chester." "You must have a violet-colored gown."

" A very delicate shade of china crêpe will do," Adelaide replied, "made up with a darker tint, and the sleeves must be puffed like that dress the princess wore to the tableaux."

" Adelaide, dear," murmured Milly, "you ought to wear angel sleeves to show your lovely arms."

"And have them flop about like a ship's pennant in a lively breeze, during that bit of rapid bowing ? That would be too grotesque."

" Puff them to the elbow," I suggested, "and then have a fall of soft lace that will float back and give the turn of your wrist as you whip the strings."

" See here, Adelaide," remarked Witch Winnie, " if you want something really fine, get that Mrs. Halsey to design it for you."

" You don't suppose that I would hire a dress for the concert at a costumer's ?"

" I didn't say that ; you could have it made wherever you pleased, but get Mrs. Halsey's ideas on the subject ; they are really remark-able."

Adelaide considered the subject and acted upon it, but, greatly to my relief, she refused to do so without explaining the entire affair to Madame.

"I'll not stand in the way of your having a nice gown," said Witch Winnie. "Come, Tib, let's confess."

I was overjoyed, and Madame, though duly shocked, was not severe. She even allowed Witch Winnie to take Adelaide to see Mrs. Halsey, stipulating only that she should be chaperoned by one of the teachers. Adelaide chose Miss Sartoris, at my suggestion, both because we liked her, and from my feeling that her artistic instinct might be of service.

The girls were disappointed to find that Mrs. Halsey was no longer at the costumer's. He had " pounced " her, he said, because she was " too much of a lady for de peesness." Fortunately he could give the girls her address—No. 1, sixth floor, Rickett's Court.

It was a very disagreeable part of town. Miss Sartoris looked doubtful as they approached it, and was on the point of getting into the carriage again as they alighted,

5

but Witch Winnie had already darted through a long dark hall which led to the court in the centre of the block, and there was nothing for it but to follow.

Evil smells nearly choked them as they ran the gauntlet of that hall, and they were no better off on emerging upon the sloppy court. The space overhead, between the buildings, was laced with an intricate network of clothes-lines filled with garments. Adelaide said she realized now where all upper New York had its laundry work done, for this was evidently not the wash of the court people. From their appearance it was only fair to conjecture that they were so busy doing other people's washing that they never had time for their own. The dirty water seemed to be thrown from the windows into the court, where it stood in puddles or feebly trickled into the sewer, from which emanated nauseous and deadly gases. Sickly children were dabbling in these puddles.

"It makes me think of Hood's 'Lost Heir,'" said Miss Sartoris—

> "The court,
> Where he was better off than all the other young boys,
> With two bricks, an old shoe, nine oyster shells, and a
> dead kitten by way of toys."

WITCH WINNIE.—*Page 66.*

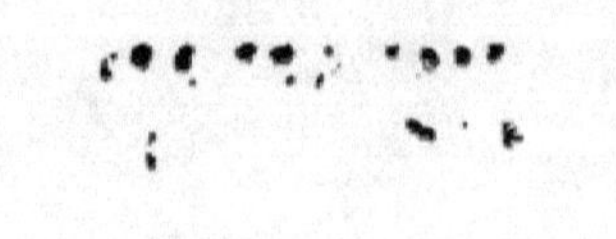

They mounted a ricketty staircase grimed with dirt. Smells of new degrees and varieties of loathsomeness assaulted them at every landing. The Italian rag-pickers in the basement were sorting their filthy wares, while a little girl was concocting for them the garlic stew over a charcoal brazier. The mingled fumes came thick from the open door. Mrs. Grogan on the first floor had paused in her washing to take a pull at a villainous pipe. She came to the door still smoking, and carrying in her arms an almost skeleton baby, who sucked at a dirty rag containing a crust dipped in gin. Winnie obtained one glimpse of the interior of Mrs. Grogan's domicile, and drew back quite pale. "Adelaide," she said, "the room literally *swarmed* with babies; that woman cannot have so many all of the same age." Inquiry of Mrs. Halsey enlightened them. Mrs. Grogan was a "baby-farmer," and boarded these children, making a good income thereby, as their mothers were servants in good families. On the next floor a family of eight were working in a hall-bedroom, at rolling cigars. The large rooms were occupied by some Chinese. Mrs. Halsey thought that they used them as

an opium den. Past more doors, up three
more pairs of stairs, and they paused at
No. 1. They knocked several times, but
they could not make themselves heard above
the buzz and whirr of a sewing-machine.
Finally Winnie opened the door, and there
sat Mrs. Halsey bent over the machine,
while the floor was piled with dainty under-
clothing neatly tucked.

She sprang up, evidently pleased to see
Winnie again, and motioned her callers to
the only seats which the room afforded—
a chair, a trunk, and a stool.

Winnie apologized for the interruption,
and explained her errand. " But perhaps you
are too busy to design this dress," Adelaide
said ; " I see you have plenty of work."

" It will not take long to make a little
sketch," Mrs. Halsey replied, "and it will be
a real pleasure for me to do it." As her
fingers moved rapidly over the paper the
girls took an inventory of the room. A
cracked cooking - stove, and a cupboard
behind it formed of a dry-goods box, but all
the utensils were scrupulously clean. A
closet, another dry-goods case on end, with
a chintz curtain in front, concealed, as Winnie's prying eyes ascertained, a roll of bed-

ding, which was evidently spread on the floor at night. Mrs. Halsey knelt before a worn table, and this, with the sewing-machine, completed the furnishing of the apartment. No, in the window there was a row of fruit-cans containing some geraniums. Miss Sartoris discovered them, and Mrs. Halsey apologized for their condition. "They were just in bud," she said, "but we were without coal for several days, and they were nipped by frost."

Poor woman! she looked as if *she* had been nipped by the frost too during that bitter experience. She coughed, and Adelaide remarked, "You ought to drink cream, Mrs. Halsey; they say it is better for a cough than cod-liver oil."

"I have plenty of milk," the little woman replied. "The milkman for whom my Jim works lets him have the milk that he finds left over in the cans when he washes them out after his rounds. Sometimes there's as much as a pint, and almost always enough for our oatmeal."

Mrs. Halsey spoke cheerily and proudly— as of a luxury which she owed her boy. The design was completed, and Adelaide was delighted.

"Would you like to have me make the costume in tissue - paper?" Mrs. Halsey asked; "the sleeve, at least, and this drapery; then any seamstress can make it."

"How much will it be?" Adelaide asked, doubtfully—wondering if her five-dollar bill would cover the charge.

"Do you think seventy-five cents too much? It would take me an afternoon."

"But you could certainly earn more than that by your sewing."

Mrs. Halsey smiled rather bitterly. "Would you really like to know the rates at which I work?" she asked.

Adelaide expressed her interest. "These pretty Mother Hubbard night-gowns sell well, I am sure, but I know you can't get very much for making them, for I bought a pair at a bargain counter for a dollar."

"It is the bargain counter which makes the low pay. I get a dollar and thirty cents *a dozen* for making them," said Mrs. Halsey, calmly.

"A dozen!" cried Winnie; "and how many can you make in a day?"

"Eight."

"Then you make—"

" Eighty-five cents a day ; but I cannot average that."

" Can't you do better with something else ? "

" I have made flannel skirts—tucked—at a dollar a dozen, but I can only make eight of those in a day, so that is less I have received a dollar and twenty cents a dozen for making chemises, which sell at seven dollars a dozen ; and seventy-five cents a dozen for babies' slips, three tucks and a hem ; forty cents a dozen for corset covers. I have a friend who works a machine in a ruffling factory ; she makes a hundred and fifty yards of hemmed and tucked ruffling a day, for which she receives twenty-five cents. So, you see, I am better off than some."[*]

" And can you live on five dollars a week ? "

" Six dollars, Madame ; Jim earns one dollar and the milk."

" You pay for rent—"

" Six dollars a month ; yes, it *is* hard to earn that."

" You must be thankful that you have only Jim to provide for."

---

[*] See "Campbell's Prisoners of Poverty" for still more harrowing statistics.

"The Sandys, on the floor below, have six children; five of them earn wages. I think they earn more than their cost."

"But," said Miss Sartoris, "I thought child labor was prohibited by law."

"Not out of school hours, or at home. Then the parents often swear a child is over fourteen, but small of its age, and get it into a factory. You wouldn't blame them, Madame, if you knew all the circumstances I do. I keep Jim at his books, but the study, with the night work, I'm afraid is killing him. They tempt him at the saloon, too, to take what they call a "bracer" as he goes out to drive the milk cart at 3 in the morning, but I get up and have tea ready for him, so that he does not yield."

"We must go now," said Miss Sartoris, kindly. "You will send Jim with the paper pattern to-night?" Adelaide slipped a dollar into Mrs. Halsey's hand, and would take no change. And the three went down the stairs thoughtful and sad.

"What can we do for her?" Winnie asked.

"I am sure I don't know," replied Miss Sartoris; "she certainly seems capable of securing better wages."

"I will speak to Madame Céleste about her," said Adelaide; and she was as good as her word. Winnie accompanied Adelaide when she took the pattern to the fashionable dress-maker. The modiste listened in rapt attention to Adelaide's explanation of the gown wanted. She examined the design with interest. "It is perfectly made," she said. "Who constructed this for you? It is the work of an expert. Ah, Miss, if I only had now in my establishment a designer who was with me last year! She had such a mind for *costumes de fantaisie!* For Greek costumes to be worn at the harp, and for Directoire dresses, I miss her cruelly, but Mademoiselle's design is so explicit that we will have no trouble."

"Was your designer a Mrs. Halsey?" Winnie asked.

"The same, Miss. Do you know her? Can you give me her address? I must try to get her back."

"I think you may be able to obtain her. She made this pattern for me; but you will have to bid high, for she has her boy with her now."

"Ah yes! the boy; that was the trouble between us. Seamstresses have no business to be mothers. Mrs. Halsey ought to give up the child entirely to some asylum for adoption; he will always be a handicap to her ; but she does not see this, and clings to him as though she thought him her only chance for fortune. There is a mystery in Mrs. Halsey's life. Her husband has deserted her, and she lives in the vain hope that he will come back some day and explain everything. She patronized me once, long ago, when she was in better circumstances. She will not talk about her husband, and I fancy that he is one of those defaulting cashiers who have run away to Canada. I am willing to take her back on the old terms, but she must give up her boy. I have an order for a set of costumes for one of our queens of the opera. Mrs. Halsey is just the one to take it in hand. Where did you say she could be found ?"

" I think you had better communicate with her through me," Adelaide replied : " I am not at liberty to give her address."

" And it is very possible," Winnie spoke up, eagerly, for she had seen a gleam in Madame Céleste's eyes, " that her friends will provide for the boy. In that case she will be more independent, and perhaps will not be willing to return at the old salary. What shall we say is the most that you will offer."

"Five dollars a week and her board; that is very good pay, Miss; fifty cents more than I paid her when she was with me."

The girls could hardly wait to reach the Amen Corner to talk the matter over. Milly was all sympathy. "I will write to papa," she said, "and get him to send Jim to a boarding-school. I'll send for several circulars, and find out how much it costs."

As an answer from Mr. Roseveldt might be expected the next day, we decided to wait for it. Adelaide regretted that her father was in Omaha, as she was sure that he would have aided in the scheme.

Mr. Roseveldt's answer was most discouraging. He regarded Milly's plan as mere sentimental nonsense, and would take no interest in it.

"You might save something out of your allowance, Milly," suggested the audacious Winnie.

"I give away three-fourths of it now," Milly replied, in an injured tone. "What with the flowers I have on the organ every day for Miss Hope, and the favors for the german, which I always furnish, and the

bonbons I give you girls, and all my other
extras—"

" But, Milly dear," I exclaimed, " we would
all ever so much rather you spent the candy
money for Jim than on us."

" But I want *some* candy for myself, and
I am not going to be so mean as to munch
it. and not pass any to the other girls."

It would have been a real deprivation
to Milly to do without her beloved candy. She gloated over luscious pasty
"lumps of delight " in the way of marsh-
mallows and chocolate creams. candied
fruits and marrons glacées, and her silver
bonbonnière was always filled with the most
expensive candied violets and rose-leaves.
Worse than this, there were certain little
cordial drops, which were a peculiar weak-
ness of Milly's ; none of us knew with what
an awful danger she was playing, or that
Milly inherited a taste for alcoholic beverages
through several generations. But Milly was
not selfish.

"Very well, girls," she said. with a sigh, " if
you will go without, I will, and we will form
a total abstinence candy society. I know
just how much that means for Jim, for I paid
Maillard eight dollars last month."

"You are a good girl," spoke up Emma Jane, "and if you hold to that resolution, Milly Roseveldt, I will deal you out a cake of maple sugar every day, from a box I've just received from some Vermont cousins. I was wondering what I should do with it, for I don't care for sweets."

Milly's face brightened; all unconsciously she was doing as great a kindness to herself as to Jim, and the pure maple sugar was a good substitute for the unwholesome concoctions of the confectioner; it satisfied her craving for sweets, and did not poison her appetite.

The rest of us added our small contributions, but the aggregate only amounted to three dollars a week, and we were unable to learn of any boarding-school to which Jim could be sent at those rates.

Winnie had communicated Madame Céleste's offer to Mrs. Halsey. "It would be just the thing if I were alone," she replied, "but what would Jim do without me?"

"Perhaps you can board him somewhere," Winnie suggested; and she told of the sum which we girls had promised.

"If I knew of any respectable place where he would have good influences, I would accept your kindness, as a loan, for a little while," Mrs. Halsey replied, "for my first earnings must go for clothes. I have friends in Connecticut; perhaps they will take Jim."

But Mrs. Halsey found that her friends had moved West. She thanked us for our interest, but said that there seemed nothing better to do than to continue as they were.

"I can't bear to tell Madame Céleste that she declines her offer," said Adelaide. "*We* must find a place for that boy."

"I don't see how," replied Winnie; but she saw, that afternoon; it came to her all by a sudden inspiration during our botany lesson.

CHAPTER V

LITTLE PRINCE DEL PARADISO.

THAT day the botany class found their teacher in a flutter of excitement. There was a fresh, pink glow in the faded cheeks, and an unusual sparkle in the kindly eyes. She seated herself in the episcopal chair, lifted her lorgnette, and began to arrange the specimens for the day's lesson, but her hand trembled so that she could scarcely adjust the microscope, and the papers on which her notes were written sifted through her fingers and were strewn in confusion on the floor.

" Are you ill, Miss Prillwitz?" Adelaide asked, in alarm.

'No, Miss Armstrong," replied the princess,

"it is not a painful in my system, and it is not a sorry ; it is a pleasant. I shall expect to myself a company, and this is to me so seldom that I find myself *égaré*—what you call it ?— scatter ? sprinkled ?— as to my understanding."

We all looked our interest, and Winnie ventured to ask—" One of your relations, Miss Prillwitz ?"

" Yes," replied the little lady ; " he is of my own family, though to see him I have never ze pleasure. It ces ze little Prince del Paradiso."

We girls pinched each other under the table, while Milly murmured, " A prince! How perfectly lovely ! "

" Yes," replied Miss Prillwitz; " ze birthright to ziss little poy is one great, high, nobilitic, *la plus haute noblesse*, but he know nossing of it, nossing whateffer. He haf ze misfortune to be exported from his home when one leetle child ; he haf been elevated by poor peoples to think himself also a poor. He know nossing of ze estates what belong his family, and better he not know until he make surely his title, and he make to himself some education which shall make him suit to his position."

"How did you know about this little stolen prince?" Emma Jane asked.

"I receive message from his older bruzzer to take him to my house *provisionellement*, till his rights and his—his—what you call—his sameness?"

"You mean his identity?"

"Yes, yes, his die entity can be justly prove."

"It seems to me," said Witch Winnie, impulsively, "that he can't be a very kind elder brother to be so indifferent."

"My dear child, you make my admiration with what celeritude you do arrive always at exactly ze wrong conclusion. Ze prince haf made great effort to recover his little bruzzer, but he must guard himself from ze false claimants, ze impostors."

"Then the little boy who is coming to you," said Emma Jane, "may not be the real prince, after all?"

"That is a possible," Miss Prillwitz admitted, "but it is not a probable. Somesing assure me zat he s'all prove his nobility."

"How very interesting," said Milly. "Was he stolen away from home by gypsies?"

"No, my child, he was not steal. He wandered himself away from his fazzer's house and was lost.

" How old is he now ? "

" Twelve year."

Witch Winnie started ; that was just Jim Halsey's age, and what a difference in the destiny awaiting the two boys! One the son of a king, the other of a criminal.

" Will you to see ze little chamber of ze petit prince ? " asked Miss Prillwitz.

We were all overjoyed by the suggestion, and the eager little woman led us to a room just under the roof, with a dormer-window looking out upon the roof of the church.

Milly ran directly to this window, and drawing aside the curtains looked out, but started back again half frightened, for a carved gargoyle under the eaves was very near and leered at her with a malicious, demoniacal expression. He was a grotesque creature with bat wings, lolling tongue, and long claws, but harmless enough, for the doves perched on his head and preened their iridescent plumage in the sunshine. The church roof just here was a wilderness of flying buttresses and pinnacles; the chimes were still far overhead, and rang out, as we entered the chambers, my favorite hymn—" Sun of my soul, thou Saviour dear."

I have not yet described the room itself. We all exclaimed at its quaint beauty as we entered.

It was papered with an old-fashioned vine pattern, the green foliage twined about a slender trellis, and this gave the room, which was really quite small, the effect of an arbor with space beyond. There was a patch of dark green carpet with a mossy pattern before the bed, which was very simple and dressed in white. In the window recess was a dry-goods box, upholstered in a fern-patterned chintz of a restful green tint, and serving, with its cushions, both as a divan and as a chest for clothing. There was a little corner wash-stand with a toilet set decorated with water-lilies and green lily-pads, and there was a little sliding curtain of green China silk with a shadow-pattern at the window, while through the uncurtained upper space one saw, beyond the church roof, the trees of the park.

" O Miss Prillwitz!" I exclaimed, "it is just Aurora Leigh's room over again. You modeled it on Mrs. Browning's description, did you not?—

> '   'I had a little chamber in the house,
>   As green as any privet-hedge a bird
>   Might choose to build in . . . . .
>   . . . . the walls
>   Were green, the carpet was pure green;
>   the straight
>   Small bed was curtained greenly,
>   and the folds
>   Hung green about the window,
>   which let in
>   A dash of dawn dew from its greenery,
>   the honeysuckle.' "

"I haf nefer ze pleasure to know zat room," said Miss Prillwitz, her eyes kindling.

"How perfectly sweet!" exclaimed Adelaide. "It is like 'a lodge in some vast wilderness.' I didn't know that there was a place in New York so like the country."

"Will the prince study botany with us?" Milly asked, as we descended the stairs.

"I fear he is not ready for ze botany. His education haf been neglect. But you s'all see him oftenly. I must beg you not to tell him zat he is a prince; zis must not divulge to him until ze proper time."

"And then," added Emma Jane, "it would be cruel to excite hopes which may be doomed to disappointment."

The princess smiled. "I do not fear zat,"

she said. "And now, young ladies, I must make you my excuse, and beg Miss Armstrong she s'all hear ze class ze remains of ze hour; I must go to ze market for prepare ze young prince his supper."

She hurried away, and we attempted to turn our minds to our lesson. Adelaide had just exclaimed that in botany the term *hop* signified small, and *dog* large, but she broke off the statement with the exclamation, "And do you see, girls, what this proves?"

"That dog-roses are large roses," replied Emma Jane.

"That the Chinese laundry man around the corner, Hop Sin, is a little sinner," said Winnie.

"No, no, I don't mean that, but she said that the Prince del Paradiso was related to her; then, of course, she must belong to the Paradiso family as well, and what we have so long suspected is really true. She is a genuine princess, and probably the daughter of a king."

"I am not so sure of that," replied Emma Jane.

"Do you suspect Miss Prillwitz of being an impostor?" Adelaide asked, coldly.

"Certainly not," replied Emma Jane; "but in many European countries every son of a prince is called a prince, instead of the eldest son only, as in England, and all the sons of all the younger sons are princes, and so on to the last descendant ; and I presume it is so with the daughters as well ; so that the title must often exist where there are no estates."

" But Miss Prillwitz said that the Prince del Paradiso was heir to immense estates," Milly insisted.

" But that proves nothing in her own case," Adelaide admitted. " Some day, perhaps she will tell us more about herself, since she has begun to open her heart to us."

At that moment the door-bell rang, and as the princess kept no servant, Winnie went to the door. She was gone a long time, and came back looking grave and distraught— giving an evasive answer when we asked her who had called. I wondered at this because, as I sat nearest the door, I had over- heard a part of the conversation, and knew that it referred to the little boy who was expected. " He cannot come," a voice had said ; " he has a situation where he can learn a trade." This was of so much interest to us all that I wondered why Winnie did not immediately report it.

As soon as we returned to the school she obtained an interview with Madame, and permission to see Mrs. Halsey in reference to the Céleste situation ; Madame stipulating that she must not ask this favor for a long time, as she did not like to have her pupils frequent the tenement district. I offered to go with Winnie, and was surprised that she declined my company. She returned glowing with suppressed excitement.

"Mrs. Halsey has accepted Madame Céleste's offer," she exclaimed ; " she leaves the court to-morrow, let us hope for good and all. O girls, it is a horrible place! I saw worse sights than when I was there before."

" And Jim ?" we asked.

" Jim is provided for. We are to pay three dollars a week for him for the present, until Mrs Halsey gets on her feet."

" Did she find a good place for him ?"

" An excellent place; but you must not ask me another question, and if any mysterious circumstances should come to your observation within a few days, you are not to say a thing, or even look surprised. Promise, every one of you."

" A mystery! how delightful!" exclaimed Milly. " It's almost as good as the little prince. You can rely on us; we will help you, Winnie, whatever it is, for we know it's all right if it's your doing."

Emma Jane was not present, and I remarked that, while the rest of us would believe in Winnie without understanding her, and even in spite of the most suspicious circumstances, I was not sure that we could trust Emma Jane so far.

" Emma Jane will see nothing to suspect, and Milly, I know, will stand by me. It's only you two that I am afraid of—Adelaide, because she has seen Jim; and Tib, from her natural smartness in smelling out a secret."

" Whatever it is, Winnie, we believe you could never do anything very bad," said Adelaide.

" But I have," Winnie replied; " something just reckless. I'm in for the worst scrape of my life, and just as I was trying so hard to be good. I shall never be anything but a malefactor, and maybe get expelled, and throw the dear Amen Corner into disgrace. I'd better have staid queen of the Hornets, for I shall be nothing but Witch Winnie to the end of the chapter."

CHAPTER VI.

RS. HETTER-
MAN came in-
to our life in
consequence of
a train of troub-
les which arose
in the board-
ing-school from
the frequent
change of the
cook. Madame
had been serv-
ed for several
years by a faith-
ful colored man,
who had suddenly taken it into his head to
go off as steward on a gentleman's yacht.
She had supplied his place by a Biddy, who
was found intoxicated on the kitchen floor.

A woman followed who turned out to be a
thief, and we were now enduring an incompetent creature who made sour bread and spoiled nearly every dish which passed through
her hands. Half of the girls were suffering with dyspepsia, and all were grumbling.
The Amen Corner was especially out of
sorts. Milly, who was always fastidious, had
eaten nothing but maple-sugar for breakfast,
and had a sick headache; Emma Jane was
snappish; Witch Winnie had stolen a box of
crackers from the pantry, which she had
passed around. Adelaide and I had regaled
ourselves upon them, but Emma Jane had
declined on high moral grounds, and was virtuously miserable. It was in this unchristian
frame of mind, or rather of stomach, that
we took our next botany lesson. We found
the princess beaming with pleasure. "My
tear young ladies," she exclaimed, "you
must felicitate me. It is all so much better as I had hoped. Ze leetle prince has
not been so badly elevated after all. He
haf been taught to be kind and unselfish;
zat is already ze foundation of a gentleman."

Miss Prillwitz had occasion to leave the
room a few minutes later. Adelaide sniffed

the air, and remarked, "Girls, don't you smell something very nice?"

"It's here on the stand in the corner," said Witch Winnie, lifting a napkin which covered a tray, and exclaiming, "Fish balls! Only see! the most beautiful brown fish balls!"

"It's the remnants of their breakfast; she has forgotten to take it away," said Adelaide. "They make me feel positively faint with longing; I don't believe she would mind if we took just one."

We ate of the dainties, even Emma Jane yielding to temptation; they were delicious, and, having begun, we could not stop until they were all devoured. Then we looked at one another in shame and dismay. "Who will confess?" asked Adelaide.

"You ought to; you put us up to it," said Emma Jane Anton.

"Let's write a round-robin," I suggested, "and all sign it."

"I'll stand it," said Winnie. "I led you into temptation."

A step was heard in the hall. Winnie stepped forward and began to speak rapidly; the rest of us looked down shame-facedly.

" Miss Prillwitz, please forgive us ; we were so hungry we could not stand it. If you knew what a dreadful breakfast we had this morning, I'm sure you would not blame us—"

But she was interrupted by a cry of dismay—" Oh ! have you eaten them all ? I bought them for Aunty."

Looking up, we saw a manly little boy with an expression of distress on his frank features.

Adelaide uttered a sharp exclamation. I thought she said, " It's him ! " and yet Adelaide seldom forgot her grammar. Winnie drew a deep breath, and caught Adelaide by the arm. The boy looked up from the empty platter to the girls' faces, and his expression changed. " Oh ! it's you," he said. " Well, no matter, only I meant 'em for a present for *her*—Miss Prillwitz, you know. She's no end good to me. Mrs. Hetterman, down at Rickett's Court, makes 'em for regular customers every Friday morning. They are prime, and mother gave me a quarter for pocket-money this month, so I got ten cents' worth for Aunty ; she lets me call her so. I thought she'd like 'em, and it would patronize Mrs. Hetterman, and show her I hadn't forgotten old friends, if I had moved up in the world."

"Here's ten cents to get some more from Mrs. Hetterman." said Adelaide, "and maybe we can get her a wholesale order to furnish our boarding - school. I'll speak to Madame about it this very day."

"And if Madame doesn't order them, we girls will club together and have a spread of our own," said Winnie.

Miss Prillwitz came in at this juncture, and explanations followed.

"If Madame is in such trouble in regards of a cook." said Miss Prillwitz, "I vill write her of Mrs. Hetterman, and perhaps it will be to them both a providence. Can she make ozzer sings as ze croquettes of codfish ?"

"Oh yes, indeed," the little prince spoke up, eagerly; "soup, and turnovers, and *such* bread ! She gave me a little loaf every baking while mother had the pneumonia. Mr. Dooley, the butcher, gave me a marrow bone every Monday, and I always took it to Mrs. Hetterman to make into soup. It made mother sick to boil it in our little room, and Mrs. Hetterman would make a kettle of stock, and showed me how to keep it in a crock outside the window, so mother could have some every day; it was what kept mother's strength up through it all. We had such good neighbors at the court! but Mrs. Hetterman was best of all. She has five children of her own, too. Bill is a messenger boy, and Jennie works in a feather factory. Mary is a cripple, but she is just lovely, and tidies the house, and takes care of the two little ones. Mr. Hetterman was a plasterer and got good wages, but he fell from a scaffolding and broke his leg, and he's at the hospital."

" And does Mrs. Hetterman support the family on ze croquettes of codfish?" asked Miss Prillwitz.

" She scrubs offices, but she could get a place as cook in a family if it wasn't for the children." He looked longingly at Miss Prillwitz as he spoke, but she did not seem to notice the glance.

" Here, mon garçon, run down to ze court, and tell Mrs. Hetterman to take a basket of her cookery to ze boarding-school. I t'ink she will engage to herself some beesness."

The lesson proceeded, but Adelaide and Winnie both blundered; they were evidently thinking of something else.

A change came over Witch Winnie; she lost her old reckless gayety and became subdued and thoughtful. The Hornets said she was studying for honors, but I knew this was not the case, for her lessons were not as well prepared as formerly. She would sit for long periods lost in reverie. Winnie had charge of the money collected for Jim's board. She reported, after one week, that his mother did not need as much; two dollars would supply the margin between what was required and the sum she was able to pay. None of us, with the exception of Adelaide, knew where Winnie had domiciled Jim, but we were content to leave the matter in her hands. A week later Mrs. Halsey only needed one dollar. Mrs. Hetterman was engaged as cook for the boarding-school, and we all rejoiced in the change. I went down to the kitchen to see her, one afternoon, and found her a buxom Englishwoman who dropped her *h*'s, but was always neat and civil. She was delighted when she found that I knew the names of her children. "It was a little boy who used to live in your court who told me about them," I said, "and who introduced us to your good fish balls."

"Oh yes, Miss, I mind; it was little Jim 'Alsey; 'e's the prince of fine fellers, 'e is."

Jim Halsey the prince! My head fairly reeled, and yet this explained many things which had seemed mysterious. Winnie's agency in the matter was still not entirely clear to me. I did not connect her remorseful remarks about another scrape, with Jim, and I believed that by some remarkable coincidence he was really Miss Prillwitz's little prince incognito. I wondered whether Mrs. Hetterman knew anything of his real history, but she preferred to talk at present about her own family. She was very happy in the prospect of introducing her oldest daughter, Jennie, into the house as a waitress. "It will be so much better for Jennie," she said, "than the feather factory. The hair there is not good for 'er lungs."

I did not understand, at first, what Mrs. Hetterman meant by the *hair*, but when she explained that it was "the hatmosphere," her meaning dawned upon me.

"It will make it a bit lonelier for Mary and the little ones," she admitted, "but I go down every night, after the work's over, to tidy them up and to see that hall's right. The court is not a fit place for the children.

If I could find decent lodgings for them, such as Mrs. 'Alsey 'as got for her Jim! I think I could pay as much, if the place was only found; I'm 'oping something will turn hup, Miss."

"I hope so," I replied; and I asked Winnie that afternoon if she thought the person who was boarding Jim Halsey would take the Hettermans, but she utterly discouraged the idea.

We saw a good deal of the little prince. Miss Prillwitz called him Giacomo, and was deeply attached to him. He did her credit too, for he was docile and bright. His mother was right in saying that he inherited his father's facility for mathematics, but with this faculty he possessed also a love for mechanics and for machinery of every sort.

"He will make one good engineer some day," said Miss Prillwitz, in speaking of him to us.

"That is a strange career for a prince," said Adelaide.

"My tear, it may be many year before he ces call to his princedom, and in ze means- time he muss make his way. Zen, too, ze sons of ze royal houses make such study, and it is one good thing for ze country whose prince interest himself in ze science."

"I wonder how he would like to study surveying by and by," Adelaide said. "I know that father could employ him in the West."

"Zat is one excellent idea," said Miss Prillwitz. "We will see, when ze time s'all arrive."

We were all fond of the little prince. After all, Miss Prillwitz had decided to let him attend the botany lessons on Saturdays. "If he s'all be one surveyor in ze West," she said, "he s'all have opportunity to discover ze new species of flower; he must learn all ze natural science."

The prince attended the public school during the week, and held his place at the head of his class with ease. It was not hard to do so, now that he could sleep all night. Emma Jane, who had had her spasms of doubt in regard to him, and had even gone so far at first as to say that Miss Prillwitz was a crank, and she had no faith in the boy's nobility, had been won over by the boy himself, and remarked one afternoon that the internal evidence was convincing; Giacomo was not like common children; he was evidently cast in a finer mold; he would do honor to any position ; birth would tell, after all. It was all that dear Milly could do not to betray the secret to the little prince. He was very fond of Milly, but deferential and unpresuming, as became his apparent position. " Some day our places may be reversed You may live in a beautiful home and have hosts of friends," Milly said to him. " Will you remember me then, Giacomo ?"

"How can that ever be ?" the boy asked. " You will grow up and be a fine rich lady ; I will be a poor young man whom you will have quite forgotten."

"Not necessarily poor," Milly hastened to reply. " If you go West you may, by working hard, become rich and famous. Will you forget your old friends then ?"

And Jim promised that he would never, never forget. Then a shade came across his face. " Maybe I will, after all," he said, " for I have forgotten Mary Hetterman for more than a week. I did not think I could be so mean."

Adelaide and I had a conference in regard to the prince. It seemed that she had recognized him as Jim Halsey from the first. " I have been wondering," she said, " whether it was not a case like that of Little Lord Fauntleroy, and whether Mrs. Halsey could not be

proved to be the wife of a prince, but I see
that cannot be the explanation of the matter ;
and I have concluded that Jim is her adopted
child. She must have taken him, when she
was in better circumstances, from the people
who brought him to this country when he
was a very little fellow, and so he has no
recollection of any other home."

"She always spoke of him as her very
own," I said, "and seemed fonder of him
than a foster-mother could be. It will be
very hard for her to part with him, if his
real relatives claim him."

"Not if he goes to high rank and great
estates," said Adelaide. "She probably had
no idea of his noble birth when she adopted
him ; and it just proves that bread cast upon
the waters returns, for he will probably care
for her right royally, when he comes into his
own, and she will find that adopting that
boy was the best investment she ever made
in her life."

Winnie came in while we were talking.

"Why didn't you tell us, Winnie," I asked,
"that Jim Halsey was the little prince ?"

"It did not seem necessary," Winnie replied, looking unnecessarily alarmed, as it
seemed to me.

"You pay his board directly to Miss Prillwitz, I suppose?" Adelaide said.

"No, I give it to his mother, and she sends
it by mail."

"Well, I don't see any harm in letting Miss
Prillwitz know that we know his mother,
and are helping in his support."

"I do, and I wish you would not tell her
this," Winnie entreated.

"Just as you please," Adelaide replied,
"but I hate mysteries."

"So do I," said Winnie, with a deep sigh.

"What is the matter with you, any way,
Winnie?" Adelaide asked.

"That is my business," Winnie replied,
shortly, and left the room, banging the door
behind her.

"Winnie isn't half as jolly as she used to
be," said Milly, in an injured tone. "I always depend on her to save me when I'm
not prepared for recitation. When Professor Todd was coming down the line in the
Virgil class and was only two girls away
from me, I made the most beseeching faces
at Winnie, who sits opposite, and usually
she is so quick to take the hint, and come to
the rescue by asking Professor Todd a lot
of questions about the sites of the ancient

cities, and where he thinks the Hesperides were situated. She gets him to talking on his pet hobbies, and he proses on like an old dear, until the bell rings for change of class. But this time she just stared at me in the most wall-eyed manner, while I signaled her in a perfect agony as he got nearer and nearer. I tried to think of some question of my own to ask him, and suddenly one popped into my head which I thought was very bright. He had just been talking about Æneas' shipwreck, and he referred to St. Paul's, with a description of the ancient vessels, and how he met the same Mediterranean storms, and I plucked up courage and said, 'Professor Todd, why is it that we hear so much about Virginia, and in all the pictures of the shipwreck we see her standing on the deck of the ship, and Paul rushing out into the surf to rescue her? Now I have read the chapter in Acts which describes St. Paul's shipwreck, very carefully, and in that, and in all the history of Paul, there is not one word about Virginia.'

"You should have heard the girls shout; I think they were just as mean as they could be. That odious Cynthia Vaughn nearly fell off the bench, and Professor Todd looked

at me in such a despairing way, as though
he gave me up from that time forth. I just
burst into tears, and Winnie came over and
took me out of the room. She acknowledged that it was all her fault, and that
she ought to have come to my rescue
sooner."

Poor Milly! we could only comfort her
with our assurances that we loved her all
the more for her troubles.

Summer was approaching, and we were
making our plans for vacation. Milly's
mother had invited Adelaide to spend the
season with them at their cottage at Narragansett Pier; and Winnie's father had consented to her spending June and July with
me on our Long Island farm. Winnie
cheered up somewhat at the prospect. "It's
the warm weather which makes me feel
muggy," she said; " I shall feel better when
we get out of the city too. The noise and
racket distract me, and seeing so many
miserable people makes me miserable and
sick at heart."

"I don't feel so at all," I replied. " It
makes me happy to see how much good
even we can do. Mrs. Halsey would not
have obtained her situation with Madame

Céleste but for us, or have been able to place Jim with Miss Prillwitz."

Winnie winced. "Don't talk about them; I am sick and tired of hearing about the little prince. Do you know, I don't believe he is a prince at all!"

"What Do you imagine that this story of Miss Prillwitz's is only a fabrication?"

"Perhaps so, or at least a hallucination on her part; and even if it is all true Jim may not be the boy. I wonder what proof she has of his identity, or whether she has written yet to his relatives. I mean to ask her —this very day."

But Winnie did nothing of the kind, for we were surprised on arriving at Miss Prillwitz's to find three new children sitting in the broad window-seats. One was a thin girl with crutches, whom I at once guessed must be Mary Hetterman; two chubby, freckle-faced little ones sat in the sunshine looking over a picture-book together, while Miss Prillwitz beamed upon them.

"My tears," she said, "you see I haf some more companie. Giacomo haf brought these small people to spend ze day."

Jim came in a little later, and introduced his friends. He was flushed and excited, and it presently appeared that the visit was a part of a deep-laid scheme of his own.

"I wanted you to know the Hettermans," he said, " because they are such nice children, and Rickett's Court is no place for them, for the family next door have the fever, and Mr. Grogan has the tremens, and scares them most to death. Mrs. Hetterman gets twenty dollars a month as cook now, and she says she can pay a dollar a week apiece for each of the children if she can board them where it is healthful and decent; and you young ladies were so kind as to help my mother at first, and now, as she don't need it any longer, maybe you would help the Hettermans, and then maybe Aunty would take them in. Mary is very handy, for all she's a cripple, and the babies' noise is just nothing but a pleasure, and—" here the tears stood in his eyes, and he looked at Miss Prillwitz, who was frozen stiff with astonishment, with piteous appealing—"and I would eat just as little as I could."

The good woman's voice trembled, " Take ze children to play in ze park," she said ; " ze young ladies and I, we talk it some over."

Mary Hetterman tied the children's hoods on with cheerful alacrity. She evidently had high hopes, while Jim threw his arms around Miss Prillwitz—" Aunty," he said, "they deserve that you should be kind to them more than I do."

"What reason is zere that I should take them in more as all ze uzzer children in ze court?"

"Just as much reason as for you to take me," replied the boy, running away.

"Bless his heart!" said Miss Prillwitz, as he closed the door; "he knows not ze reason zat draw me to him, ze cherubim. But I did not know you to help his muzzer until now."

Adelaide explained matters, and the case of the Hettermans was discussed, Miss Prillwitz agreeing to take them in if we would assist in their support. "I shall leaf zem in my apartement for ze summer," she said, "for it is necessaire to me zat I go ze shore of ze sea, and I s'all take Giacomo with me, for I cannot bear to separate myself of him. Zis is so near to your school zat Mrs. Hetterman can sleep her nights here. But I have not decided to myself where I shall repose myself for ze summer."

I spoke up quickly, referring her to Miss Sartoris for the beauties of our part of Long Island and for mother's low price for board.

Miss Prillwitz was evidently pleasantly impressed. She thought she would like to study the seaweed of that part of the coast, and when she heard of the lighthouse, against which the birds of passage dashed themselves, and how the keeper had kept their skins, waiting for some one to come that way and teach him to stuff them, she was quite decided in our favor.

I noticed that Winnie grew suddenly silent. As we left the house she pinched me softly. "You didn't mean any harm, Tib," she said, "but if they go, it will take every bit of pleasure out of my summer."

CHAPTER VII.

WILHELM KALB-FLEISCH, the butcher's boy, was one of the most uninteresting specimens of humanity that I have ever seen. That any of us would ever give him even a passing glance seemed quite beyond the range of probability, and yet Wilhelm's stolid, good-natured face haunted Winnie's dreams like a very Nemesis, and came to acquire a new and singular interest even in my own mind.

We passed a little Catholic church on our way to the boarding-school.

"We are early," said Winnie. "Let's go in."

It was Lent, and the altar was shrouded in black, and only a few candles burning dimly. We stood beside a carved confessional. A muffled murmur came from the interior, and the red curtains pulsated as though in time to sobs.

"Let us go out," whispered Milly; "I am stifling."

She looked so white that I was really afraid she was going to faint. "I feel better," she gasped, when we reached the open air.

"It was frightfully close," Winnie said, "and the air was heavy with incense."

"It was not that," said Milly, "it was the thought of it all; that there was a poor woman in that confessional telling all her sins to a priest. I never could do it in the world."

"It would be a comfort to me," said Winnie, fiercely. "I only wish there was some one with authority, to whom I could confess my sins, that I might get rid of the responsibility of them."

'There is," I said, before I thought; "'He hath borne our griefs and carried our sorrows.'"

Winnie gave me a quick look. "You

don't usually preach. Tib," she said, and burst into a merry round of stories and jokes, which convulsed the other girls, but did not in the least deceive me. I could see that she was troubled, and was trying to carry it off by riding her high horse. " Girls," she said, " I want you to come around to the butcher's with me. They have such funny little beasts in the window. I mean to get one, and the butcher's boy, Wilhelm, is such a princely creature—just my *beau ideal*—I want you to see him."

The funny little beasts proved to be forms of head-cheese in fancy shapes. Strange roosters and ducks, with plumage of gayly colored sugar icing, and animals of uncouth forms and colors. Winnie bought a small pig with a blue nose and green tail, all the while bombarding the butcher's boy, who was a particularly stupid specimen, with keen questions and witty sallies. He was so very obtuse that he did not even see that she was making sport of him.

As we hurried home to make up for our little escapade, Winnie amused us all by asking us how we thought Wilhelm would grace a princely station. "Just imagine, for an instant, that he was the lost Prince Paradiso ! What a figure he would cut in chain armor, or in a court costume of velvet and jewels ! Did you notice the elegance of his manners and the brilliancy of his wit ?"

" Winnie, Winnie, have you gone wild ?" Adelaide asked. " Why do you make such sport of the poor fellow ? He is well enough where he is, I am sure."

" Is he not ?" Winnie replied, a little more soberly ; " I was only thinking what a mercy it is that people are so well fitted for their stations in life by nature. Now, think of Jim as a butcher, growing up to chop sausage-meat and skewer roasts !"

" Jim never could be a butcher," Adelaide replied ; " even if Miss Prillwitz's dreams do not come true, the education she is giving him will do no harm. He will carve a future for himself."

We went into the house, and the subject was dropped. The next morning a message came from Miss Prillwitz that one of the Hetterman children was sick. It was the fever, contracted in their old home, and we were told that our botany lessons must be interrupted for the present. We heard through Mrs. Hetterman that the child was not very sick. It was one of the chubby lit-

tle ones that had looked so well. She was
quarantined now in Jim's room, the green one
up under the roof, and had a trained nurse
to care for her. Mrs. Hetterman did not see
the child, but talked with her daughter Mary
in the basement every evening She thought
it was a great mercy that they had completed their moving before the child was
taken sick. This did not seem to me to be
exactly generous to Miss Prillwitz, but I
could not blame the mother for the feeling,
for under the careful treatment the child
speedily weathered the storm, and came out
looking only a little paler for the confine-
ment. We were expecting a summons to
return to our lessons, when Mrs. Hetterman
told us that Jim was sick. We were not
greatly alarmed, for the little girl's illness
had been so slight that we fancied we would
see our favorite about in a fortnight.

Milly sent in baskets of white grapes and
flowers, and Adelaide carried over a beautiful set of photographs of Italian architec-
ture. "It may amuse him to look them
over," she said, "and it is just possible that
his ancestral palace figures among them."

Adelaide hoped to go to Europe as soon
as she graduated. "If Jim is established in

his rights by that time, I shall visit him," she said, "so, you see, I am only mercenary in my attentions to him now."

Winnie looked up indignantly, "Then you deserve to be disappointed."

Adelaide laughed merrily. "I thought you knew me well enough, Winnie, to tell when I am in fun. I like Jim so much, personally, that I would do as much for him if he had no great expectations; but I do not see that there is any harm in thinking of the kindnesses which he may be able to do me."

"If you don't count too surely on them. Miss Prillwitz has had time to notify his relatives, and they do not seem to take any interest in him."

It is the unexpected that always happens. That very evening Mrs. Hetterman brought us this note from Miss Prillwitz. She wrote better than she spoke, for on paper there was no opportunity for the foreign accent to betray itself:

"My dear young ladies:

"The elder brother have arrived, and I fear you will have no more opportunity to see little Giacomo, for I think he will take him away very shortly to his father's house.

"You must not be too sorry, but think what

a so great thing this is for poor little Giacomo, to be called so soon to his beautiful estate; no more poorness or trouble, in the palace of the King. Giacomo desire me to thank you for all you kindness to him. He hope some time you will all come to him at his beautiful country of everlasting spring-time, and the elder brother invite you also. Mrs. Halsey is here. She is much troubled. She forget that Giacomo was not her very own, and the pain of parting from him is great. She can not rightly think of the good fortune it is to him. She wish to go with him, but that is not possible for now. Giacomo hope you will comfort her. He hope, too, we will continue our care to the children Hetterman. Come not to-night, dear young ladies, to bid him farewells; I fear you to cry. and so to trouble his happiness.

" Your at all times loving teacher,

" CÉLESTINE PRILLWITZ."

" The idea of our crying, like so many babies !" said Emma Jane Anton; " why, it's the best thing that possibly could happen to him, and I, for one, shall congratulate him heartily.

" I suppose so," Milly assented, doubtfully, " but I shall miss him awfully, he is such a nice little fellow."

" So much the better," said Adelaide ;

"how glad the prince must be to find that his little brother is really presentable. As Winnie was saying, 'Fancy his feelings if he had found him a coarse, common creature like Wilhelm, the butcher's boy!' And now, Winnie, what do you say to my being too sure about visiting him some day? Here is the invitation from the prince himself. I wonder just where in Italy they live!"

So the girls chatted all together, but Winnie was strangely silent.

"I ought to see Miss Prillwitz at once," she exclaimed, suddenly.

"It's too late, now," replied Emma Jane; "there! the retiring-bell is ringing, and if you look across the square you can see that Miss Prillwitz's lights are all out; besides, she particularly requested us not to come until morning."

"Then I must run over before breakfast," said Winnie, "for it is very important."

She set a little alarm-clock for an hour earlier than our usual waking-time; but she was unable to sleep, and her restlessness kept me awake also. She tossed from side to side, and moaned to herself, and at last I heard her say, "Oh! what wouldn't I give if some one would only show me the best way out of it."

"Winnie," I said, softly, "I am not asleep. What is the matter? Are you in trouble?"

"Yes, Tib."

"Do you need money?"

"No."

"Are you in love?"

"The idea! A thousand times no."

"Are you going to be expelled?"

"Not unless I tell on myself; perhaps not even then. But oh, Tib, I told you I was in for a scrape. I thought I could stick it through, but it's worse than I thought. I can't keep the secret; I've got to tell."

"I would, and then you'll feel better."

"No, I will not, for telling will not do any good. I'm not sure but it will do harm."

"You poor child, what can it be?"

"Just this—Jim is *not* the prince."

"I don't see how you know that, or, if you do, what business it is of yours."

"Because I deceived Miss Prillwitz, and got Jim in there by making her think he was the boy she had heard about, while the real boy is somewhere else. I've *got* to tell her before his friends take him away, and before that other boy disappears from view entirely."

"That is really dreadful, but if you know where the true prince is, it can't be quite irreparable. What ever made you do such a thing? and how did you manage to do it?"

"Why, you see, I hadn't any faith in this story of a lost prince at all. I thought that Miss Prillwitz was just a little bit of a crank, who had been imposed on by designing people, and I was sure, when I saw the woman at the door who came to tell Miss Prillwitz that her boy had a situation and could not come, that she had been in league with the person who had told Miss Prillwitz about the lost prince, but had backed out of the plot because she was afraid. Miss Prillwitz had evidently not suspected that she knew anything of the boy's supposed expectations, for she had merely promised to take him to board, teach, and clothe, for whatever the mother could give her, the woman having said that she was going into a family as German nursery governess, and agreeing to send a trifle toward her boy's support whenever she received her salary. It was just the time that Mrs. Halsey was looking for a place for Jim. It was so easy to have him

come at the time agreed upon and
take the place of the other boy. I was
afraid, at first, that Miss Prillwitz would be
surprised by the regularity of our pay-
ments and the amount we sent, but she
didn't seem to suspect anything, and she
is so fond of him, and he deserves it all—
and everything worked so well up to the
coming of the prince."

" But, Winnie, why didn't you tell her the
whole story at first ? I think she would have
taken him, all the same, and then you would
not have got things into this awful mud-
dle."

" Indeed she would not have taken him, a
mere pauper out of the slums, unless she
had thought that he was something more.
She is a born aristocrat, and she never could
have taken Jim to her heart so if she had
not believed that he was of her own class—
of her family, even. Why, even Adelaide
would never have seen half the fine qualities in him which she thinks she has discovered if she had not thought him a
noble ; and it has thrown a fine halo of romance over him for Milly ; and even Emma
Jane, who was hard to convince at first, is
firmly persuaded that he is made of a little

finer clay than the rest of us. And you, Tib, confess that you are disappointed yourself."

"I am bitterly disappointed," I admitted; "but that is nothing to the extent that Miss Prillwitz will feel it. I wouldn't be in your shoes, Winnie, for anything."

"I know it; I know it. I have been wicked, but I had no idea that the family would ever look him up. I hardly believed the story that there had been any prince lost. And, Tib, if there had not been, where would have been the harm in what I did?"

"It would have been wrong, all the same, Winnie, even if it had seemed to turn out well. Deception is always wrong, and I did not think it of you. But there, don't sob so, or you will make yourself sick, and you need all your wits and strength to carry you through the ordeal of setting things straight to-morrow. I'll stand by you. I'll go with you if it will be any help."

"No, you shall not; Miss Prillwitz might think you were implicated in the affair. The fault was all mine, and I will not have any one else share the blame; only be on hand at the door, Tib, with an ambulance to carry away the remnants, for I shall be all broken into smithereens by the interview."

I tried to soothe the excited girl, and fancied that she had fallen asleep, when she suddenly began to laugh hysterically.

"I haven't told you who the real prince is," she said. "Aren't you curious to know?"

"Have I ever met him?"

"Yes, indeed; it's Wilhelm the butcher's boy."

"Impossible!"

"Isn't it too absurd for anything? That was the situation which his mother, or foster-mother, preferred to Miss Prillwitz's care. What will Adelaide say now about blue blood telling even in low circumstances? There is *blood* enough about Wilhelm if that is all that is desired. And won't that foreign prince be just raving when he is introduced to his long-lost brother! But poor Miss Prillwitz!—that's the worst of all. No doubt she has been writing with pride and delight the most glowing letters in reference to Jim's fitness for his high position. How chagrined and mortified the dear old lady will be! Tell me now, Tib, that things were not better as I managed them."

"It does seem as if there must be a mistake somewhere. Still, the truth is the truth, and I believe in telling it, even if the

Heavens fall. This matter is all in the hands of Providence, Winnie, and I believe you got into trouble simply by thinking that you knew better than Providence, and that the world could not move on without you."

"I must say you are rather hard on me, Tib, but perhaps you are right. Do you suppose that if I hand the tangle I have made right to God, he will take it from my hands and straighten it out for me? I should think He would have nothing more to do with it, or with me."

"That is not the way our mothers behave when we get our work into a snarl."

This last remark comforted her. She laid her head upon my shoulder and prayed:

"Dear Heavenly Father, I have done wrong, and everything has gone wrong. Help me henceforth to do right, and wilt Thou make everything turn out right. For thy dear Son's sake, I ask it. Amen."

Then trustfully she fell asleep, her conscience relieved of a great weight, and with faith in a power beyond her own.

CHAPTER VIII.

OTWITHSTAND-
ING Winnie's pro-
testations to the
contrary, I insist-
ed on going with
her the next morn-
ing when she went
to make her con-
fession.

The little alarm-
clock made its
usual racket, but
Winnie slept
peacefully, and I
was dressed be-
fore I could make
up my mind to
waken her. But I knew how disappointed
she would be if she could not make her call

on Miss Prillwitz before breakfast, and I wakened her with a kiss, and made her a cup of coffee over the gas while she was dressing. Then we put on our ulsters and hoods, and slipped out of the house just as the rising-bell was ringing.

We knew that Miss Prillwitz was habitually an early riser, or we would not have planned to call at such an hour, but we were surprised to find a cab standing before her door.

"I wonder whether the prince and Jim are just about to leave," Winnie exclaimed. "I did not know that any of the ocean steamers sailed so early in the morning. What if they have gone and we are too late!"

Something was the matter with the door-bell, and just as we were about to knock, the door opened and a stout gentleman came down the steps, and drove away in the carriage. Jim was not with him, and Miss Prillwitz stood inside the door.

Winnie caught her arm and asked, "Was that the prince, the elder brother?"

"No, tear," said Miss Prillwitz, gravely. "Why haf you come, when I write you you must not?"

"Oh Miss Prillwitz, it was because I have

something so particular, so important, to tell you. Do not tell me that Jim has gone, and that it is too late!"

"No, tear, Giacomo haf not gone already. I think ze elder brother take him very soon, and we keep our little Giacomo not one leetle longer. Go in ze park by ze bench and I vill come and talk zare wiz you."

We wondered at her unwillingness to let us in, but obeyed her directions, and presently she came out to us with a shawl thrown about her and a knitted boa outside her cap. Even then she did not sit near us, but on a bench at a little distance, having first noted carefully that the wind blew from our direction toward her. All this might have seemed strange to us had we not been so thoroughly absorbed in what Winnie was about to say. The poor child blundered into her story at once, and told it in such broken fashion that Miss Prillwitz never could have understood it but for my explanations. When we had finished, the tears stood in Miss Prillwitz's eyes.

"My tear child," she said, kindly, drawing nearer to us, "how you haf suffer! Yes, you have done a sin, but you are sorry, and God he forgive ze sorrowful."

"But do you forgive me, Miss Prillwitz?" Winnie cried, passionately. "Can you ever love me again?"

"Yes, my tear, I forgive you freely, and I love you more as ever."

"And the elder brother and Jim? Have Jim's expectations been raised? Will he be greatly disappointed, and will the prince be very angry?"

"My tear, in all zis it is not as you have t'inked. See, you haf not understand my way of talk. I t'ink Giacomo will, all ze same, pretty soon go to his Fazzer's house. Ze elder brother is may be gone wiz him by now. You have not, then, understand zat dis elder brother is ze Lord Christ? zat ze beautiful country is Heaven? Our little Giacomo lie very sick. Ze doctor, whom justly you did meet, he gif no hope. His poor muzzer sit by him so sad, so sad, it tear my heart. She cannot see he go to ze palace to be one Prince del Paradiso."

We sat bolt upright, dazed and stunned by this astounding information.

"Do you mean to say," Winnie said, slowly, grasping her head as though laboring to concentrate her ideas, "that Jim is dying, and that he is no more a prince than any of us?

I mean that the other boy is not a real prince, and that no child ever strayed away from its father's house, or elder brother has been seeking for a lost one? Oh Miss Prillwitz, how could you make up such a story?"

"My tear, my tear, it is all true, and I t'ought you to understand my leetle vay of talk. Giacomo is a prince in disguise; you, my tears, are daughters of ze great King. Zat uzzer boy, ze butcher, he also inherit ze same heavenly palace. All ze children what come in zis world haf wander avay from zat home, and ze elder brother he go up and down looking for ze lost. He gif me commission; he gif effery Christians commissi a to find zose lost prince—to teach him and fit him for his high position. I did not have intention to deceive you, my tear. It was my little vay of talk."

"Oh! oh!" exclaimed Winnie, "I feel as if my brain were turning a somersault, but I cannot realize it. Then I did not really deceive you, after all, Miss Prillwitz, though I was just as wicked in intending to do so. And Jim—do not say there is no hope!"

"No, my tear. I know all ze time zis was not ze boy I expect. But I say to myself,

9

'How he come I know not, but he is also ze child of ze King.' Ze elder brother want him to be care for also. May be ze elder brother send him, and I take him very gladly. And surely, I never find one child to prove his title to be one Prince of Paradise better as Giacomo. So gentle, so loving, so generous and soughtful. I not wonder at all ze elder brother want him. I sank him, I sank you, too, Winnie, I have privilege to know one such lovely character."

Miss Prillwitz looked at her watch. "I can no longer," she said quickly, and hurried back to her home. We crossed the park thoughtfully and entered the school. There was just time to tell the girls the news before chapel. The knowledge that dear Jim was lying at death's door overwhelmed every other consideration, and yet we talked over Miss Prillwitz's little allegory also.

"We were stupid not to see through it at first," said Adelaide. "She is just the woman to create an ideal world for herself and to live in it. I have no grudge against her because we misunderstood her meaning, and yet there certainly is something very fine in Jim's nature."

"Now I think it all over," said Emma

Jane, "she has said nothing which was not true."

"I understand her letter better now," I said. "We have all been parts of a beautiful parable, and we have been as thick-headed as the disciples were when Jesus said, 'O fools, and slow of heart to believe.'"

Milly was silently weeping. "All the beauty of the idea doesn't change the fact that Jim is dying," she said.

"I have never loved any one so since I lost my mother and my baby brother," said Adelaide. "I can't remember how he looked —it was ten years ago, and I have no photographs, only this cameo pin, which father bought because it reminded him of mother. Not the face either, only the turn of the neck. He said she had a beautiful neck— and as he came home from his business at night he always saw her sitting in her little sewing-chair by the window looking every now and then over her shoulder for him with her neck turned so, and her profile clear cut against the dark of the room like the two colors of agate in this cameo."

It is not natural for girls to talk freely on what stirs them most deeply, and little more was said on the subject that morning, but we each thought a great deal, and if our hearts could have been laid bare to each other, we would have been startled by the similarity of the trains of thought which this event had roused. All through the morning's lessons our imaginations wandered to the house across the park, and we wondered whether all was indeed over, and dear, cheery, helpful Jim had gone. We did not remember that we had declared we would gladly let him go to an earthly princedom, and yet this was far better for him. Our imaginations saw only the white upturned face upon the pillow, the grief - stricken mother, and Miss Prillwitz flitting about drawing the sheet straight, and placing white lilacs in his hands.

Adelaide confessed to me, long after, that all of her worldly thoughts in reference to visiting Jim some day came back to her in a strange, sermonizing way. She said that in her secret heart she had rather dreaded the visit because she knew so little of the etiquette of foreign courts, and was afraid she might make some mistake. She had even studied several books on the subject, and knew the sort of costume it was necessary to wear in a royal presentation, just the

length of the train, the degree of décolletée,
and the veil, and the feathers. The thought
came over her with great vividness that she
had never studied the etiquette of Heaven
or attempted to provide herself with
garments fit for the presence of the King.
Mrs. Hetterman had a habit of singing
quaint old hymns. There was one which
we often heard echoing up from the basement—

> "At His right hand our eyes behold
>   The queen arrayed in purest gold;
>   The world admires her heavenly dress,
>   Her robe of joy and righteousness."

This scrap was borne in upon Adelaide's
mind now. "A robe of joy and righteous-
ness," she thought to herself; "I wonder
how it is made! it surely must be becoming."
Then she thought again of her mingled
motives, of how glad she had been that she
had befriended Jim because she could claim
him as an acquaintance as a prince, in that
foreign country, and how she had wished
that she might entertain more traveling
members of the nobility in his country in
order to have more acquaintances at court.
"If the poor are Christ's brothers and sisters," she said to herself, "I have abundant

opportunity to make many friendships which may be carried over into that unknown country;" and a new purpose awoke in her heart, which had for its spring not the most unselfish motives, but a strong one, and destined to achieve good work, and to give place in time to higher aims.

Afternoon came, and no message had arrived from Jim "Girls," said Adelaide, as we sat in the Amen Corner, "if Jim dies, I propose that we carry this sort of work on of fitting poor children for something higher, and broaden it, as a memorial to him. I don't exactly see my way yet, but we can do a good deal if we band together and try."

"Oh! don't talk about Jim's dying," said Milly, "we'll do it, anyway."

"I can't see why we don't hear from Miss Prillwitz," said Winnie, impatiently. "It is recreation hour; let us go out into the park, and perhaps she will see us and send us some word."

We walked around and around the paths which were in view from Miss Prillwitz's windows. Presently we saw Mary Hetterman coming toward us with a note in her hand.

"I know just what that note says," exclaimed Milly, sinking upon a bench. "The little prince has gone to his estates."

"Hush!" exclaimed Adelaide. "See! is it a ghost? We looked as she pointed, and saw at Jim's window a perfect representation of Adelaide's cameo. A white face against the dark interior. It vanished as she spoke, leaving us all with a strange, eerie sensation, a feeling that this was certainly an omen of Jim's death. But our premonitions, like so many others, did not come true. The note was not for us. Mary Hetterman passed us with a smile and a nod, and a moment later Miss Prillwitz herself came out to us.

We knew by her face that she brought good news, but none of us spoke until she answered our unuttered question.

"No, tears, Jim haf not gone. Ze prince haf been here, but I sink he not take him zis time already. The doctor sink we keep him one leetle time longer. I cannot stay. It is time I go give him his medicine, and let loose ze nurse, for I care for him ze nights. Good-bye, my tears. Ah! I am so happy zat ze little prince go not yet to his estates; so happy, and yet so sleepy also." And we noticed for the first time the great dark rings which want of sleep and anxiety had drawn around Miss Prillwitz's eyes.

"Good-bye, princess," I cried; "surely no one deserves that title more than you, for you have proved yourself a royal daughter of the King. We have called you so a long time among ourselves—our Princess del Paradiso."

She smiled, waved her hand, and vanished into the queer house which she had made a palace.

It was some time before Adelaide could recover from the shock of the apparition at the window, though we assured her that it was probably only the trained nurse; and we afterward ascertained that it was in reality Mrs. Halsey, who had come to the window for a moment to greet the glad new day, and who was now as joyful as she had been despairing. So much tension of feeling, so great extremes of joy and sorrow, had affected her deeply, and she wept out her gratitude on Miss Prillwitz's sympathizing heart. "You have been very good to him," Mrs. Halsey said, with emotion. "Some time, when the past all comes back to me, as I am sure it will some day, I may be able to return your kindness."

Mrs. Halsey had made several mysterious allusions to the past, and Miss Prillwitz, who had a kindly way of gaining the confidence of everyone, said sweetly, "Tell me about your early life, my dear."

"It is a strange story." Mrs. Halsey replied. "I had a happy childhood and girlhood, and a happy married life up to the time that my dear parents died, and even after that, for my husband was the best of men, and I had a sweet little daughter. Their faces come back to me, waking and sleeping, though I have lost them, I sometimes fear, forever."

"Did they die?" Miss Prillwitz asked.

"No, dear, I think not; but now comes the strange part of my story: I remember a journey vaguely, and a steamer disaster, a night of horror with fire and water, and then all is a frightful blank; a curtain of blackness seems to have fallen on all my past life. I am told that I was rescued from the burning of a Sound steamer, with my baby-boy in my arms, and given shelter by some kindly farmer folk. I had received an injury—a blow on the head—and had brain-fever, from which I recovered in body, but with a disordered mind, my memory shattered; I could remember faces, but not names. I could not tell the name of the town in which I had lived, or my own name. I remained with the kind people who first received me for several months, but I did not wish to be a burden to them, and I hoped that I might find my home. I knew that it had been in a city, and I felt sure that if I ever saw any of my old surroundings, or old friends I would recognize them at once. It was thought, too, that New York physicians might help me, so I came to New York, and my case was advertised in the papers. But months had passed since the accident, and my friends either did not see the advertisement, or did not recognize me in the story given. The doctors at the hospital pronounced me incurable, and I was discharged. I wandered up and down the streets, but although I felt sure that I had been in New York before, I could not find my home. I read the names on the signs, hoping to recognize my own name, but I never came across it. Meantime I took the name of Halsey; it was necessary for me to live, and I knew that I could sew, and that I had a faculty for designing; and seeing Madame Céleste's advertisement for a designer. I applied at once for the situation. It seemed to me at first that I had seen Madame

Céleste before, but she was repellent in manner, and I did not dare question her, and gradually that impression faded. I hired a woman to take care of Jim, and though he was not well cared for, he lived, and we got on until he was large enough to play upon the streets. Then I took him home to the little room in Rickett's Court, and finding that I could not be with him as much as he needed, I gave up my place at Madame Céleste's and worked at first for the costumer, where the young ladies found me, and afterward tried to keep soul and body together by taking sewing home. It was the life of a galley-slave, but I did not care so long as I could keep my boy at school, and with me out of school hours. But I could not do that, for to earn the money which was absolutely necessary for our support Jim had to work too, and driving the milkman's cart in the early morning was the best we could find for him out of school hours. He was so proud and happy to do it, and to help earn for us both; but, as you know, it cut into his hours for sleep, and left him no time to study. Oh! I was nearly in despair, when God sent you as angels to my help and Jim's."

"And have you never been able to guess

what your old name was?" Miss Prillwitz
asked.

"Never; sometimes it seems to me that I
remember it in my dreams, but when I
awake it is gone; still, I cannot help feeling
that I shall find my own again. Sometimes
there comes a great inward illumination, and
the curtain seems to be lifting. I cannot
think they have forgotten me—my husband
tender and true, and my little girl with the
great questioning eyes."

Miss Prillwitz did not share Mrs. Halsey's
confidence, but her sympathy was enlisted,
and she caressed and comforted Mrs. Halsey.
"It shall be as you hope, my tear; if not
just now and here, zen surely by and by,
and zat is not very long. And meantime
you have found some friends, ze young
ladies and me, and ze Elder Brother have
found you, and we are all one family, so
you can be no longer lonely and wizout
relation, even in zis world."

CHAPTER IX

THE KING'S DAUGHTERS AND THE VENETIAN FÊTE.

"O ladies, dear ladies, the next sunny day,
Please trundle your hoops just out of Broadway,
From its whirl and its bustle, its fashion and pride,
And the temples of trade which tower on each side,
To the alleys and lanes where Misfortune and Guilt
Their children have gathered, their city have built.

Then say, if you dare,
Spoiled children of fashion, you've nothing to wear!"

MILLY ROSE-VELDT made an important entry in her diary a few days after this. She was very exact about keeping her diary, recording for the most p a r t, however, very trivial matters, but the day that she wrote "We have organized a 'King's Daughters Ten'" was a day with a white stone in it, and deserved to be remembered.

Jim had passed the crisis of the fever, and recovered rapidly. Neither of the other Hettermans was taken ill. The house was thoroughly cleansed and disinfected, and after a few weeks we took up our interrupted botany lessons. But Jim's illness had made more than a transient impression, and Adelaide's suggestion that we should broaden and deepen our work was talked over amongst us.

"There is a society," said Emma Jane, "which I have heard of somewhere, which is called 'The King's Daughters.' I think they have much the same idea that Miss Prillwitz has expressed. It is formed of separate links of ten members, bound together by the common purpose of doing good. Now, I think, we might form such a link, with Miss Prillwitz for our president. There are five of us, but we need five more. Whom shall we ask?"

"Girls," said Winnie, "I'm afraid you won't agree, but there is real good stuff in those Hornets."

"The Hornets! Oh, never!"

"What an idea!"

"Why, they hate us!"

"No, they simply think that we despise them."

"Well, so we do. I am sure, the way that Cynthia Vaughn behaves is simply despicable."

"Perhaps so," Winnie admitted, " but the other three girls are not so bad. Little Breeze"—that was our nickname for Tina Gale—" is a real good-natured girl, and a perfect genius for getting up things. When I roomed in the Nest she was devoted to me; so they all were, for that matter. I could make them do whatever I pleased, and Rosaria Ricos, the Cuban heiress, is just as generous as she can be. Trude Middleton is a great Sunday-school worker when she is at home, and Puss Seligman's mother has a longer calling-list than Milly's, I do believe. Don't you remember what a lot of tickets she sold for the theatricals? If we are going to get up a charitable society we must use some brains to make it succeed, and those girls are a power. You know very well that it is the Hornets' Nest and the Amen Corner which support the literary society, and when we unite on any ticket-selling or other enterprise it is sure to succeed."

" Yes," replied Emma Jane Anton, " that is because we appeal to entirely different sets of girls—between us we carry the entire school."

"I will take all in," said Adelaide, "except Cynthia. She has been too hateful to Tib and Milly for anything !"

"Oh, don't mind me," murmured Milly; "I dare say she could not help laughing when I made that mistake about Paul and Virginia."

"I don't believe she will join us," I said, doubtfully ; "but I am sure I would a great deal rather have her for a friend than an enemy."

"She will be so surprised and flattered that she will be as sweet as jam," said Winnie, confidently. "You have no idea what a lofty reputation you girls have. I used to reverence and envy you until it amounted to positive hatred. That is what made me behave so badly. I knew we couldn't approach you in good behavior, and I determined to take the lead in something. That's just the way with Cynthia. She imagines that you would not touch her with a ten-foot pole, and she wants you to think that she doesn't care, but she does."

Milly promptly furnished the wherewithal for a spread, and the Hornets were invited.

Adelaide said that they acted as if a sense of gratification were struggling with a sneaking consciousness of unworthiness, and it was all that she could do not to display the scorn which she was afraid she felt. But Milly was as sweetly gracious as only Milly knew how to be, and Winnie put them all at their ease with her rollicking good-fellowship. I was sure that Cynthia at first suspected some trick, but even she succumbed at last to our praise of her banjo-playing, which was really admirable. They melted completely with the ice-cream—little ducks with strawberry heads and pistache wings; and when Winnie told them the entire story of the little prince they were greatly interested.

" Now," said Winnie, " I have been talking with Jim, and he says that the tenement house in which he lived swarms with children who ought not to pass the summer there, who will die if they do ; and what I want to propose is, that we club together and have some sort of entertainment, to send them to the country, or do something else for them."

The proposition met with favor, as did the plan for the King's Daughters society, which was organized at once, and officered as follows, the "spoils" being divided equally between the Amen Corner and the Hornets:

President—Miss Prillwitz.

Vice-Presidents—Adelaide Armstrong and Gertrude Middleton.

Secretary—Cynthia Vaughn.

Treasurer—Emma Jane Anton.

Executive Committee—The foregoing officers and the rest of the society.

"Little Breeze" then made a practical suggestion: "You know," said she, "that the literary society is always allowed to give an entertainment the week before the graduating exercises, to put the treasury in funds, or, rather, to pay old debts. We have no debts this year, and I am sure that the society will let us have the occasion. Whatever we ten favor is sure to be carried in the literary society."

"That is what I said," remarked Winnie.

"So if Miss Anton will get Madame's permission for the change, I have no doubt we can make at least three hundred dollars."

"Nonsense! we will make twice that," said Puss Hastings."

"But what shall we have?"

"I know the sweetest thing," said Little Breeze. " A Venetian Fête! It is really a fair, but the booths are all made to represent gondolas. They are painted black, and have their prows turned toward the centre of the room. We can have it in the gymnasium. The gondolas are canopied in different colors and hung with bright lanterns. We must all be dressed in Venetian costume, and have music and some pretty dances. It will be lovely !"

The fair was planned out : each girl had a gondola assigned her, with permission to work other girls in, and enthusiasm had reached a high pitch, when the retiring-bell clanged and the Hornets took their departure, the utmost good feeling prevailing between what had been until this evening rival factions of the school.

After our next botany lesson we lingered to inform Miss Prillwitz of what we had done, and to ask her to accept the Presidency of our ten. She listened with much interest.

" My tears," she said, " I sink perhaps you s'all do much good. I have justly been sinking, sinking ; but ze need is great. I know not how we s'all come at ze money which we do need."

Then Miss Prillwitz explained that she had visited Rickett's Court, and had found so many little children in those vile surroundings; some of them, whose mothers were servants in families, and received good wages, were "boarding" with Mrs. Grogan, the baby-farmer. She had met one such mother in the court — a waitress on Fifth Avenue, who had three children with Mrs. Grogan.

"I pay her fifteen dollars a month," she said; "it is cheaper than I can board them elsewhere, and all that I can pay; but it makes my heart sick to see them sleeping and playing beside sewers and sinks, and to have them exposed to language of infinitely worse foulness. I know that if they do not die in childhood, of which there is every likelihood, they will grow up bad; and I don't know which I would choose for them. I wouldn't mind slaving for them, if there was any hope, if I could see them in decent surroundings, with some prospect of their turning out well in the end; but now, when I ask myself what all my toil amounts to, it seems to me that the best thing which could happen to us all would be to die."

The waitress knew of other servants who could have no home of their own for their children, but who could pay something for their support, and whose maternal love and feeling of independence kept them from giving their children up to institutions; who had entrusted their little ones to bad people, who hired them to beggars, beat and half starved them. And now the summer was approaching, and it was dreadful to think of those closely packed tenement houses under the stifling heat.

Miss Prillwitz said that it had seemed to her positively wrong for her to go away to the seashore for the summer while so many must remain and suffer.

'I don't see that," said Adelaide, "unless by staying you can make their condition better."

" Perhaps I can so." replied Miss Prillwitz, " if ze King's Daughters will help me." And then she developed a plan of Jim's. He had noticed the vacant floors in her house, which had remained unlet all the winter. " If you could rent them for the summer, Miss Prillwitz," he had suggested, " we wouldn't need much furniture, but could just invite a lot of the children in and let them camp down. The rooms are so clean, and there is such lovely fresh air and no smells, and such beautiful bath-tubs, and the park for the little ones to play in, and Mary Hetterman could watch them."

"You forget," Miss Prillwitz had replied, "zat zose children are use probably to eat somet'ings."

No, Jim had not forgotten that, but Mrs. Hetterman would be out of a place for the summer vacation, and would cook for them, and the children's mothers would pay something, and he would do the marketing. After the public school closed the older children could earn something, he thought. He was all on fire with the idea, and his enthusiasm had communicated itself to our princess. "I haf even vent to see my landlord," she confessed; "he is von very rich man. I sought maybe he let me use ze rooms for ze summer, since he cannot else rent them. But no, he did not so make his wealths. We can have them von hundred dollar ze months; six months, five hundred. We cannot else. Now do you sink you make five hundred dollar from your fair?"

"Oh, I think so; indeed, I am sure of it!" Adelaide exclaimed; "dear little Jim, what an angel he is! We will go right to work and see what we can do."

Of course the fair was a success, as fairs go. I have since thought that a fair is a poor way for Christian people to give money to any charitable purpose. So much goes astray from the goal, so much is swallowed up in the expenses, that if people would only put their hands in their pockets and give at the outset what they do give in the aggregate, more would be realized, and much time, vexation, and labor saved. But people do not yet recognize this, and we knew no better than to follow in the old way. I had charge of the Art gondola, with Miss Sartoris and all the Studio girls to help me. We decided that, as it was a Venetian fête, we would make a specialty of Italian art. Miss Sartoris suggested etchings, and one of the leading art dealers allowed us to make our choice from his entire collection, giving them to us at wholesale, as he would to any other retail dealer, we to sell them at the regular retail price, thereby taking no unfair advantage over our purchasers, and yet making a handsome profit on each etching sold, while we ran no risk, as all unsold stock was to be returned.

We were surprised to find how many Venetian subjects had been etched. There were half a dozen different views of St. Mark's Cathedral—exteriors and interiors; San Giorgios and La Salutes ; there were Rainy Nights in Venice, and Sunny Days in Venice, canals and bridges, shipping and palaces, piazzas and archways and cloisters.

Then we obtained a quantity of photographs of the Italian master-pieces, chiefly from the works of Titian and the Venetian school, though we included also the Madonnas of Raphael. Miss Sartoris found an italian curiosity-shop, which was a perfect treasure-trove, for here we secured, on commission, a quantity of Venetian glass beads, the beautiful blossomed variety, with tiny smelling-bottles of the same material, together with sleeve-buttons of Florentine mosaic, ornaments of pink Neapolitan coral, and broken pieces of antique Roman marbles, all of which we sold at immense profit. We had not thought of having any statuary, until Jim came to us, one afternoon, saying that Miss Prillwitz had told him that we intended to have an Italian fête, and as several of the families whom he wished benefited were Italians, who lived in Rickett's Court, he thought they might help us.

"What do they do?" I asked.

"The older Stavini boys peddle plaster-of-paris images, and some of them are very pretty. Pietro will bring you a basket of them, I am sure, and take back all you don't sell."

The plaster casts proved to be artistic and new. There was a set of five singing cherubs which we had seen on sale in the stores at twenty-five dollars a set, which Pietro offered us at fifty cents each, and others in like proportion. We sold his entire basketful at advanced prices, and received several orders for duplicates.

Winnie had charge of the refreshment department, and had a troop of the "preparatories" dressed as contadinas, who were to serve Neapolitan ices in colored glasses. Jim enabled her to introduce a very taking novelty by telling her of Vincenzo Amati, a cook in an Italian restaurant, who had three motherless little girls who were candidates for the summer home. Vincenzo agreed to come and cook for us while the fair lasted, Mrs. Hetterman kindly giving him place in the kitchen, so that we were able to add to our other attractions that of a real Italian supper, served on little tables in an adjoining recitation-room. Vincenzo brought us several dozen Chianti wine flasks, the empty bottles at the restaurant having been one of his perquisites. They were of graceful shapes, with slender necks, and wound in wicker, which Miss Sartoris gilded and further ornamented with a bow of bright satin ribbon. These flasks, empty, decorated each of the little tables, and one was given to each guest as a souvenir.

The menu consisted of—

Riso con piselli, }
Minestra Zuppa, } (Soup).
Olives.
Bistecca (Beefsteak).
Macaroni al burro (with butter).
Macaroni a pomidoro (with potatoes).
Testa de vitello (Calf's head).
Carciofi (Artichokes).
Cavolifiori (Cauliflower).
Salami di Bologna (Bologna Sausage).
Crostata di frutti (Fruit tarts).
Formaggio (Cheese).

Adelaide was musical director, and led the singing class in " Dolce Napoli " and other Italian songs. The girls were dressed in costume, and there was one fisher chorus, which made a very effective tableau with a background of colored sails and nets. Vin-

cenzo allowed his little girls to appear with
a neighbor's hand - organ, and when they
passed their tambourines they gathered a
goodly harvest of pennies.

Little Breeze arranged the tableaux and
the dances, Mrs. Halsey sending in designs
for the costumes ; and Cynthia Vaughn ran
a side show of stereopticon views, Professor
Todd kindly working the lantern.

Milly had the flower gondola, or booth of
cut flowers, supplied from her father's conser-
vatory, and Miss Prillwitz contributed to this
department a quantity of little albums and
herbaria containing pressed flowers and seaweed from different Italian cities.   Our dear
princess was present, beaming with happiness, and the " ten " introduced her proudly to their parents and friends. Mr. Roseveldt
seemed much interested, in an amused way,
in what we were trying to do. " Go ahead,
my dear," he said to Milly, " and if you don't
come to me to shoulder a lot of bad debts
before the summer is over, I shall be greatly
surprised, and have a far higher respect for
what little girls can do than I now possess."

" ' Little girls,' indeed!" Milly repeated, with
scorn. " There are younger gentlemen, sir,
who consider us young ladies, if you do not.

But we will compel your respect, and we will not ask you for one penny either."

This was rather hard, for we had secretly hoped, all along, that Milly's father would help us, and now she had made it a point of pride not to ask him. He behaved very well, however, for although he bantered us cruelly on our Utopian enterprise, he bought a button-hole bouquet of his own violets from Milly, paying a five-dollar bill for it and neglecting to ask for change, and then took Miss Prillwitz, Madame, Emma Jane Anton, Miss Sartoris, and Miss Hope successively out to supper. He purchased, too, an alabaster model of the Leaning Tower of Pisa, which Madame had contributed on condition that it should be sold for not less than twenty dollars, and which we had feared would not be disposed of, as we had voted that there should be no raffling. Madame was greatly interested in the fair; it drew attention to her school, and she smiled on everyone—a self-constituted reception committee. She was even gracious to the cadet band which had serenaded the school in the fall term. The cadets to a man invited Milly out to dinner. She went with each of them in succession, and as the viands were sold *à la carte*, she bravely ordered the

WITCH WINNIE.—*Page 155.*

more expensive dishes over and over again, enduring a martyrdom of dyspepsia for a week in consequence.

Of course Jim was present, and his mother. Adelaide was attentive to both; there seemed to be a mutual attraction that kept them together, and whenever Adelaide left Mrs. Halsey, and taking up her baton (Milly's curling-stick), led her ochestra. Mrs. Halsey's eyes followed her with a strange wistfulness. Winnie, with her usual heedlessness, had neglected to introduce Adelaide to Mrs. Halsey when she called on her in the court, and she now turned to Jim and asked her name. It happened that Jim thought that she referred to the pianist instead of to Adelaide, and he replied that the young lady in question was Miss Hope. the music-teacher. Mrs. Halsey gave a little sigh of disappointment, and continued her spell-bound gaze. I was about to correct the mistake which I was sure Jim had made, when it was announced that Mrs. Le Moyne, the celebrated interpreter of Robert Browning, would kindly recite a poem of Mrs. Browning's. Mrs. Halsey and Jim moved nearer the rostrum, and my opportunity for explanation was lost. If I had known the

effect that the name of Adelaide Armstrong
would have had upon Mrs. Halsey, chains
could not have kept me in my gondola—so
many invisible gates of opportunity are
closed and opened to us all along life's pathway!

The poem recited was, most appropriately,
"The Cry of the Children." Tears welled
into the eyes of many a mother as the
practiced art of the speaker rendered most
feelingly the pathetic words

> "But these others—children small,
>   Spilt like blots about the city
> Quay and street and palace wall—
>   Take them up into your pity !
>
> Patient children—think what pain
>   Makes a young child patient yonder ;
> Wronged too commonly to strain
>   After right, or wish or wonder·
>
> Sickly children, that whine low
>   To themselves and not their mothers,
> From mere habit, never so –
>   Hoping help or care from others;
>
> Healthy children, with those blue
>   English eyes, fresh from their Maker
> Fierce and ravenous, staring through
>   At the brown loaves of the baker,

Can we smooth down the bright hair,
  O my sisters, calm, unthrilled in
Our hearts' pulses?   Can we bear
  The sweet looks of our own children?

O my sisters! Children small,
  Blue-eyed, wailing through the city—
Our own babes cry in them all;
  Let us take them into pity!"

That poem was worth a great deal to our cause. Those of the mothers of our Ten who were present were won to us at once.

Mrs. Middleton, our vice-president's mother, and the wife of a clergyman, entered into our scheme with enthusiasm, and felt sure that her husband's church would assist us.

Mrs. Seligman and Mrs. Roseveldt put their heads together and planned to interest their society friends. One of hers. Mrs. Roseveldt was sure, would contribute the coal, and another the flour, while Mrs. Seligman would provide the blankets, and a friend of her acquaintance would certainly assume the butcher's bill. Madame Céleste, the dressmaker, who was present, was about to refurnish her parlors, and would contribute curtains. Madame Céleste bought a quantity of my photographs of old Italian

11

portraits, and I have no doubt that they were very serviceable to her in the way of suggestions for æsthetic costumes.

We knew before the evening closed that the fair must have realized more than we had hoped, and Emma Jane, the Treasurer of the new society, announced at our next meeting that the fair had cleared six hundred dollars. Vociferous applause followed, and we immediately adjourned to Miss Prillwitz's to report the unexpectedly happy result.

Our princess had talked over the scheme with such of our mothers as were present at the fair; and she now advised that we create them a board of managers of the proposed Home, to carry it on for us, as we were all minors, and lacked the necessary experience, we to labor for it harder than ever. This was immediately done, and after this, affairs marched with great rapidity. The Home of the Elder Brother was licensed and fitted up for its little guests within a week. The vacant floors in Miss Prillwitz's house were rented—not for the summer only, as we had at first planned, but, to our great surprise, for a year. An "unknown friend," who had admired our efforts, sent in a subscription of nine hundred dollars, thereby more than doubling the amount obtained by the fair, and guaranteeing that amount annually as long as the Home was continued.

Mr. Roseveldt had been better than his word, and the Home was placed on an assured basis for a year. What it would be after that we could not tell. It was only permitted to see one step ahead, but that step we could take with thankful assurance.

Madame sent over a quantity of furniture, as she intended to refit the students' rooms during the summer vacation. Donations of every kind poured in, and twenty-five little iron bedsteads were dressed in white, and set in the sunny rooms which were to be used as dormitories. Madame Céleste had said that she would not require Mrs. Halsey during the three summer months, and the little woman offered her services for that interim as nursery care-taker.

Another surprise came when Emma Jane Anton announced that she had written home and obtained permission to remain as matron. She had a talent for housekeeping, and she gave her services freely. "I am not rich," she said. "I can't give money, but I can give myself. I am not used to children; I don't believe they will like me, for I don't

care for them overmuch ; but Mrs. Halsey
will mother them, and I can keep the house
sweet and clean ; I can market economically,
and keep accounts exactly, and I mean that
the princess shall not give up her visit to
Tib She must go to the country for a part
of the summer at least."

" And when she comes back," I said, " you
must take your turn, Emma Jane ; we will be
so glad to have you !"

" Oh, immensely ! I am a genial, sweet
creature, I know, an addition to society; but
I thank you, all the same, and if I feel run
down, I will come and get a sniff of sea air."

The King's Daughters' Ten held their last
meeting before the breaking up of the
school. The money gained was entrusted to
Emma Jane's care for the summer, and each
of the members bound herself to carry the
scheme with her wherever she went, to
interest others, to gather and forward funds,
and to work for the Home in every possible
way.

Then we paid our last visit, for that term,
to Miss Prillwitz, and our first to our little
guests, and returning, packed our trunks,
attended the graduating exercises of the
senior class (the Amen Corner and the

Hornets were all juniors and sophomores, with the exception of Emma Jane, who graduated), hugged and wept over each other, and elected Winnie corresponding secretary for the summer, and promised to write to her every month, reporting work done for the Home, and separated with mingled hilarity and depression of spirits.

Mr. Roseveldt called at the Home with Milly and Adelaide before they left town. It was a little plan of the girls to interest him in Jim, and it succeeded admirably. After a number of other questions, Mr. Roseveldt asked Jim if he could drive.

"I managed the milkman's nag," the boy replied, "and he was an awfully hard-mouthed, ugly brute."

"Then I fancy you will have no trouble with Milly's pony, which is as gentle as a kitten," Mr. Roseveldt replied. "I want a boy in buttons just to sit in the rumble while the girls drive about the country." And so Jim was engaged to go to Narragansett Pier, and would have a happy summer with Milly and Adelaide.

CHAPTER X.

THE LANDLORD OF RICKETT'S COURT.

OLOMON MEY-
ER, who collect-
ed the rents at
Rickett's Court,
was looked upon
by the tenants
as the landlord,
though he dis-
tinctly disclaim-
ed that honor,
explaining that
he was only the
agent, empower-
ed merely to
receive money,
never to disburse. According to Mr. Meyer

the landlord was a heartless miser, whom
he had entreated to make repairs and to
lower rents, but who always turned a deaf
ear to such appeals. If he, Solomon Meyer,
only owned Rickett's Court, there would be
no end to the reforms which his tender
heart would cause him to institute ; as it
was, there was no hope for anything of the
kind ; his orders were explicit—if tenants
could not pay, they must leave.

Many of the tenants believed that Mr.
Meyer was really the owner of their building, and that the landlord whom he represented as responsible for all their discomfort was purely imaginary, but in this they
wronged the agent. Solomon Meyer had
no scruples against telling a lie whenever
it would serve his purpose, but here the
truth did very well. Rickett's Court had a
landlord who, although he was not the in-
human wretch which Solomon represented
him, still cared nothing for his tenants, and,
while the agent had never suggested any
reforms or repairs, might well have guessed
that they were needed. Adelaide Armstrong would have been shocked beyond
expression if she had known that the true
landlord of Rickett's Court was no other

than her own father. Mr. Armstrong would have been no less shocked if he had known of the abuses for which he was really responsible. He had never seen his own property. It had been represented to him as a profitable investment, and had proved so. He was only in New York for brief intervals each year, and he left the entire management of Rickett's Court to Solomon Meyer, well pleased with the returns which he rendered, and not suspecting that they were less than the sums wrung from the tenants.

He had mentally set aside Rickett's Court as Adelaide's property, and he used its proceeds to defray her expenses. There was a neat little surplus left over each quarter-day, which he placed in the savings bank to her credit, and with which he intended to endow her on her marriage. But of all this Adelaide of course knew nothing. Mr. Armstrong's more important business ventures were in western railroad speculations. These absorbed his attention, and needed the closest application of his faculties. He was glad of this. The East had grown distasteful to him since the loss of his wife and infant son. He felt that he might have been a different man if his wife, whom he tenderly loved, had lived; and Adelaide had never ceased to mourn her mother, whom she could not remember. "What shall I ever do," she frequently asked, "when I finish school? If I only had a mother to be my companion and counselor! but I shall be so lonely, and so unfit to take care of myself!"

The circumstances which I relate in this chapter because they belong here in sequence of time, did not come to my knowledge until long after their occurrence.

Mr. Armstrong came on from the West the evening of our fair. He was weary and much occupied by matters of business, and he did not attend it, much to our regret. He lent a kindly ear to Adelaide's description of it, for he was fond and proud of his beautiful daughter, and he liked to see her a leader in everything.

He manifested apparently little interest, however, in what she had to tell him of Rickett's Court. "There, there, Puss!" he said, lightly, "you must not get fanatical, and rant. I hardly think things are as bad down there as you make them out."

"But, papa," Adelaide interrupted, "I went there myself. I saw it with my own eyes. It is horrible to think that human beings should be obliged to live in such filth and misery. I think the landlord of Rickett's Court ought to be prosecuted. I wish I knew that old Rickett! I would give him a piece of my mind."

"I've no doubt of it; but spare me, Puss, since my name is not Rickett."

He must have felt a sharp twinge of conscience as he spoke, while his daughter's words could not have failed to make an impression on the false Rickett. He had read in the cars a little book entitled "Uncle Tom's Tenement," by Alice Wellington Rollins, and Helen Campbell's "Prisoners of Poverty." He wondered if their pictures of tenement life were indeed true. A few days later he listened to some remarks of Mr. Felix Adler's on tenement reform. He knew what Mr. Charles Pratt was doing in Brooklyn, and his better man told him that now was his opportunity. Why should he not put the plumbing in his tenement in decent repair; it might not cost much more, after all, than to bribe the inspector to report it as all right—a proceeding which Solomon Meyer advised. He could at least drain the sink in the court, and do away with the unchristian smells which now drove the chance visitor from the vicinity. And if he should have the rooms cleaned and whitewashed, he might even pose before the public as a humanitarian landlord, and so gain the co-operation of some of the philanthropists of the day for some other schemes which he had in mind.

He visited the court with a plumber, and found it in worse condition than he had imagined. There was a leak from the sewer in the back basement. All of the rooms were foul with vermin, and rats scuttled back into the walls through great holes. Many of the tenants had left, for various reasons. The opening of the Home of the Elder Brother was in great part responsible for the emptying of Rickett's Court, for the better class of its tenants had embraced this great opportunity to place their children in good surroundings. So many children had been transferred from Mrs. Grogan's care to the Home by their mothers that Mrs. Grogan, finding her occupation gone, betook herself to petty larceny and was arrested.

The Italian rag-pickers had taken to the road, with a monkey and an organ as tramps

for the summer, leaving their filth behind
them.

Mr. Armstrong looked into their vacated
den, and found it impossible to imagine what
it could have been when occupied.

The windows had been stoned by the
street boys until hardly a pane remained,
and the staircase had rotted so that he
thrust his foot through it. The house would
need plastering and glazing as well as re-
plumbing. It began to look like a great undertaking. However, he bade the plumber
make and send him his estimates, and hurried
out of the court, not taking a full breath until he was fairly on Broadway. Then he
sent a mason and a carpenter to look at the
building. "I must make some repairs," he
said to himself, "or I shall get no tenants
whatever."

He had noticed another defect : there was
but one staircase. He must add a fire-escape,
for the place was a death-trap. He had a
feeling of responsibility in regard to en-
dangering the lives of human beings by fire,
and he was trying to invent a scheme for
heating and lighting railroad cars in such a
manner as to do away with the danger of
fire in case of accident. So far, the full com-

pletion of the invention escaped him, but he worked at it by night and day, not so much because it would be an immense boon to the age, but because he was sure that, if introduced only on his own railroad, it would boom the line above a rival route, and if patented, would make his fortune. Solomon Meyer, in enumerating the tenants of the court, had mentioned a Mr. Trimble, a poor inventor, who occupied the back attic, whom it would be well to turn out, as he had paid no rent for some time, though he had promised well, saying that he had just invented a scheme for the safe heating of cars, from which he hoped to realize a large sum. Mr. Armstrong thoughtlessly displayed before his agent the interest which he felt. "Bring the man to me," he exclaimed; "if he has really worked out the problem, it is just what I want."

The agent at once paid a visit to the poor inventor and possessed himself of his plans and model, promising to do his best for him.

Mr. Armstrong saw at a glance that the inventor had compassed just what had baffled him so long.

"What will he take for this invention?" he asked, eagerly.

"Not one cent less as five t'ousand dollar," replied Mr. Meyer.

"That is a good round sum," remarked Mr. Armstrong. "but the right to it is worth more than that to me. Arrange the papers for me, get the gentleman to sign them, give him this check for a thousand dollars, and I will send him another, soon, for four thousand."

Mr. Meyer saw his opportunity here. He returned to Mr. Trimble, assured him that his contrivance had been anticipated and already patented by another man: he was too late. The poor man's disappointment was intense ; his head and hands trembled.

"I thank you for trying for me," he said ; "there is nothing for me now but the river. I have occupied this room in the hope of paying my rent when I realized from that invention, but I have no longer any expectations, and I had better go and drown myself."

Then for the first time Mr. Meyer realized that there was another person in the room. Jim had come down to the court to see his old friends, and had dropped in to inquire after Mr. Trimble's son, a merry little fellow who had been a playmate of his in the old days. Jim had retreated into a corner when the agent called, but he now sprang forward and threw his arms around the poor inventor's neck.

" No, no !" he cried ; " Mr. Meyer will beg Mr. Rickett to let you stay until the first of the month, and something may turn up by that time."

Some sense of shame prompted Solomon Meyer to yield to this request, though in his secret heart he knew that his own plans could be more safely carried out if his victim did drown himself; and the sooner the better. Then he hurried away to collect rents of the new tenants, with the money which Mr. Armstrong had sent Stephen Trimble burning like a coal in his pocket.

The contract for the new invention was returned to Mr. Armstrong at the same time with the estimates of the different mechanics for the improvements of Rickett's Court. It would cost three thousand dollars to put the tenement in decent repair, and this did not include the fire - escape. Mr. Armstrong whistled as he added up the items. It was really not convenient for him to place his hand on so much ready cash ; certainly not without using the money which he had placed in the savings bank to Adelaide's

credit. Mr. Meyer stood cringing before
him, and Mr. Armstrong explained the situation.

The agent promptly disapproved of the
improvements. They would be a great
waste of money. No one would rent the
tenements after they were repaired, for it
would be necessary to charge a higher rent,
and tenants able to pay it, or desiring bathrooms and sanitary plumbing, would not
occupy such a quarter of the city.

" But suppose I do not charge any more
rent, but simply try to educate my old tenants to better habits of life ? "

Mr. Meyer explained that Mr. Armstrong
could throw away his money in that way if
he wished, but that the class of tenants who
patronized Rickett's Court could not be
educated. They preferred filth to cleanliness, and, however respectable their quarters
were made, would soon convert them into
sinks again.

Mr. Armstrong reminded his agent that
his best tenants had left him, that the house
was practically deserted, and that something
must be done to attract new occupants.

Mr. Meyer assured him that applications
had already been received for the rooms in

their present state. A ship-load of emigrants had just arrived: Polish Jews and exiled Russians, who had been imprisoned as Nihilists, and who had suffered such barbarities that Rickett's Court, horrible as it was, seemed positively comfortable to them."

Mr. Armstrong hesitated. He did not like to give up his scheme of renovation; still, there were the papers waiting for his signature for the transfer of the invention, and this he had decided he must have; it was sure to bring in a great deal of money, and another year he could much better afford to make these improvements. He decided, reluctantly, that he would put them off for the present.

"I will have a fire-escape put up," he said to his agent, "and we will do the rest as soon as possible."

Solomon Meyer shrugged his shoulders. "There is no danger of fire," he said, "and I was about to propose that you take out a fire insurance policy on that building; that cost about the same, and much more sensible."

Mr. Armstrong thought a moment. "If the danger of fire is sufficient to warrant me in insuring, it is also great enough to make furnishing the fire-escape an imperative duty. I insist on your seeing that one is adjusted immediately. You may also take out an insurance policy for twenty thousand. See if Mr. Trimble can wait for the rest of his money until the first of the month. (The agent's face fell.) You have given him my check for one thousand ; he ought to be willing to wait a few days for the rest. If he is not satisfied, tell him to come down and see me, and we'll come to some agreement."

This was exactly what Solomon Meyer did not wish. " I will try my best to make him sign the papers on those terms," he said, and carried them away to his own den, where he forged the name of Stephen Trimble to both contract and check. He found no difficulty in cashing the check, for Mr. Armstrong's name was well known, though Stephen Trimble's was not.

And in the mean time the poor inventor sat in his garret trying to think. His wife was in the hospital, and his little son busied himself with washing the supper dishes. It was not a heavy task, for their supper had consisted only of some cold griddle-cakes which the flap-jack man had given them. When the boy had finished his work he crept close to his father and laid his head on his knee.

"Why don't you light the lamp?" Mr. Trimble asked, rousing himself.

"There isn't any oil, daddy."

"No matter. I can think better in the dark, and you had better go to bed."

"I am going out pretty soon to help the flap-jack man wheel his cart."

"Very well, Lovey, if he is a good man; I don't want you to do anything wrong."

"He's good to me, daddy."

"I'm glad of that; you need a friend, and you may need one more." He kissed his little boy as he went out—an unwonted action on the father's part—and waited until he was sure that the child had left the building, then rose, with a desperate look upon his face, and stepped out on the landing. The house was very full now; people had been coming for two days past with great bales of foul clothing, offensive with odors of the steerage, and had packed into the already dirty rooms. It was an unusually warm night for spring, and the house was unbearably close. The tenants had resorted to the roof, and were sitting under the stars, trying in vain to find fresh air, and screaming and scolding at one another in a strange, harsh language.

Stephen Trimble was about to descend the staircase, when two men of unpleasant aspect stopped him.

" You are the machinist who lives on the top floor ? "

" Yes."

" Have you time for a little job ? "

" Plenty of time. Thank God!" he added, mentally, "who has sent me help in time."

'Then come down-stairs with us : we are your neighbors, and are just under you."

" What do you want me to do ? "

" We'll show you."

The men admitted him to their room, and carefully locked the door behind them. One of them struck a light, and in so doing dropped a match upon the floor. The other sprang upon it quickly, ground it out with his heel, and cursed him for his carelessness. Stephen Trimble looked about him, and saw that one end of the room was piled with boxes and tin cans, one of which was open, showing a compound slightly resembling maple sugar. A table stood before the low window, and on it was apparatus or machinery of some sort The first man placed his candle on the table, and drew up a packing-box for Mr. Trimble to sit upon. There was no other furniture in the room.

" You do not live here ?" said the inventor.

" No," replied the first man, who constituted himself the spokesman for both ; " it isn't a sweet place to live in We hire it as a workshop. You see, we are perfecting a sort of torpedo. You've heard of the submarine torpedoes that did such good service in blowing up the Turkish ships in the Russo-Turkish war ?"

" Oh yes," replied Stephen Trimble, much interested. " I thought that stuff looked like dynamite! So you are inventing a new torpedo, which you mean to sell the Government ? That's a good idea. They are thinking of increasing the navy, and it's always better to deal with the Government than with private individuals."

The silent man nudged his partner and remarked, " Yes, we're agoin' to deal with the Government. That's a good way to put it."

The other man made an impatient gesture, and proceeded to explain a small machine to

Mr. Trimble. "You don't exactly understand my friend," he said, "but no matter. This kind of a torpedo isn't of the submarine kind; we pack the explosives here, matches here, friction paper just beside them; but just here we are stuck, and we need you or some other mechanic to show us how the thing can be set off by electricity, the operator to touch a button at a distance."

Mr. Trimble bent himself to an examination of the contrivance. He asked several questions, and as his scrutiny continued, his expression of satisfaction changed to one of mistrust and alarm. Suddenly he sprang from his seat and pushed the model from him. "That is an infernal - machine!" he exclaimed.

"That's about the long and the short of it," said the man, calmly.

"Then I will have nothing to do with it," and he turned toward the door.

"Hold on, my friend, ain't you a trifle in a hurry? All we want you to do is to fix that attachment for us, and if you won't do it some other man will, but we're willing to pay you a hundred dollars for the job. That's a goodish sum to pay, if the job is a little queer, but I take it you're used to doing queer things by the big checks that pass through your hands."

"What do you mean?" Stephen Trimble asked, with some indignation.

"Oh! you needn't pretend innocence and poverty. A man doesn't scatter round thousand-dollar checks who's as poor as you pretend to be, or as good, either."

"Tell me what you mean."

"Now don't tell us you know nothing of a check for a thousand dollars which we happened to see in the pocket-book of the agent of this building when he dropped in here to collect the rent."

"I never saw a check for a thousand dollars in my life."

"If you don't believe me, ask that sharp little boy of yours. It was he who first let me know there was a scientific man in the building He saw me unpacking my machine. I happened to leave the door open just a minute. I never saw such a sharp little fellow. In he comes and says, 'My father makes machines too. He's going to make us awful rich some day.'

"After that he got in the way of knocking at the door and asking to see my machinery. I thought it would be a good idea to let him, for he is too little to suspect any-thing, and I could stuff him with the idea that I was making a new kind of telegraph, for I was pretty sure that he would tell it around, and that people would believe it and think there couldn't be anything shady in what I was doing if I let anybody and every-body have the freedom of the room.

"Well, the day I'm speaking of, your little chap was sitting there turning the crank of that machine just as cheerful as if it wouldn't have blown him to kingdom come if the attachment had only been on, when in come another little feller who had been looking for him. 'See here,' says my partner, 'there's getting to be too many children here; we don't keep a Sunday-school, we don't.' They were just going to leave, when the agent he come in with the rent contract for us to sign. Well, the boys lingered round, full of curiosity, as boys are, and we signed the paper and handed over the cash. Mr. Meyer in stuffing it away in his pocket-book brought to light that thousand-dollar check I was telling you about. He fumbled to hide it, but it dropped on the floor, and a little gust of wind carried it over to where the boys were. The oldest boy—Jim, I think your son called him—picked it up, and took a good look at it. 'Hullo!' says he, 'here's your father's name, Lovey. "Pay to the order of Stephen Trimble one thousand dollars"!' The agent he just made one dive for that check, with his fist lifted as though he were going to strike the boy, who dropped the check, and both the little shavers scooted, and none too soon either, for Meyer looked mad enough to kill the youngster, though he tried to laugh it off, and turned the check over and showed me that it was his fast enough, for it was endorsed on the back, 'Pay to the order of Solomon Meyer.'"

Stephen Trimble put his hand to his head in a dazed way. "You are fooling me," he said.

"Not we, but somebody is, if you don't know anything about it. Well, if you are not the bloated bondholder we took you for, perhaps you'll consider our little offer?"

"No, gentlemen, not to-night at least; give me time to think it over. One bad man may have wronged me, but I've no call to go against the law."

"Oh yes, take plenty of time"—and they opened the door. Some one was knocking at Stephen Trimble's own room. It was the flap-jack man, and he had a white, scared face

"What is the matter?" asked the inventor.

"Lovey's been—"

"Run over?" gasped the poor father.

"No; arrested."

Stephen Trimble gave one exclamation of horror—then asked, "What's he done?"

"Nothing but wheeling my cart; they'd have caught me, too, but I cut and run. This is a pretty country where one is arrested for trying to earn an honest living!"

This was the last straw. Stephen Trimble had said that he had no reason to resist the law, but he could not hold to that now. He staggered feebly down-stairs, knocked at the door of the dynamiters, and said. "I've come back sooner than I thought I would. Give me five dollars in advance, and I'll undertake that business of yours to-morrow, and maybe I'll get up a little infernal-machine for my own use at the same time, but just now I must find my boy."

The man handed him some greasy bills. "You look sick," he said. "You had better go down to the free-lunch counter at the saloon, and have a good square meal."

Stephen Trimble went and ate and drank

to excess. **He** did not look for his little son, and he did not return to the dynamiters' the next morning, for he was drunk—and drunk for three days thereafter. Then he sobered down and applied himself to the task which they had set him—a task intended to bring ruin to the class which had wronged him. He knew the aims, now, of the men for whom he was working, and he believed that he sympathized with them. They told him how they had borne imprisonment and torture for no wrong in Russia, and had come to this country expecting to find it the land of justice and kindness, but had met only the same tyranny of the rich over the poor—the rich, who cared for nothing but their own pleasures, and ground the poor under their chariot wheels.

As he worked he thought of his own private wrongs, and determined that as soon as his task was done he would seek out the man who had defrauded him. He was sure now that the check which the men had seen had something to do with his invention, but he believed that the true criminal was some one behind Solomon Meyer, the man to whom the agent said he had given his invention—the landlord of Rickett's Court. It was

like a man who would compel human beings
to live in such a state as this to commit such
a fraud. He would hunt him down presently, and in the name of his tenants, as well as
in his own cause, wreak such revenge that
the ears of those who heard should tingle.

The landlord of Rickett's Court, all unconscious of the volcano upon which he was
treading, attended the closing exercises of
Madame's school, and listened with pride
to his daughter's prize essay on "The Dangerous Classes."

There was a quotation from Ruskin at the
close which pricked his heart a little, and
made him regret that it was not convenient
to carry out his good intentions just at present. How charming she looked in the
white India silk, and how well she read that
final quotation!

"If you can fix some conception of a true
human state of life to be striven for—life for
all men as for yourselves—if you can deter-
mine some honest and simple order of existence following those trodden ways of wisdom, which are pleasantness, and seeking
those quiet and withdrawn paths, which are
peace; then, and so sanctifying wealth into
'commonwealth,' all your art, your literature,

your daily labors, your domestic affection, and citizen's duty, will join and increase into one magnificent harmony. You will know, then, how to build well enough; you will build with stone well, but with flesh better— temples not made with hands, but riveted of hearts, and that kind of marble, crimson- veined, is indeed eternal."

Mr. Armstrong entirely ruined a new pair of kid gloves in applauding his daughter.

He consigned her to Mrs. Roseveldt for the summer, and in reply to that lady's urgent request that he would visit them, ex- plained that Narragansett Pier was fraught with so many memories that he had never been able to revisit it. "I own a cottage a little distance from the town," he said. "It was there that both my children were born. We were in the habit of occupying it every summer, but since my wife's death I have neither been able to bring myself to go there, or to rent it, and it has remained closed."

"O papa, will you not let me have it for the summer?" Adelaide asked.

"Certainly, Puss, if you want to fit it up for a studio or that sort of thing; but it is in a lonely wood, and you must have suitable company with you if you think of staying there. If you manage to change the place and infuse new life in it, I may bring myself to look in upon you there. At all events, I will join you at the Roseveldts' as soon as I can; just now important business detains me."

The business, as we know, was the securing and putting in service of the new invention for heating and lighting cars. It was necessary for him to go to Washington to arrange for the patent, and it was on this trip that a clue most unexpectedly fell into his hands which seemed to lead to a startling discovery—a discovery which was more to him than any fortune which the invention could bring.

It all came about through a scrap of paper which fell in his way as he was looking about his hotel bedroom for a piece of wrapping-paper with which to cover the model of the machine which he was about to carry to the Patent Office. He could find nothing for this purpose but an old newspaper which lined a bureau drawer. In this he wrapped his machine, and took his seat in the street-car, the package resting on his knees. His fellow-passengers were uninteresting, and he fixed his gaze upon his package. A heading to one of the shorter articles in the old newspaper attracted his attention.

" Remarkable Case of Loss of Identity ; the Doctors Puzzled."

He read on aimlessly.

"The physicians of —— Hospital have an interesting case. One of their patients, a lady, was injured at the burning of the *Henrietta* in the Sound in October last. This accident has resulted in a partial loss of memory, and total confusion as to her identity. The unfortunate lady is unable to give her own name or that of her friends. A remarkable circumstance in the case is the fact that, through all the horror and suffering of the accident, which has resulted in a partial loss of her reason, the poor lady kept her infant boy safely clasped in her arms, and the child, entirely uninjured, was rescued with her. Any person who believes that he recognizes a lost friend in this case is requested to communicate with Dr. H. C. Carver, of the —— Hospital."

Mr. Armstrong read this item over and over again. He had believed that his wife and child were lost in the burning of this steamer. Was it possible that they still lived ? and what had ten years of separation done for them ?

The horse-car passed the Patent Office, but he did not see it. He sat staring at the newspaper until the car brought him to the end of the route and the conductor touched him on the shoulder. " Pardon me, sir; I forgot you wished to stop at the Patent Office."

Mr. Armstrong woke from his reverie. "No," he exclaimed, " at the railway station. I want to catch the next train for New York—none until 4 o'clock ? Then I *will* go to the Patent Office ; but, first, tell me where I can send a telegram."

CHAPTER XI.

THE GUESTS OF THE ELDER BROTHER.

"And man may work with the great God; yea, ours
This privilege; all others, how beyond!

   *   *   *   *   *   *

Effectually the planet to subdue,
And break old savagehood in claw and tusk;
To draw our fellows up as with a cord
Of love unto their high-appointed place,
Till from our state barbaric and abhorred
We do arise unto a royal race,
To be the blest companions of the Lord."
—HENRY G. SUTTON.

A FEW days before school closed saw the Home filled for the summer.

The gathering in was achieved principally by Jim, Mrs. Hetterman, and Vicenzo Amati.

Vincenzo was an Italian of the better sort. He had lived in America long enough to acquire

some of our ways of life. He earned a fairly
good salary as cook, and he had kept his
little family in comparative comfort in the
best apartment which Rickett's Court had to
offer, until the death of his pretty wife Gio-
vanina. Since then the three little girls had
done their best, but there was a woeful
change. They became slatternly in appearance, and the two rooms grew dirty and
cheerless. Worse than this, the girls affiliated
with a lower class of their own nationality,
the children of the rag-pickers in the basement, already referred to, who lived upon the
chances of garbage barrels and beggary, and
who spent much of their time in picking
over and assorting the old bones, rags,
paper, and other refuse dumped each night
upon the floor of their sleeping and living
room, as the result of their father's daily toil.
These children were sickly and miserable,
tainted morally as well as physically ; and
their parents, who were contented with their
disgusting lives, were laying up money, in
fact, for a return to Italy. But Vincenzo was
not contented that his children should live in
such fashion or have contaminating associ-
ates. He was one of the first applicants to
place his children in the Home, paying

cheerfully the highest sum asked for board, it having been early decided that the rates for each child should be proportioned to the wages of the parent.

Then several children previously "farmed out" to Mrs. Grogan, whose mothers were servants in good families, were received on similar terms.

A German woman, a Mrs. Rumple, brought her two children, saying that she was going West, but, as she knew not what fortune awaited her there, wished to place her children in the Home until she could send for them. She paid their board in advance for the summer, taking the money in coin from her petticoat pocket.

"Why do you leave New York?" asked Emma Jane Anton.

"It ish not de guntry. De guntry ish a very goot guntry. It ish de beeples," said Mrs. Rumple.

"What is the matter with the people?" asked Emma Jane.

"I comes de seas over a pride, mit my man Heinrich Rumple; dat is ten years aco already. Heinrich is one very goot man; he trinks only one mug of lager every days; he comes every Saturday home mit his moneys, and oh, mine fraulein, how he luf me! Pretty soon py und py de peer ish not coot, and he takes one leetle glass of schnapps instead. Den de leetle babies come, one, tree, four, six, and it cost all de time more to live, and he pring all de time less moneys mit de Saturdays. But he trinks all de time more schnapps—one, two, tree, four glass de every days, and I know not how much de Sundays, and I tink he not luf me now so much as sometimes. Den de sickness comes, de shills and de fevers, and we all de time shake, shake, and first one little children die, and den anudder, all but Carl and de little Gracie; and mine man not haf any moneys to py medicines, put he haf blenty to py schnapps, and he all de time trink more as is goot for him, and one night he comes home and he knows not vat he does, and he sthrikes de leetle Gracie, and she is long time very sick. Mine soul! I tinks she vill die, and Heinrich Rumple—dot ish my man—he puts his name mit de bledge, and says he vill not any times trink any more, und de Gracie gets vell, und ve are all wery happy, but he all de same trinks again shust so pad as ever. Py und py pretty soon I says, 'Heinrich Rumple, I cannot sthand dis nonsense any more ain't it. I cannot haf dose childer all their bones broke any more; I put dem in one 'sylum avay from you, and I goes in dot Western land seek my fortune.'"

" And so you left your husband ? " asked Miss Anton.

" Ya. I left mine man," replied the woman.

" And don't you suppose he will ever reform, and send you money to come back to him ? "

"No, I s'pose so. He said to me dat day: ' Barbara, it is de beeples. I haf too many friends, and I trinks mit dem all de time, too often ; I tinks if I am in de West, where I know nobodys, I would be a petter husband to you alretty.' And so he goed away mit me."

" Do you mean to say that you and your husband are leaving New York for the West together ?"

" Ya. I left him, and he say, ' Barbara, you has right ; I leaf myself, too.' But I cannot trust him alretty mit de chillern. I leaf dem one six month, to try what come of it all."

"I hope your husband has indeed left his worst self behind him," said Emma Jane ;

and on suitable security being provided, the Rumple children were admitted.

In almost all cases it was not the desperately and hopelessly pauperized and vicious— who were provided for by reformatories and the city charities—whom they helped, but the class just above them, who were slipping over the brink, and would surely have fallen and contributed to swell the dangerous classes, if not reached by this timely assistance.

" Prevention is better than cure," and it was the hope of the " King's Daughters " to rescue the innocent children of decent and struggling parents before they should need reformation.

Rosaria Ricos, the Cuban heiress, endowed a bed to be used for some child whose parents could do nothing whatever toward its support. She wished to have more free beds, but Miss Prillwitz showed her how much better it was for the parents to do something, however little it might be, for their children, and not be pauperized by having every feeling of independence and ability to care for their own taken from them. Exceptional circumstances might arise, when a mother out of employment, could wisely be helped over a great exigency, but she advised that Miss Ricos's "Emergency Bed" be given for short periods only. It was first occupied by Lovell Trimble, familiarly, but most inappropriately, nicknamed by the other children, Lovey Dimple. He was a homely, unprepossessing boy, with a pug nose and a disproportionately large head. His father was the unsuccessful inventor of Rickett's Court, with whom we are already acquainted. He spent all his former earnings in securing patents for various great inventions which were to make all their fortunes. His mother had been a shop-girl in a large dry-goods store, and had supported the family until long-continued standing had sent her to the hospital. Lovey had tried to take her place in supporting his father by wheeling "the machine" of a hot-flap-jack seller, while the flap-jack man devoted his attention to frying the cakes, flipping them on to a plate, and serving them up with a dab of butter and a lake of molasses. They did their best business winter nights after the theatres were out—sheltered from the snow by an awning or a convenient door-way, and they knew which places of amusement were out first, and would

race at ambulance speed from Harrigan
and Hart's to the Bowery, to secure the cus-
tom of each. Lovey liked the business, for,
besides the pay, after the day's trade was
over the flap-jack man let him eat whatever
was left, for the batter would not keep, and
he had always a few cakes to carry home
to his father of the full brain and empty
stomach.

But one night a member of the Society
for the Prevention of Cruelty to Children,
who had had his eye on the flap-jack man as
employing too young a child for labor in-
volving so much privation, descended upon
the cart with a policeman; and the flap-jack
man having discreetly absconded, they arrested Lovey in default of his employer.
Miss Prillwitz appeared in court at Jim's
request, for in some way Jim had
heard of his friend's apprehension, and having ascertained that Mr. Trimble had gone
upon a spree, she rashly, but not unnaturally,
decided that nothing was to be expected
from such a father, and next paid a visit to
Mrs. Trimble, at the hospital. Learning
there that there was a prospect of her cure,
she offered Lovey the hospitality of the
Emergency Bed until his mother should be

able to work once more. This case established relations between the Society for the Prevention of Cruelty to Children and the new Home; and a little girl—who had been forced to sell lead-pencils on the street at night by a drunken mother, though her father was a brakeman, who could well afford to support her—was committed to the Home through the agency of the Society ; and the father, on being notified, approved the action, and paid her board regularly.

One desirable result of the Home was its effect on Emma Jane's character. From being, as she had truly said of herself, an unlovely and unloving girl who disliked children, her nature sweetened by contact with them ; and taking them one by one into her heart, it broadened and softened, till an expression which was almost madonna-like trembled in a face which had been grim and repellent. Lovey Dimple was the first to scale the fortress of Emma Jane's affections. He inherited his father's aptitude for mechanics. Among the old books and papers contributed to the Home were, strangely enough, some bound volumes of the *Scientific American* and a few stray Patent Office reports, and over these he pored until his head seemed full of revolving cog-wheels and pulleys, and pistons, and his heart beat like a stationary engine. He was certain that he would be an inventor some day, like Ericsson or Edison; indeed, he was an inventor already, for had he not constructed unnumbered mill-wheels and windmills, weathercocks and whirligigs, besides taking to pieces the clock (which he could not get together again), and adapting his mother's sewing-machine to fret-saw purposes? He had studied every machine which he had seen in the stores, from the corn-sheller to the great patent mower, and believed that he understood the action of each. "Patent" was a word that stirred his soul, though he had but a dim conception of its meaning. It was something, his father had said, that the Government would give him if he invented a really useful, labor-saving machine, one which would "supply a felt want."

Lovey knew what a felt hat was, but it was several days before he really knew what his father meant by a felt want. As soon as he had grasped the idea he began in earnest. "Mother Halsey," he asked, "what part of your work bothers you most?"

Mrs. Halsey looked hot and flustered. Half an hour before this she had put her room and the nursery in order, had dressed the twenty-five children; from combing their hair and scrubbing the little ones, and introducing them into each separate garment, to merely tying apron-strings and buttoning the " behind buttons " of the older ones, and giving them a final dress review before starting them to the public school.

In view of this state of affairs, it is not to be wondered at that Mrs. Halsey said that dressing the children gave her more bother than anything else. Lovey, with a pencil and paper, sat down to invent a machine which should do this for her. He reflected that such a machine would be hailed with delight in nearly every family, and if he could manage to sell them at a dollar apiece his fortune was assured. He took as his models the washing - machine, a cross - cut saw, and a corn - sheller, and in a few moments had made his drawing of a combination of the three machines. The motive power, he decided, should be furnished by the father of the family, who could turn the crank; and on days when this was not convenient the smoke from the cooking-stove could be utilized, the stove pipe being turned so that the smoke should strike the paddles of the main wheel, and the continuous stream passing across the edge of the wheel and up the chimney, he felt certain, would turn it. Just back of the machine, and above it, there was to be a great hopper into which the naked children could climb by means of a ladder, and where the clothing could be tossed promiscuously, the machine sorting it and robing each child properly. The cross-cut saw near the mouth would shingle each child's hair, and save the trouble of curling, while the children, completely dressed, would be poured through this spout into their mother's arms.

Lovey exhibited this drawing to Mrs. Halsey and to Miss Antos, and begged them to show it to President Harrison and obtain a patent for him as soon as possible ; but, somehow, though the invention was received with applause and approbation by the entire family, nothing was ever done about it.

The droll conceit attracted Emma Jane to the boy. "Perhaps some day he may become an inventor of something more practical," she said, and ever after watched him with increasing interest.

Lovey had had great trouble with his arithmetic, and he had decided that a grand labor-saving machine would be one which would save a boy the trouble of studying. He thought that it would be a good idea to bore a hole in a boy's head when he was asleep, introduce the end of a funnel into the opening, and then with a coffee-mill grind up the usual text-books and stuff his brains. He made a drawing of this machine also, and Merry Twinkle and he came very near trying it practically, but they never could quite agree as to who should be the operator and who should be operated upon. Lovey had another brilliant inspiration. He noticed that his rubber ball, which had a hole in it,

had a remarkable power of suction, and that
if he held the orifice to his cheek and
squeezed the ball, when he let go it would
pucker his cheek in a way to remind one
distantly of a kiss. He imagined that if the
ball were drawn out into a tube, and that
tube continued indefinitely the action would

still be the same. Here was a discovery.
How many separated friends and lovers
would be glad to patronize a kissaphone, an
instrument by which kisses could be sent
and actually felt. He imagined the establishment of offices on both sides of the
Atlantic, and the laying of a submarine
tube.

A young physician, a friend of Mrs. Roseveldt's, was visiting the Home just as Lovey
completed this triumph. " Another invention of Lovey Dimple's," Emma Jane explained, as the child handed her the drawing. Dr.
Curtiss came oftener than the sanitary condition of the Home really demanded, and he
was well acquainted with Lovey's genius in
this direction.

" Yes, sir," promptly replied Lovey, " and
I have met a felt want now, sure," and then
he explained the kissaphone.

" Try it on me, Lovey, and let me see how
it feels," asked the doctor.

Lovey did so, and Dr. Curtiss made a wry
face. " It strikes me that is a very poor substitute for the genuine article," he said, " but
perhaps I am not qualified to judge.

"Now if you could have a nice looking
lady operator, and could attach your tubing
to the back of her head, and have her trans-
mit the kiss as the mouthpiece of the machine,
I should think your invention might be very
popular."

Lovey received this suggestion with entire
good faith. " Miss Anton," he said, beseech-
ingly, " won't you act as mouthpiece and let
me send a kiss to Dr. Curtiss ?" And he

could never quite decide why Emma Jane, who was usually so kind, declined in great confusion to render him this trifling service.

There was another little boy in the Home who made remarkable drawings—the one already referred to as Merry Twinkle. All of his family, even the female portion, were sea-faring people; his grandfather had been a sailor, and was now an inmate of the Sailors' Snug Harbor. His mother sometimes took Merry to visit him when she was back from a voyage, for she was stewardess on an ocean steamer. His father had been engineer on the same boat, but had been killed by a boiler explosion, and Merry had been *boarded* hitherto with Mrs. Grogan.

One evening, after a visit to his grandfather, Merry handed Emma Jane a series of wonderful marines.

"Grandfather sang me a very old song to-day," he said. "It went this way:

> Two gallant ships from England sailed;
> Blow high, blow low, so sailed we:
> One was the *Princess Charlotte*, the other *Prince of Wales*,
> Cruising down on the coast of Barbaree.

"This is a picture of the *Princess Charlotte*," handing Emma Jane his drawing.

"It is night, and the captain is pacing the lonely deck; he has set his lantern on a small stand, and has put his hands in his pockets to keep them warm. The second verse goes this way :

"Up aloft! up aloft!" our gallant captain cried ;
    Blow high, blow low, so sailed we.
"Look ahead, look astern, look aweather, look alee,"
    Cruising down on the coast of Barbaree.

"Oh, I've seen on ahead, and I've seen on astern,"
    Blow high, blow low, so sailed we;
"And I see a ragged wind and a lofty ship at sea,"
    Cruising down on the coast of Barbaree.

"Ahoy ! ship ahoy !" our gallant captain cried,
    Blow high, blow low, so sailed we;
"Are you a man-of-war, or a privateer ?" says he ;
    Cruising down on the coast of Barbaree.

"Oh ! I am no man-of-war or privateer," says he,
    Blow high, blow low, so sailed we ;
"But I am a jolly pirate seeking for my fee,"
    Cruising down on the coast of Barbaree.

"This is the picture of the pirate ship and the fight. Captain Kidd has cut off the head of one of the men who boarded his ship. One of his men is firing a cannon, the rest of his crew may be seen between-decks.

14

"'Twas broadside to broadside, so quickly then came we ;
  Blow high, blow low, so sailed we ;
Until the *Princess Charlotte* shot her masts into the sea,
  Cruising down on the coast of Barbaree.

Then " Quarter ! oh, quarter !" the pirate captain cried;
  Blow high, blow low, so sailed we ;
But the quarters that we gave them were down beneath
    the sea,
  Cruising down on the coast of Barbaree.

" Grandfather called it the story of Captain Kidd, because he thought he must have been the pirate whose ship the *Princess Charlotte* sunk. Captain Kidd was taken to London and hanged in chains, and I've made a picture of that too."

Emma Jane hardly approved of the sanguinary spirit displayed by these drawings, but she could not expect that the boy's antecedents and surroundings would produce an angel. She endeavored to draw his attention to gentler subjects for his pencil, recited tender and loving ballads, and changed the current of the boy's thought and aspiration, realizing that here was material which, in the fostering atmosphere of Rickett's Court, might easily develop into an anarchist—a menace to the state.

The Sandy girls were the last to be re-

ceived from the court. The father had been
a truckman, but a heavy box had fallen upon
him, and he had lived in pain and misery for
a year and had then died. Mrs. Sandy, by
making men's clothing, managed to keep the
wolf from the door—no, only snarling *at* the
door with fierce, hungry eyes. All of her
six children helped her. The oldest girl did
the ironing and finishing ; the next child,
a boy, carried the great bundles back and
forth in the intervals of his profession as a
bootblack ; the second girl did all of their
poor housework ; the twins sewed on buttons and pulled out basting threads, and the
youngest boy sold newspapers, while Mrs.
Sandy herself ran the sewing-machine ten
or twelve hours in the day.

When Mrs. Hetterman asked her why she
did not give up this desperate battle with
the point of the needle, and leave her vile
surroundings to take service in some good
family, she replied that she had often thought
of this, but she must keep a home, however
poor, for the children. "The two boys could
live at the Newsboys' Lodging-House, for
they earn enough to support themselves, but
what would I do with my four girls ?"

When Mrs. Hetterman assured her that

there was a Home where they could all be cared for in cleanliness, health, and comfort, and have time for study and schooling and industrial education, which would fit them to earn their own living in future, and all for a sum quite within the means of any domestic, she brought her cramped hand down with a heavy blow upon the sewing-machine.

"I don't mind if I break every bone in yer body, ye Satan's grindstone!" she said to the machine; "it's the last time that Mary Sandy'll grind soul and body thin at ye, praise be to a delivering Providence!"

Mrs. Hastings, one of the managers of the Home, had had great trouble with incompetent and ungrateful servants, and she gladly took the faithful Scotch woman into her family.

These, then, were the guests of the Elder Brother, for that first summer, from Rickett's Court:

1 Jim Halsey, American.
3 Hettermans, English.
3 Amatis, Italian.
4 Babies from Mrs. Grogan's, Irish.
2 Carl and Gracie Rumple, German.

1 Lovey Dimple, American.
1 Merry Twinkle, American.
4 Sandy Girls, Scotch.

In all, nineteen children transplanted from
the filth and vice, hunger and ignorance, of
the court, and six more from other localities as bad, to sweet, wholesome surroundings. It was thought best that those children
of school age should attend a public school
to avoid "institutionizing" them ; and for
this end they wore no uniform, and mingled
freely with other well-behaved children in
the park under Mrs. Halsey's motherly super-
vision. Their birthdays were celebrated
with a little party, with cake and candles,
and everything was done to cultivate a home-
like feeling. They drew their books like
other children from the children's new free
circulating library, and were taught to
guard them carefully. They had a sewing
society—in reality a sewing-class—where
boys and girls were alike taught to mend
and darn, to sew on buttons, and to make but-
ton-holes—all but the Sandy children, who, it
was judged, had served a long enough ap-
prenticeship in this department, and were
sent to Mrs. Hetterman to learn how to cook.

Miss Prillwitz was anxious that the boys should have industrial training, and brought the matter before the board of managers, who entirely agreed with her, and voted that a subscription sent them by Mr. Armstrong be used to secure a suitable teacher.

It was just at this time that a letter was received from Adelaide announcing that she had fitted up the cottage which her father had placed at her disposal, and would like to have Mrs. Halsey occupy it with the youngest children for the heated term. Miss Prillwitz was delighted. Jim was already at the Pier with the Roseveldts, and it would be pleasant for his mother to be near him, and a fine thing for the little girls and the babies. This would leave the nursery vacant, and it could be fitted up as a workshop for the boys, She had a chat with Mrs. Halsey the day before she left, and asked her if she knew of anyone who could teach the boys carpentry.

"Mr. Trimble, Lovey's father, is a perfect jack-of-all-trades," replied Mrs. Halsey.

Miss Prillwitz was doubtful. "Mr. Trimble is a drunkard," she said.

"Not irreclaimable, I am sure," said Mrs. Halsey. "He was a sober man when I knew him. Despair alone could have driven him to drink. I wish you would send and ask him to call and see you."

So a letter was sent, and none too soon, for affairs were now at their worst with Stephen Trimble.

CHAPTER XII.

WITH THE DYNAMITERS.

" While we range with Science, glorying in the time,
City children soak and blacken soul and sense in city slime ;
Where among the glooming alleys Progress halts on pal-
    sied feet,
Crime and hunger cast out maidens by the thousand on
    the street;
Where the master scrimps his haggard seamstress of her
    daily bread,
And a single sordid attic holds the living and the dead."
—Anon.

THE anarchist of Rickett's Court, under whose influence the inventor had fallen, was a thoroughly bad man, and the writer has no sympathy to waste upon him or his methods, but with his deluded and desperate victim we should all sympathize.

212

Stephen Trimble had brooded over his
troubles and wrongs until he was half crazed,
and the men for whom he worked added
fuel to the flame.

" Why should you be so precious careful
of the rich?" his employer said. " What have
the rich ever done for you? They've mur-
dered your wife, as I make out, insisting on
her standing all day long, when she was not
able to do so, and might have done her work
just as well sitting, They've sent your innocent little boy to jail along with common
pickpockets. They've robbed you of your
money—"

" Stop !" cried Stephen Trimble; " you've
said that over and over, until I believe it,
though I don't know why I should take
your word any quicker than that of any one
else. You've made much of your kindness
in telling me, though I don't see what good
it does me, unless you are willing to go into
court and testify for me as to what you've
seen."

The men shook their heads. " No going
into court for us ! We want to keep as far
away from the law as possible."

" Then I don't see but you are as much
against me as the rest. I've worked with

you long enough to know what your aims
are ; your machine is now in working order,
ready to blow up the finest house, the largest audience, in New York, church or arm-
ory, bank-vault or prison ; and if all you say
is true, you may blow away, for all I care,
and blow yourselves up with the rest, and
me too.   If the world is the Sodom and
Gomorrah it seems to me, we have Bible
warrant for its destruction.   My work for
you is done ; give me my money, and we
are through with each other."

"See here, Trimble," said the anarchist,
"we have already paid you fifteen dollars, and you ought not to be too close
with us."

"You promised me a hundred ; do you
mean to say—"

"Don't be so touchy ; what I mean to say
is this : We cannot help you by testifying in
court, as you suggested ; it wouldn't do you
any good if we did ; but find out the man
who has wronged you, and we will help you
to your revenge.   In a few days our society
will begin its operations.   We are out of
funds now, but there will be a new deal
soon.   We begin with the banking-house of
Roseveldt, Gold & Co., and as soon as the

fireworks are over we will be rich enough, and you shall have a fair share."

Stephen Trimble sprang to his feet. "I thought you were anarchists! do you acknowledge that you are common burglars?"

"No, my friend, we acknowledge nothing of the kind. Be good enough to attend to your own business."

"It is time that I did," replied the inventor; "I have neglected it long enough."

Stephen Trimble walked out of the building. He had three things to do—to discover the landlord of Rickett's Court; to see his wife for the last time; and to free his little son, whom he believed to be still in prison.

There was quite a commotion in the court; some men were putting up a fire-escape. "What ever put it into Solomon Meyer's head to do that?" he asked.

"'Tain't Solomon Meyer," a workman replied; "it's the landlord himself. He ordered it done some time ago, and was mad as a hornet because Meyer hadn't attended to it."

"See here, my friend," said Stephen Trimble, "if you know who the landlord of this tenement is, you will do me a favor by directing me to him."

"Armstrong's the man—Alexander Armstrong, President of the —— R. R. Co.; his office is over the banking-house of Roseveldt & Gold, No. —— Broadway. He rooms there too, when he's in town—back of his office."

Stephen Trimble stood very still for a moment. The information which he thought would be so difficult to obtain had come to his door. The vengeance which he had fancied might take long days and nights of plotting, hung now over the man who had wronged him. He need do absolutely nothing, and Alexander Armstrong was doomed. He must inevitably be killed in the explosion and conflagration which was planned to cover the robbery of the bank beneath him.

They had changed places, and the landlord of Rickett's Court was his victim. One-third of his task was accomplished. He walked now in the direction of the hospital, and asked to see his wife. He hardly expected to be admitted, but he would at least make the attempt. To his surprise he was shown into a cheerful parlor, and Mrs. Trimble was sent for. She came down, looking pale, but happy.

"O Stephen," she cried, "it has been so

long since I have seen you! but never mind,
I am almost well now, and we shall soon be
together again. The doctor tells me I may
leave next week. They have been so very
kind to me here, it has been like Heaven.
The rich are thoughtful and generous to provide such places for the poor. I am so grateful ; and I have rested so that I shall be able
to take hold with new courage."

He listened in a stupefied way, and seeing
that he was not inclined to speak, she ran
on, "And isn't it beautiful about Lovey?"

This stung him to speech. "Beautiful?
To be arrested and sent to prison?"

"Why, no, dear. Haven't you heard? A
sweet, kind woman—Miss Prillwitz—called,
and told me that he is being cared for at a
little Home, for nothing, Stephen ; and they
will keep him there until we are on our feet
again. If that isn't brotherly love, I don't
know what is. It makes me believe that
there is such a thing as Christianity, after
all."

Still Stephen Trimble was silent. She
was happy, and he would not dispel her
illusion, at least not now. Evidently there
were *some* good people in New York, and
she had experienced their kindness. He had

expected to find her suffering from neglect
and cruelty. He would not have been surprised if she had died. He could hardly believe that a *charity patient* had received such
attention. That their little son had been
also tenderly cared for passed his belief, but
he would see for himself, and he took the
address of the Home. He bade his wife
good-bye gently. "I shall come back to
you very soon, Stephen," she said, "and
things will go better then." He could not tell
her of his deep despair. He tried to smile,
but only succeeded in giving her a pitiful,
longing look. He walked on toward the Home
of the Elder Brother, sure that its name was
a lie, and that he would find Lovey abused.
But he was met at the door by Mrs. Halsey,
whom he had known at Rickett's Court, who
called his little son to come down and see
his papa, and who told him of the plan
of which she had just been speaking
to Miss Prillwitz. And a moment later
Lovey, well dressed, clean, fat, and jolly,
tumbled into his arms with a cry of rapture.

"Do you want to come home, Lovey?" he
asked.

"No, daddy, I want you to come here.
Please, Mrs. Halsey, mayn't he come?"

"We would like to have him very much to teach our boys the use of tools for a few hours every day. It is just what I have been telling your father."

"A week ago," said Stephen Trimble, "your offer would have been heaven to me ; now I am afraid it is too late."

"Don't say so," urged Mrs. Halsey; and she called Miss Prillwitz to talk the matter over with him. Miss Prillwitz's first argument was to ask him to luncheon. He ate the nourishing food—the first good meal that had passed his lips for many days—and he said, as he bade them farewell, "I will come to you if I can, and teach your boys mechanics ; if I don't come it will be because something has happened to me, and if anything happens to me I want to ask you to lend a helping hand to my wife—and may God bless you." A new impulse stirred within his heart, gratitude, which he had not felt toward any human being for years. He was softened, and tears stood in his eyes. He could almost forgive the landlord of Rickett's Court now.

An impulse to see the man, though not with any hope of gaining anything from the interview, came over him. It was still early, and he walked down Broadway to the building designated, and looked into the bank. How wealthy and strong it looked, with the clerks busily at work calling off fabulous sums to one another, and handling the piles of bills and coin! The safe-doors stood open, and he could see the great bolts and bars, and complicated combinations; and he smiled scornfully as he thought how easily the little machine upon which he had been working would open them all.

A policeman saw him staring in at the window, and asked him his business.

"I want to find Mr. Armstrong, the R. R. president."

"Then you must go up-stairs. There is the door."

He walked up and saw another room, with gentlemen sitting in easy attitudes in comfortable chairs. He asked a clerk for Mr Armstrong, and was told that he was in Washington, on business.

"Business connected with a patent?"

"Yes; I believe so. What did you want of him?"

"Nothing. Say only that Stephen Trimble called."

"What! is this Stephen Trimble?" exclaimed a hearty voice behind him; and, turning, the inventor saw an earnest but kindly looking man, who had just entered carrying a hand-bag.

"That is Mr. Armstrong," said the clerk, and Stephen Trimble stared fascinated.

"Step into my private office," said the financier. "I am glad you have come. It is always better to transact business at first hand, and I was sorry you could not come when Mr. Meyer asked you to do so."

"I do not know what you mean, sir."

"Did not Solomon Meyer tell you that I wanted you to call, with reference to the four thousand dollars still unpaid on our patent transaction?"

"Solomon Meyer told me that I was too late, and that you did not care for my invention."

Mr. Armstrong sprang from his chair. "And he never gave you my check for a thousand dollars?"

"Never; though I heard that he had it;" and Stephen Trimble related what the anarchist had told him.

Mr. Armstrong unlocked a safe, and took
15

from it the contract in regard to the patent. "Is not this your signature ?" he asked.

"No, sir : I never saw the paper.

"Then Solomon Meyer is a swindler."

" Very likely, sir."

"Go home ; say nothing, and I will have him arrested. Stop—a little money may not come amiss to you just now. Here is fifty dollars on our account. I will see you again to-morrow, but I have an important appointment now."

" I don't know how to thank you, sir, or what to say," said Stephen Trimble, utterly confounded.

"There are no thanks due ; on the contrary, I owe you a small matter of five thousand dollars—perhaps more—for it seems you have not signed this paper, and perhaps may not be willing to sell your invention for so small a sum."

As he spoke, the confidential clerk tapped at the door and remarked, " Dr. Carver, sir, of ——— Hospital, says you telegraphed to him from Washington to meet you here."

Instantly Stephen Trimble saw that Mr. Armstrong had forgotten his existence ; his entire expression changed from kindly benevolence to intense eagerness and anxiety.

"What has he got to worry about, I wonder!" thought the inventor, as he gave place to the physician, and descended the stairs. Force of habit led his steps toward Rickett's Court, but he walked like a different man, and the workman who had seen his cringing, crouching manner as he slouched out of the court that morning, did not recognize the man who entered with buoyant, determined step. The change had begun when he left the door of the Home of the Elder Brother. There his faith in his kind had been restored. Had the good fortune of the afternoon befallen him before that experience he could not have believed it, or the stupendous change would have driven him insane. But it had come upon him, mercifully, by degrees, and he was rapturously happy, and clearer in mind than he had been for months. It was as if a great and crushing weight had been lifted from heart and brain. Suddenly, as he crossed the threshold, he remembered the infernal-machine. The anarchists would probably use it that night, and Alexander Armstrong, his benefactor, was doomed. He wondered how he could ever have been so mad as to aid them. There was only one thing to be done:

he must undo his work, render the contrivance harmless, and save his friend. He knocked at the door; there was no answer; the men were probably out. He tried to open it, but it was locked. He could easily have picked the lock, but people were coming and going. The new fire-escape suggested itself to his mind, and he decided to go to his room and, as it was already dark, descend by it to the workroom. This resolution was quickly accomplished. He lighted a candle and was just reaching toward the machine, when the door opened and the anarchists entered.

"What are you doing? I thought you had finished your work," said his former employer.

"No, I have not finished," replied Stephen Trimble, nervously taking up a tool and beginning to remove a screw.

"You are tampering with the machine; put it down!" and the man seized it angrily.

"Let go!" shouted Stephen Trimble, "you touch it at your peril; the button is under your hand!"

The warning came too late—there was a blinding flash, then a crash as though the heavens had fallen; then blackness and silence.

" Her father sent her in his land to dwell,
　　Giving to her a work that must be done ;
And since the king loves all his people well,
　　Therefore she, too, cares for them, every one.
And when she stoops to lift from want and sin,
The brighter shines her royalty therein.
" She walks erect through dangers manifold,
　　While many sink and fail on either hand ;
She dreads not summer's heat nor winter's cold,
　　For both are subject to the king's command.
She need not be afraid of anything,
Because she is the daughter of a king."　　*Anon.*

WHILE all these sad things were happening Winnie and I were enjoying a happy summer at my beloved home in the blessed country.

It is not to be imagined that Winnie dropped all her wild ways and became a saint at once. She had been sobered by her sad experience in plotting and scheming for the little prince; but since her full forgiveness her elastic spirits rose to the surface, and her cheerful disposition asserted itself in many playful pranks and merry, tricksy ways.

We did not forget our promise to work for the Elder Brother, but for a time we did nothing but rest fully and completely.

She was delighted with the country. The fresh air and free, wholesome life acted upon her like wine. She climbed walls and trees, leaped brooks, whistled, shouted, rode on the hay-carts, helped in the kitchen and in the garden, drove Dobbin about the country roads, went berrying, and was a prime favorite with all the boys, though I regret to say that at first, perhaps on this very account, the country girls were a little jealous and envious of her. But not a whit cared Winnie for this. She tramped over the fields and through marshes, with her botanist's can swung across her shoulder by a shawl-strap, searching for specimens. She boated and bathed, taking like a duck to the water, and learning to swim more quickly than any other person I had ever known. She loved to work in our old-fashioned garden, pulled weeds diligently, and seemed to love to feel the fresh earth with her fingers. Our flowers were all such as had grown there in my grandmother's time. It seemed to me that she must have modeled it on Mary Howitt's garden, for we had the very flowers which she describes in her poems.

> " And there, before the little bench,
>   O'ershadowed by the bower, ,
> Grow southernwood and lemon thyme,
>   Sweet-pea and gillyflower ;
>
> " And pinks and clove carnations,
>   Rich-scented, side by side :
> And at each end a holly-hock,
>   With an edge of London-pride.
>
> " I had marigolds and columbines,
>   And pinks all pinks exceeding ,
> I'd a noble root of love-in-a-mist,
>   And plenty of love-lies-bleeding."

There was a bed of herbs, too, which my mother cherished—sweet-marjoram and summer savory, sage, rue, and rosemary.

Winnie took a great interest in all of these plants. The country girls thought it odd that she should care for the wild plants which were so common in our vicinity, not knowing Winnie's enthusiasm for botany, and her desire to make a large collection to show the princess. An unusually ignorant girl met her on one of her botanizing expeditions, and Winnie asked her if maiden-hair grew in our region. "Of course it does!" the girl replied, indignantly; "you didn't s'pose we all wore wigs, did you?"

It was some time before Winnie could control herself and explain that the maiden-hair of which she was in search was a kind of fern.

"Do you want it for a charm?" the girl asked.

"No," replied Winnnie; "what will it do?"

"If you put it in your shoe and say the right kind of a charm, you will understand the language of the birds."

"Then I shall certainly try it," said Winnie, "for that would be great fun."

Another day mother brought the same girl into the garden, where Winnie was at work, to give her some vegetables.

"Did you try the charm?" the girl asked.

"Yes, indeed," Winnie replied.

"And did it work?"

"Oh, famously! There is a wood-pecker in the old tree just outside of my window, and he wakes me by his drumming every morning. This morning I understood for the first time just what he has been saying. It was 'Wake up, wake up! little rascal, little rascal, little rascal!'"

The girl stared at Winnie in open-mouthed astonishment. "You must be a witch," she said.

"That's what they call me—Witch Winnie.'

They were standing beside mother's bed of herbs, and the frightened girl pulled up a stalk of rue and held it at arm's length, as though it were a protection. "Don't come nigh me! don't work any of your tricks on me!" she said.

Winnie explained that she was only in sport, but the girl was only half reassured, and still clung to the spray of rue.

Miss Prillwitz afterward explained that rue, like vervain, was supposed to "hinder witches of their will," probably from the fact that it was once used in the Church of Rome, bound in fagots, as a holy-water sprinkler, and is spoken of in old writings as the "Herb of Grace."

In this way Witch Winnie's name was revived again, and was applied to her by her new friends, even though they did not believe in her uncanny powers.

The princess came to us later in the season for a visit of a month, and we came to know her intimately and love her dearly. She brought five of the boys from the Home with her, for mother was pleased with the enterprise, and father had said that he guessed it wouldn't break him to give those city children a taste of what the country was like, and if we women folk could stand them he supposed he could.

Winnie took the boys in charge and led them off with her on her long tramps and to row in the safe, flat-bottomed boat. They had great sport, crabbing, bathing, swimming, and fishing, and their vacation did them a world of good. These were the boys for whom the princess had planned the industrial classes, but Mr. Trimble lay at the hospital injured, it was thought, unto death by the explosion at Rickett's Court, and that plan was postponed for the present.

The boys attracted much attention in the Sabbath-school and wherever they appeared. Many questions were asked, and Miss Prillwitz was requested to explain the plan of the Home, in public and in private, at the sewing society, and at the Fourth of July picnic.

WITCH WINNIE.—*Page 230.*

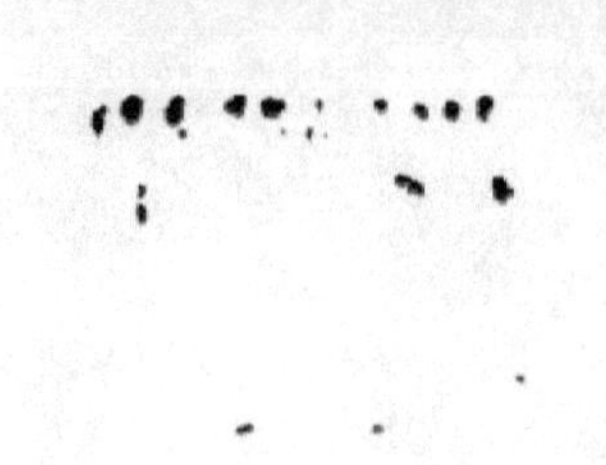

We were not all ignorant country bumpkins at Scup Harbor, and we were not all poor. There were plenty of farmers, who dressed coarsely and fared plainly, who had bank accounts that would have bought out many a New Yorker of fashion. They were not selfish either. I have heard somewhere of a stingy deacon who, on hearing of a case of heart-rending distress, prayed for it in this wise:

"O Lord, 'giving doth not impoverish Thee, neither doth withholding enrich Thee,' but giving doth impoverish us, and withholding doth enrich us; therefore do Thou attend to this case, good Lord; do *Thou* attend to this case."

Now this story may not be exaggerated, but I can only say that he did not live in our section of the country. Our deacons were soft-hearted, though horny-handed men, and though they had the poor of their own church and vicinity to look out for, and performed that office well, they decided that Scup Harbor was rich enough to extend a helping hand to New York, since New York was either too poor or too hard-hearted to care for its own.

Accordingly a collection was taken up in

church that made Miss Prillwitz's heart sing for joy; and the Ladies' Benevolent Sewing Society voted to have a box of clothing ready for the Home by cold weather.

The grown people were not the only ones interested; there were girls among us of gentle manners and hearts, and who were far better educated than Milly Roseveldt. Some of these heard of Miss Prillwitz's eminence as a scientist, and helped me to organize a class for her in Natural History, and the remainder of the summer took on an aspect of mental improvement as well as of physical recreation. Miss Prillwitz mapped out a course of work and reading for each of us to carry on after her return to the city, and the circle arranged to meet at the homes of the members, and read essays and discuss different scientific subjects.

Winnie was surprised at the amount of intelligence and information displayed, and soon acquired a sincere respect for country girls. It was at one of our meetings after the princess had returned to New York that she noticed that Ethel Stanley, the daughter of a wealthy dairy farmer, wore a little silver cross with a purple ribbon knot.

"Has it come here, too?" she asked; "are you a King's Daughter?"

"Oh yes," replied Ethel; "I belong to the Helpful Ten, and there is a Cheer-Up Ten at the Corners What do you call your link?"

"The Seek-and-to-Save Ten," Winnie replied; and she explained the mission of our Circle, and how we hoped to help the Elder Brother in his search for the little lost princes. Ethel was delighted. "I think we might help you," she said; "we are Methodists, but we don't mind working for you if you will let us. I suppose you are all Episcopalians in New York?"

"Oh dear, no!" exclaimed Winnie, "we are everything; Tib is a Congregationalist, and Emma Jane is a Unitarian; Adelaide is Presbyterian; Trude Middleton is a Dutch Reformer; Rosario Ricos is Catholic; Puss Seligman is a Jewess; Little Breeze comes from Philadelphia Quaker stock, though she is so gay you wouldn't think it; Cynthia Vaughn is a Baptist; Milly Roseveldt is the only Episcopalian; and I'm a —heathen."

"No you are not," I protested; "you are a follower of the Elder Brother, Winnie, and that means you are a Christian." She gave my hand a little squeeze, and Ethel exclaimed, "I should think your society would go to pieces; I don't see how you can work together with such different views."

"That depends," said Winnie, thoughtfully, "whether in future we all pull in different directions, and tear our charity to pieces between us, or whether each of us uses all her force to bring in people from our different church organizations to help in the work, and make it widely and purely undenominational. I mean to write a little parable on that subject some day, for I feel full of it."

"Do!" we all exclaimed; "write it for the next meeting at Ethel's."

"I don't know; it would hardly be a scientific essay, you know."

"I am not sure about that," replied Ethel; "I think it might be called a scientific method of carrying on charitable enterprises. Please write it, and I will invite our Ten, and the Cheer-up Ten from the Corners, and the Loyal Legion, and the Missionary Society, and all the girls I know generally."

The plan was carried into effect, and at the next meeting Winnie read us this fable, which she called

A FISH STORY.[*]

Once upon a time the fishes and salt-water animals down in the bay decided to organize a Home for Sea-urchins.

The circumstances of the remarkable agitation which suddenly spread among the peaceful denizens of the deep became known to me by my inadvertently getting a spray of sea-fern in one of my bathing-sandals. I suddenly discovered that I could understand the voices of the little creatures that I had so often watched from Tib's father's dory, or sported among when I took my sea-bath. I lay in the dory one afternoon, looking down into the clear depth of the water, watching the tricks and manners of a sea-anemone, and thinking how similar her behavior was to that of a reigning belle at a popular watering-place, when it dawned upon me that she *was* the belle of the cove, surrounded by a circle of obsequious masculine admirers, prominent among whom were the hermit-crab, the oc-

---

Note. — This allegory was first published in *Good Company*, of 1880.

16

topus, the jelly-fish, the lobster, the conger-
eel, the king-iyo, and the stickleback—

"Now, Winnie," I objected, "you never
saw an octopus or a king-iyo in our cove, and
you can't make me believe it!"

"My dear Tib," Winnie replied, "didn't I
tell you this was a fish story? Pray do not
interrupt again. The animals that I have
mentioned were all aspirants to the hand
of the Sea-Anemone, and the first remarks
which I overheard and comprehended were
her confidences to her friend the Gold-Fish,
in which she intimated that she considered
the Jelly-Fish the most amiable, the Lobster
the richest, the King-iyo (a titled foreigner
from Japan) the most *distingué*, and the
Conger-Eel the most polite; but, after all, the
Hermit-Crab was really the best, and she
liked him more than any of the others, with
the exception of the Octopus, who was so fas-
cinatingly wicked.

The next time that I looked into the cove
was during a meeting of the managers of
the Sea-Urchins' Home.

The Sea-Anemone had just been unanimously elected to the presidency on account
of her popularity.

The Cuttle-Fish had been created secretary

in recognition of his remarkable facility in
throwing ink, while all official documents
were stamped by the Seal.

The Electric-Eel was made visiting physician ; and the Shark, surgeon and lecturer
on vivisection.

The Hermit-Crab, who had been detailed to
make observations on the *modus* in which
such societies were carried on among human
beings, made the following report :

" Miss President and Fellow-Fishes :

" Your committee have made a careful
investigation of the subject assigned them,
and agree that while man's faculties have
not been cultivated to so high an extent as
those pertaining to fishes, he is still a moral
and intellectual animal. We believe that if
he were put in possession of the advantages
accorded to our race, and were submerged
in salt-water for several centuries, his brain
would undoubtedly become so pickled as
to reduce it in size and intensify its quality. Favorable conditions of brain-pickling
are all that is necessary, in our opinion, to
develop some of the most advanced specimens of this *genus* into a low form of *mol-
lusk*.

" The opinions of the Hermit-Crab were

considered a marvel of liberality and generous thinking. He proceeded to explain the society-forming instinct of the human race as a professor of our own species might lecture on the concretions of deep-sea corals, and continued swimmingly, as fishes usually do, until a white-whiskered Sea-Lion begged leave to make a motion, in the language of a motto of conduct which he had often heard shouted to seamen by their commanders: 'When you are in the navy, do as the knaves do.' 'Let us,' he added, ' act upon this principle of conformity, by doing amongst men as the many do, and immediately organize a fair to meet the salaries of our officers and pay the debt on the society building.'

" ' But none of us need salaries,' objected the Lobster, ' and we have no debt.'

" ' As to declining a salary because I do not need it,' replied the Sea-Lion, ' I can only say that I find no such example set by the race whose customs we are following; and without a debt, or at least a deficit in the accounts of our treasurer, the respectability of our society may well be questioned.'

"A committee of Codfish aristocrats was at once authorized to secure a debt of magnificent proportions, at whatever cost, and the salary of each member of the society was set according to his own estimates. Frequent meetings of the managers were appointed for the purpose of drawing the salaries, and as the care of the Sea-Urchins could with the utmost ingenuity be made to take up but a small portion of the time, each of the managers seized upon these meetings as opportunities to air their own particular opinions. The Lobster, who was something of an autocrat, and had determined from the outset to run the concern, took the entire business management into his own claws, greatly incensing the ladies on the debt committee by intimating that they knew nothing of business, and that his office-boy, the Craw-Fish, could have devised a debt of far nobler proportions. The King-iyo, or three-tailed fish of Japan, trusted that the philosophy of the Orient was to have its full recognition in the principles of the society, and that the Sea-Urchins would be instructed in Buddhism. The Octopus, who had been one of the most desperate characters in the bay, carried his change of heart so far as to assert that no one could be considered as religious, or even respectable, who had not been ex-

tremely wicked, and urged that only the
most depraved and hopeless young Sea-Urchins be admitted into the Home. While the
Octopus raved over essential wickedness,
and the King-ivo of philosophy, the Jelly-
Fish dabbled in humanitarianism, and asserted that brains were not to be tolerated,
thought was to be considered a crime, and a
heart the only organ necessary for the spiritual body. All books on theology and philosophy should be sold for old paper, and the
proceeds invested in charlotte russe for
tramps and criminals. Every measure in
the least savoring of logic or common sense
must be vetoed.

"The Stickleback, who luxuriated in contro-
versy, and in making himself generally disagreeable, summed up the remarks of those
preceding him as the merest vaporing of
idiocy, and denounced every system of belief held by his fellow - managers, before
hearing it, with the same impartiality. An-
tagonism, he asserted, was the only rational
attitude for any fish under all circumstances.
The Conger-Eel, managing to gain possession of the floor, endeavored to pour oil on
the troubled waters. He was sure that if the
heterogeneous, and even antipathetic, ideas

held by the different managers were only presented in writing, they would, properly mingled, blend as sweetly as lemon juice and loaf sugar in a cooling summer libation. The Cuttle-Fish, was unanimously elected chairman of a committee for eliciting and reconciling the opinions of the managers in a printed constitution. He opened the ball with a statement of his own views, which he passed to each member in turn, asking them to add their several criticisms and corrections. When the paper had gone the rounds it was read in open session by the Hermit-Crab, who summed up everything that had gone before, in a paper entitled 'A Historical Review of the Documents, beginning with the King-iyo's criticism of Mr. Snapping-Turtle's attack on Mr. Shrimp's vindication of Mr. Jelly-Fish's Apology of Mr. Conger-Eel's Deprecatory Answer to Mr. Lobster's satire on Mr. Stickleback's Challenge to Mr. Octopus's Dogmatic Denunciation of Mr. Shark's strictures on Miss Sea-Anemone's conciliatory explanation of Mr. Cuttle-Fish's exposition of the views of the society.'

"Of course this paper satisfied no one, and the meeting plunged at once into a whirlpool of ruinous discussion.

"The Stickleback bristled his spines and glared angrily about him, shrieking, 'Antag- onism! Nihilism!'

"'Fanaticism, Sensationalism!' yelled the Octopus.

" 'Dogmatism! Absolutism!' replied the Lobster. hurling clams about him in the belief that they were works on combative theology.

"' Asceticism! Monasticism!' groaned the Hermit-Crab, retreating into a pipe bowl and blocking the entrance with a pearl-oyster.

"'Humanitarianism!' warbled the Jelly- Fish, as he choked three sea-melons and a quart of sea-mushrooms into the mouth of a sick Grampus.

"'Paganism! Barbarianism!' retorted the King-iyo, punching the Jelly-Fish.

"'Optimism! Universalism!' sweetly chanted the Conger-Eel, but as he spoke the entire convention broke up and floated away, leaving the little Sea-Urchins crying for their supper, and only a debt of colossal propor- tions to mark the site of the proposed Home."

"And how do you propose to avoid the fate of the Fish Society?" Ethel asked, after the storm of applause which followed Win- nie's paper had subsided.

"By recognizing, from the first, that we unite only for this special purpose, and that we all have very varied and contradictory opinions, which we will make no attempt to reconcile or ventilate. I think we can make our very differences an element of strength, if it is acknowledged from the outset that we are to be different. As Corresponding Secretary of our Ten I have received the most encouraging reports from the girls. They are all working hard for the Home, and all working in different ways, and each seems to think that the Home belongs to her individually—as it really does—and that her organization is responsible for its success. I am sure that when we next meet, the girls will accept Mrs. Middleton's proposition to have the Home of the Elder Brother entered as one of the Dutch Reformed charities, and I hope that each of the other girls will take measures to have it recognized as one of the charities of her particular church organization. I have a letter from Little Breeze, saying that the Friends' Meeting in Philadelphia, of which her mother is a member, propose to own a bed in the Home; and Puss Seligman writes that the Hebrew Charitable Association, of which her brother is Vice-President, have voted to hold themselves responsible for every child of their race whom we entertain. Cynthia Vaughn reports that the Church of ——burgh, Pennsylvania, will keep us in coal on condition that a delegation of the children go to the Baptist Sunday-school. Miss Prillwitz has already divided the Home into detachments, sending the children, as far as possible, to the churches which their mothers prefer, and there is a strong division of Baptists."

"I think," said Ethel, "that our Methodist Church would like to have a share in the work. I am sure that father will be glad to supply you with milk and butter as his own private subscription."

The President of the Loyal Legion then spoke up, and proposed that their organization furnish barrels and make the rounds of the farms in procession, soliciting apples and potatoes, which they would freight to the Home, on condition that a Loyal Legion Temperance Society be organized among the children of the Elder Brother, to be considered as a branch of the Scup Harbor Legion.

The Cheer-up Ten from the Corners held a brief meeting in the orchard, and returned to report that they had decided to adopt one of our children to clothe. They desired that the child of the poorest parents be assigned them, and promised that if the proper measurements were sent, they would keep it respectably dressed in garments of their own make.

I suggested little Georgie, a child rescued from Mrs. Grogan, whose mother could only furnish fifty cents a week from her scanty earnings for his support; and our convention broke up for that day, after partaking of strawberries and cream, singing a good old hymn, slightly altered for the occasion by Winnie.

> " Here we raise our Ebenezer,
>   Hither by God's grace we come;
> And we hope, by His good pleasure,
>   Long we may remain a Home."

Note.—The Messiah Home, 4 Rutherford Place, New York, a charity founded for children by children, whose beautiful work suggested to the author this simple story, has been greatly helped by circles of the King's Daughters, several of whom have adopted children to clothe after the manner of the Cheer-up Ten. The writer commends this work to any other circles of the King's Daughters eager to do the work of the Elder Brother.

CHAPTER XIV.

"When smale foules maken melodie,
    That sleepen alle night with open eye,
    Than longen folk to gon on pilgrimages."
        Chaucer, Prologue to " Canterbury Tales."

IT must not be imagined that our entire summer was given over to works of charity and mercy. There were times when we quite forgot the Home of the Elder Brother in merry romping and girlish enjoyment ; and one of the pleasantest experiences of that season was an excursion in two tin-peddler's carts, or rather, in two carts belonging to one tin-peddler; a pilgrimage which was undertaken solely and simply as a lark, and most successfully realized its aims.

Toward the end of June, while Miss Prillwitz was still with us, father fell into a state of body or mind which he called "the malary." It was the fashion for everyone in our region to dub every disease with which they might be afflicted, from indigestion to inherited insanity, malaria ; and the prescription given by our wise old physician for this disease of many manifestations was always the same.

"I don't know exactly what has caused this trouble," he would say, "but I know what will cure it. You need a change. If you've been living high, diet. If you've been starving yourself, have Thanksgiving dinner every day. Take a change of air and a change of scene, a change of occupation, and, above all, a change of habits, and somewhere we'll hit the nail on the head that has done the mischief."

The prescription pleased my father. He decided that he needed a change from the coast to the interior, and from exercise to a sedentary life. "Instead of tramping around this farm," he said, "I would like to be driving over the western Massachusetts hills. I

am as sick of this eternal pound, pound of
the surf on the shore as of the sea-fog in my
throat."

"Take the horses, father," said mother,
cheerfully, "and drive through Connecticut
up to your brother Asahel's farm in Hawley.
I can run this household well enough without you."

"It would be a rather lonesome drive,"
father demurred, though his eyes shone with
longing.

"Zen why not to take us wiz you, Mr.
Smiss?" asked Miss Prillwitz. "We would
each stand her share of ze expenses, and such
a tour of *diligence* would be most delightful."

Upon this the matter was thoroughly can-
vassed, and it was finally decided that
mother should remain at home with the five
little boys, whom Ethel Stanley and the Helpful Ten had agreed to amuse during our absence; and that Miss Prillwitz, Miss Sartoris, Winnie, Mr. Stillman, and I should
accompany father. Mr. Stillman was a sum-
mer-boarder from New York, who came to
us every season to fish and hunt. Hearing
that Miss Prillwitz was fond of ornithology,
and that the lighthouse-keeper sent her dead
birds, he tried to please her by shooting

others and bringing them to her, but she soon made him understand that she preferred studying them alive and at liberty.

"Zese poor leetle tears zat haf cast zemself on ze lighthouse," she explained, "zey have not been kill for me, zey could not else, but I wish I could hinder zem of it."

"It is not much fun to shoot birds, after all," Mr. Stillman admitted, "only the exultation in hitting a difficult mark. I hate to pick them up afterward."

"If it is only ze chase and ze difficulty which make you admiration," said Miss Prillwitz, "why do you not buy to yourself a camera of detective for ze instantaneousness, whereby you can photograph ze bird on his wing? Zey tell me it shall be much more difficult to do zat zan to shoot him dead."

And so Mr. Stillman had sent to New York for an amateur photographer's outfit, and had fitted up a dark-room in the old smoke-house, where he developed his negatives. He was a man to whom almost everything he tried was easy, and he tried his hand at many things. He had traveled much, and assured us that wherever he went he tried to learn some new accomplishment. In China he had learned the art of

making fireworks, and earlier in the season
the smoke-house had served as a chemical
laboratory for the manufacture of rockets.
Before Miss Prillwitz had suggested amateur
photography, Mr. Stillman had amused us
by setting off fireworks on the beach at
night, but the new craze seemed destined to
supersede every other ; pyrotechnics were
neglected, and the shot-gun and rifle rusted
from lack of use.

A tin-peddler lived not far from us—an enterprising man, the proprietor of two carts,
one of which his wife was accustomed to
conduct. following him in caravan style on
his summer journeyings ; but this season the
man was sick, his wife busied in his care, and
the great carts, piled with wares, stood waiting in the sheds.

" I've a notion," said father, " to buy Eben
Ware's stock and hire one of his carts.　I
can hitch my span of horses to it, and I will
make enough selling tinware, as we go, to
pay the expenses of the whole trip."

This plan did not strike me pleasantly at
first, but before I had time to object Mr.
Stillman joined in enthusiastically.

" A capital idea, Mr. Smith, but you know
our board is to be paid regularly to Mrs.

Smith during our absence. Miss Sartoris, Miss Prillwitz, and I all insist upon that. I will take the peddler's horses and his second cart, which I will load up with my photographic outfit, the ladies' baggage, camp supplies, etc., and I will fill in any spare space with fireworks, which I will offer for sale along the route, all profits to be devoted to the charity in which the ladies are interested. The Fourth of July is so near that I fancy the rockets will meet with a ready sale."

All joined in the plan with zest. Our wardrobe was reduced to a minimum. It was discovered that the two carts were arranged to turn into ambulances for camping at night, and would furnish comfortable accommodation for the feminine portion of the party, while a small tent was provided for father and Mr. Stillman. In reality we camped but one night, preferring to stop at wayside inns, but it was pleasant to know that we could do so whenever we wished. A roll of army blankets and comfortables, a few kitchen utensils, and some canned goods were stored away in Mr. Stillman's cart, with Miss Prillwitz's botanizing equipments, Miss Sartoris's sketching materials, his own belongings, and all the fireworks which he could manufacture in time; and still there was room in the capacious interior. The rifle was added at Winnie's urgent request, as a defense against wild beasts, though we all joined in ridiculing her fears that bears might be found in the Massachusetts woods, little thinking that we should have a thrilling adventure with a grizzly bear. At the last moment Mr. Stillman added another camera and more chemicals.

"This means," he replied, in answer to our questions, "that I have rented a tintype outfit of a photographer over at the Corners, and propose to add to our resources by taking tintypes as we go."

Mr. Stillman's ready invention, so fertile in expedients, received hearty applause, and the gypsy caravan set out in high feather. We took the steamboat with the carts to New Haven, and from that point struck into the interior by turnpikes and country roads, father leading the way with his jingling coach, Miss Prillwitz and Winnie perched high beside him, and Miss Sartoris, Mr. Stillman, and I, who called ourselves the Art Contingent, bringing up the rear. How beautiful the roads were, shaded by willows or arched by elms! Often fascinating lanes led off from the highway toward comfortable farm-houses, or grass-grown, deserted roads mounted through shady gorges to the lonely hills, tempting us from the beaten track. But the highway was beautiful enough. Sometimes it followed the curves of some vagrant stream, or wound around gently undulating hills. Miss Sartoris pointed out the fact that it was most frequently a succession of curves, while French highways are laid out as straight as the surveyor can make them, and do not compose as well in landscape paintings. The Connecticut roads we found easy to travel, well kept, and for the most part level or of easy grade. It was not until we reached western Massachusetts that we walked up the hills to lighten the load, or that the driver pressed his foot hard on the brake as the cart coasted down the steep inclines like a toboggan.

Winnie was delighted with a bit of gorge road which played at hide and seek with a wayward brook. " It seems to me," she said, " that the wood is a matter-of-fact business man, and the brook is his sweet but willful little wife. See how he tries to adapt himself to her whims and pranks, keeping as close to her as he can, while the side which she does

not touch is stern with rock and shadow!
And she, coquettish little thing, wanders
away from him into the deepest part of the
ravine, where he cannot follow, and hides
herself in a tangle of fern and wild-flowers,
till, just as the lonely old road, quite in despair
at having lost her, crosses the ravine on a
bridge of logs, apparently for the sole purpose
of seeking her, the merry little brook flies
under the mossy bridge and is close beside
him on the side which he thought farthest
from her."

"That is a very good parable," said father.
" You've struck the nail pretty fairly. That's
the way it has always been with my wife
and me. My daughter, too, is one of the
brook kind, but you needn't conclude that
the old road doesn't enjoy all the company
of blackberry vines and laurel and ferns
that the brook attracts to itself, and which
never would have come near the road but
for the brook. I mean you and Miss Sartoris
and the rest."

"And sometimes," Winnie added, "the
road has its grains of corn or wheat dropped
from a passing cart, you know, to give to the
sparrows, and the brook likes that ever so
much."

Father always called the boys from the Home "the sparrows," and he was pleased by this allusion to his generosity.

We found ourselves following the circus at one stage of our journey, and we pitched our tent and made camp not far from the fair-grounds. We chose for our camp a site which had once been occupied by a house that had been burned to the ground. The only out-building which had escaped the conflagration was a root-house, or cellar, excavated, cave-like, in the side of a hill. It struck Mr. Stillman as a particularly good "dark-room," and we at once pre-empted it. Miss Sartoris painted a sign-board for the photographic studio, and Winnie and I arranged a bower with a flowery background for Mr. Stillman's sitters. We had a rich harvest that day, Winnie acting as cashier, and Miss Sartoris, as assistant, posing the groups. Mr. Stillman was quite exhausted when evening fell. He said he had never done such a day's work in his life, and his tintype material was nearly used up. We were patronized not only by the country people who came to see the show, sheepish lovers who wished to have their portraits taken together, and parties of merry young

people, but also by the showmen themselves. The living skeleton and the fat lady,
the strong man supporting a great weight
by his teeth, the lion tamer with his pets,
and the snake charmer, were all among Mr.
Stillman's patrons. When it was understood that he had an instantaneous camera
with him, the equestrienne desired him to
take a photograph of her while performing
her famous feat of riding five horses at once,
and the acrobats challenged him to catch
their rapid evolutions. He surprised them
by his remarkable success in obtaining a
perfect negative. It was our most successful day, from a financial point of view, for
we realized over twenty dollars.

Father had a rather annoying experience
which made him desire to avoid the circus
in the future. Among the articles which
the tin-peddler had given him was a soldering furnace and irons, for mending old tinware. Father made his first attempt to use
these tools on this afternoon. The door-
keeper of one of the tents brought him his
japanned tin strong-box to mend, and father
attacked the task laboriously, succeeding in
making it firm by a rather too plentiful application of solder. He was so interested in

his task that he did not notice that an organ-grinder, one of the followers of the circus, had pressed quite near and was regarding the coins, which the door-keeper had temporarily turned into his handkerchief, with hungry eyes. Suddenly the monkey, which had been tied to the organ, became loose, and springing straight to the little furnace, seized and brandished the heated soldering-iron. A great excitement ensued, for no one dared to take the formidable weapon from the mischievous creature. The owner of the monkey seemed at his wits' end He raged, stamped, tore his hair, commanded and entreated the monkey to bring back the iron, all to no avail. The monkey, having burned himself, finally dropped it, but, frightened by the pain or by his master's threats, continued his flight into the woods, followed by the organ-grinder. When the excitement occasioned by this event had subsided, a still greater one ensued on the discovery that the door-keeper's handkerchief and money had disappeared. The man angrily charged father with its theft, but Mr. Stillman came running from his dark-room with a negative which he had just developed. He had been standing at

the door, with his detective camera in his
hand, and, quite unintentionally, had done
real detective work, for, intending only to
catch the monkey with the soldering-iron,
he had focused upon it at the very first, and
the unerring eye of the camera had seen and
recorded what every one else had been too
preoccupied to discover—the organ-grinder
snatching the gate-keeper's money. The
negative was a sufficient witness, and the
organ-grinder was at once sought for, but
the earth seemed to have swallowed him.
The monkey was found nursing his burned
paw in a tree, but his master and the money
were not to be found. There was such a
train of beggars and questionable characters
in the wake of the circus that it was decided
not to pursue our moneyed advantage by
following with them ; and the next day we
stood back from the road to let the heavy,
shambling elephants and long train of
gaudily decorated wagons pass by. Mr.
Stillman had his detective camera out, and
took some interesting views of the procession. Father had taken a dislike to the
soldering outfit, and congratulated himself
that the monkey had lost the iron, but the
last in the procession, a gypsy fortune-teller,

handed it to him, saying that it was a lode-
stone, which would bring evil fortune to the
person who possessed it, and advising him
to give it to his worst enemy. "I am a
witch," Winnie laughed, "and can reverse
all omens—so we need not fear." Turning
from the highway, we now struck across the
country, through chestnut woods, where
Miss Prillwitz taught us to recognize the
song of the thrush, the sweetest of New
England songsters, and cousin of the mock-
ing-bird. Mr. Stillman was vexed that he
could not obtain a single photograph of a
thrush, but she is a shy bird, and keeps hidden in leafy thickets, and though we heard
her song frequently, we never saw her. Mr.
Stillman became very skillful in photograph-
ing other birds, even fixing the agile little
fly-catchers in their eccentric movements,
the watchful bobolink atilt on a mullein-
stalk, the swallows skimming the river's
surface, and the sagacious crows, who, having proved that a very natural scarecrow
was harmless, were less suspicious of him.
The withered limbs on certain old apple-
trees were favorite perches for the birds, for
there was no foliage here to impede their
flight, and outlined against the sky they

were capital targets for the camera. Mr. Stillman secured a gentlemanly king-bird in such a position, his white breast and black back and tail feathers reminding Winnie of a dandy in full evening dress.

Miss Prillwitz remarked on the brilliant plumage of the New England birds, and said that it was a mistake to imagine that those of the South were more beautiful. She pointed out the black and gold orioles, the lovely bluebird, the scarlet tanagers, as brilliant as flamingoes, the beautiful rose-breasted grosbeaks, with a rich crimson heart upon their breasts, and the red-winged blackbirds, with their scarlet epaulets, reminding one of brisk artillerymen. It was the last of June—the most perfect of all the months—and as we rode we repeated all of the poets' praises of the month that we could remember. We agreed that Lowell had sung the season best :

> " The bobolink has come, and, like the soul
>   Of the sweet season vocal in a bird,
>   Gurgles in ecstasy we know not what,
>   Save June ! Dear June ! Now God be praised
>   for June."

But Margaret Deland pleased us nearly as well in her homage to the queen month :

" The dark laburnum's chains of gold
   She twists about her throat ;
Perched on her shoulder, blithe and bold,
   The brown thrush sounds his note !

" And blue of the far dappled sky,
   That shows at warm, still noon,
Shines in her softly smiling eye—
   Oh who's so sweet as June ?"

Father was not a very successful tin-peddler. The thrifty New England housewives were not pleased because he was unwilling to exchange his wares for rags, after the manner of other itinerant venders. He was uncertain as to the prices which he ought to charge; asking so little for his brooms that one patron purchased all his stock, at a decided loss to himself, as he afterwards learned, and demanding so much for nutmeg graters that a sagacious purchaser showed him the door with scorn. The soldering outfit, too, caused him much woe. It seemed that the original peddler was a clever tinker; and all sorts of broken articles, from clocks to umbrellas, were brought out for father to mend. At first father good-humoredly tried his best, but having burned holes in his clothing, as well as blistered his hands, and succeeding in no instance in satisfying his patrons, he was tempted to throw the little furnace away, but his sense of economy would not allow him to do this, and he stowed it away vindictively in the depths of his cart.

Shortly after this we spent two very interesting days in visiting Mt. Holyoke and Smith colleges. They gave both to Winnie and me a desire for a higher education than that which we were receiving at Madame's. Miss Sartoris wandered slowly through the Art Building of Smith, looking longingly at its superb equipment. The college is charmingly situated in the old town of Northampton. We were told that the students had just acted a Greek play, the " Electra " of Sophocles, very successfully, and we looked at one another in envy as we thought how impossible it would have been to present such a drama at Madame's.

We passed the Holyoke range on July 1. This barrier marks as distinct a climatic change as Cape Cod in the Atlantic currents, for, just as, south of the Cape, and apparently threatened by her bent arm, the Gulf Stream sweeps to the north the tropic sea-weeds, and north of it, and gathered close in its embrace, the Arctic mosses cling to the cold heart of New England; so, south of the Holyoke range the air may be tepid and lifeless, while beyond it invigorating breezes from the Northland are dancing cheerily.

We had eaten the last native Connecticut strawberries, but they were just in their glory north of the barrier, and though the almanac said July, it was June weather still.

Mount Tom and Mount Holyoke stand as sentinels at the entrance of a lovely region, through whose elm-covered villages we drove at leisurely pace, resting over a Sabbath at old Hadley, one of the most charming places, with its principal street a double cloister of elms and maples, and where a Sabbath peace and stillness brooded even on week-days. Mr. Stillman found, for the next few days, a ready sale for his fireworks, exhausting his stock and adding twenty-five dollars to the treasury. About twelve miles north of Mount Holyoke rises Mount Toby, a noble mountain, which assumes, from certain directions, the shape of a crouching camel. The resemblance is even more marked than that of the Rock of Gibraltar to a lion. It dominates the country round about, and from its summit nearly a score of nestling towns and villages are visible. Among these Mr. Stillman sold his rockets, and proposed that we should spend Fourth of July night on its summit, and there watch the little fire-fountains on the plain below. It was an attractive plan, but Mr. Stillman had not counted the weather into his reckoning. It had been a sultry day. As we stopped at a farm-house on our way from Sunderland to Mount Toby, the good woman told us to look out for rain. "The grass has been waiting two days to be cut," she said, "but it looks kinder lowry, and the men-folks daresn't begin haying."

There were two superb cumulus clouds in the west, shaped like elm-trees, or wine-glasses touching rims, and there was a blue rain-cloud in the southeast, with fringes trailing the landscape, and blurring it from our view.

"The rain may not reach Mount Toby at all," father said; "showers travel about among those hills in a curious fashion. I have seen it raining hard on one side of Sugar-Loaf, while the other was dry and dusty. There is a deserted railway station at the foot of Toby, where we can spend the night. There were picnic grounds laid out on the mountain at one time, but the enterprise failed, and trains no longer stop there."

A view of the station, which we reached early in the afternoon, confirmed father's recommendation of it. The roof was weather tight, and it was a roomy, comfortable building, a good refuge should a shower overtake us. We picnicked beside a beautiful cascade, and leaving the horses picketed beside the carts, proceeded to climb the mountain on foot. It was glorious with masses of white and pink laurel, which I had never before seen in its perfection, and Miss Prillwitz introduced me to many other plants and flowers new to me. The Amherst basket-fern, shaped like a Corinthian capital, grew in perfection, the Columbine blew her flame-colored trumpets, and the harebell rang her inaudible chimes from mossy clefts in the gray rocks. Miss Prillwitz said she had last picked harebells in Austria.

"You know," said Miss Sartoris, "that Mary Howitt calls the harebell

> 'The very flower to take
> Into the heart, and make
> The cherished memory of all pleasant places;
> Name but the light harebell,
> And straight is pictured well
> Where'er of fallen state lie lonely traces.

> Old slopes of pasture ground,
> Old fosse and moat and mound,
> Where the mailed warrior and crusader came;
> Old walls of crumbling stone
> With ivy overgrown,
> Rise at the mention of the harebell's name.'"

Miss Prillwitz pointed out more obscure plants, and gave us interesting bits of information in regard to them. Some had strangely human characteristics. The cassia, a shrinking sensitive-plant with yellow blossoms, was one of these, while the poison-ivy in its unctuous growth had an evil and malignant appearance which seemed to hint at its inimical nature. She told us how to tell the poisonous sumac from the harmless variety, the poisonous kind being the only one that has pendant fruit. She gave us also a little chat about parasitic plants, suggested by a *gerardia*, a little thief which draws its nutriment from the roots of huckleberry.

"I did not know that plants had so little conscience," said Winnie. "It reminds me of a guest a Southern gentleman had, who remained twelve years, and after the death of the host married his widow."

"Plants seem also to be cruel," said Miss Prillwitz. "Zere is ze *apocynum*, a carnivorous plant which eat ze insect. You should read of him by Darwin. He set a trap for ze fly wiz some honey, and when Mr. Fly tickle ze plant, quick he is caught, and Mr. Apocynum he eat him, and digest him at his leisures."

"Miss Prillwitz, you should write a book for young people, and call it 'Near Nature's Heart,'" I suggested.

"I would so like," replied Miss Prillwitz, "but if I waste my time to write, how should I earn my lifes? I have know many author, and very few do make their wealths by—by their authority."

Miss Prillwitz brought out the last word triumphantly, quite sure that she had achieved a success in our difficult language. I turned aside to Mr. Stillman, that she might not see my smile. "How interesting she makes our climb," I said, "and all these wayside weeds! 'She illustrates the landscape.'"

"In my humble opinion it is Miss Sartoris who 'illustrates the landscape,'" he replied. "See what a picture she makes reaching after those sweet-briar blossoms! I wish I had not left my detective at the station."

Miss Sartoris was indeed very pretty. It seemed to me that she grew younger and more bewitching with every day of our trip. Each changing pose as she leisurely picked the wild roses was full of grace, but I could hardly understand why Mr. Stillman should greatly regret not securing this particular view, when she had figured in at least half of the photographs which he had taken.

We reached the top of the mountain just at sunset. The west glowed with a yellow-green color. The strange clouds, which had been as white as curds in the afternoon, were now dark blue, lighted by flashes of heat lightning. They moved forward like the pillar which led the Israelites, great billowy masses piled one on the other and toppling at the summit, while they melted at the base into a mist of rain. Behind them was the background of the sunset, like a plate of hammered gold dashed with that sinister green. There were threatening rumblings in the east also, and Amherst and its college buildings were blotted out by the rain clouds, which resembled the petals of a fringed gentian, and seemed to be traveling rapidly in our direction.

Father took a rapid view of the horizon. "There will be no fireworks display for us to-night," he said. "There are two showers which will meet in an hour's time, and Toby will be just about in the centre of the fracas. We had better hurry down the mountain if we want to escape a wetting."

Miss Sartoris gave a longing look at the beautiful panorama of nestling villages, forest and winding river (a view unsurpassed in Massachusetts), and now glorified by the magnificent cloud effects. "Can we not rest for half an hour?" she asked.

" I think not," father replied, and we reluctantly retraced our steps. When half-way down the mountain the wind, which preceded the march of the cloud battalion, caught up with us. The chestnuts crouched low and moaned, the poplars shivered and shook their white palms, and the hemlocks writhed and tossed their gaunt arms as though in agony. Then there was a hush, when they seemed to stand still from very fear, and a minute later the storm burst upon us. We were but a short distance from the station when this occurred, and the foliage which roofed the road was so dense that we were not very wet when we reached our shelter. There was an invigorating scent of ozone in the air, and a certain exhilaration in being out in a storm, and in hearing the crash of falling limbs far back in the woods. We noticed the gentleness of the rain, which, though apparently fierce, did not break a single fragile wild-flower. Each leaf, sponged free from dust, brightened as though freshly varnished, and each blade of grass threaded its necklace of crystal beads. The cascade, swollen and turbid, roared angrily at our side, and a shallower rivulet made the path slippery as we hurried on; but a few moments of laughing scramble brought us panting into the dry station, safely housed for the night from the storm.

Father and Mr. Stillman arranged shelter for the horses by spreading the tent between the two carts, and we ate our supper at what had formerly been a refreshment counter. Then the ticket-office was assigned to the gentlemen as their dormitory, and hammocks were hung for the rest of us in the ladies' waiting-room. We told ghost stories for a time by the light of a spirit-lamp and a few candles, but retired early, as we were thoroughly tired from our long walk, and were soon asleep, lulled by the monotone of the falling rain. We were not destined, however, to enjoy a night of undisturbed repose, for the principal adventure of our journey occurred that night.

I do not know how long we had slept when we were all suddenly awakened by a startling scream.

"What is it? Oh, what is it?" gasped Winnie.

"Is it a catamount?" asked Miss Sartoris.

I thought of the railroad track, which ran close beside us, and suggested that it might be the shriek of a passing engine, when suddenly it came again on the side of the station opposite to the track. Father sprang up, exclaiming, "Something is the matter with the horses!"

The rain was still pouring, and a dim light from the swinging lantern illumined the room. As father spoke, one of the windows, which had been left open for ventilation, was suddenly filled by an uncouth form, which, with much scrambling and snorting, was proceeding to force an entrance.

"It is a bear!" shrieked Winnie; and so it was. Mr. Stillman rushed forward with his rifle. There was a loud report, and a heavy fall on the outside.

"Horses can scent bears at a distance," said father, as he took down the lantern;

"but who would have thought there were any such creatures in these woods?"

" Perhaps it has broken away from the circus," suggested Mr. Stillman, reloading his rifle; for there was an ominous growling outside. Human voices were presently heard whose intonations were almost as harsh as those of the brute. Father unbarred the door, and we saw two men bending over the wounded bear, which he now saw was muzzled, and the property of the men, who had evidently heard of the old station, and had thought to take refuge in it from the storm.

"Here's a pretty state of things!" father exclaimed, with a whistle. " You have shot a performing bear, Stillman, and these show-men will probably make us pay dearly for the mistake."

We had all been terribly frightened; but we recovered instantly on this announcement, and hurriedly dressing, we peered out at the men as they stood about the wounded animal and discussed the situation. One of the showmen was a foreigner, who swore and grumbled in some strange language, which Miss Prillwitz afterward told us was Russian. The other was unmistakably a Jew, and he took a Jewish advantage of the accident.

"You haf ruined our pizness—dot bear he wort one, two hundert dollar!"

"Nonsense!" replied father, as confidently as if he were accustomed to trade in that species of live-stock; "he's dear at fifty. Besides, he isn't dead, nor anything like it. Hold him with this halter, you two, and I'll examine him. There! I told you so; it's only a flesh wound in the right foreleg. There are no bones broken. He will be ready for travel in a week. All you've got to do is to stay here for a few days—and where could you be better off? We leave in the morning, and no one will dispute your possession of this house. I will leave you enough provisions to keep you until you are ready for the road again."

The men talked it over in Russian, and seemed far from satisfied, though Mr. Stillman offered to give them twenty dollars as an equivalent for what they would have gained during the next week, and father added his remaining stock of small tinware, which, he explained, they could easily sell from door to door at the farm-houses and villages in the vicinity. He was tired of his occupation as a tin-peddler, and glad to get rid of the obnoxious soldering furnace, as well as the patty-pans and muffin-rings. A settlement was finally effected when, in addition to this, Mr. Stillman agreed to their demand for fifty dollars cash indemnity.

There was no more sleep for us that night, and it was with rueful countenances that we discussed the adventure among ourselves.

"To think," lamented Winnie, "that, just as we were congratulating ourselves on gaining so much money for the Home, we should be obliged to pay it all out, and more besides, to these wretched men, and all for nothing too!"

"Yes," replied Mr. Stillman, "that is the provoking part. If I had only killed the creature we might have bear-steak for breakfast (though it would have been pretty expensive meat), and I could have had his hide mounted as a rug, and have exhibited it to my friends with truthful braggadocio as one of my hunting trophies."

I sympathized with Winnie in regard to the depleted condition of our treasury; but Miss Prillwitz remarked, enigmatically, that the adventure might not prove to be such a losing one as we imagined. We begged her to explain; but she bade us wait until we were at least ten miles from our encampment.

We relinquished the station to the showmen after a very early breakfast, and drove away with lightened carts and subdued spirits.

The rain had ceased, but was likely to begin again at any moment, for the sky was thickly overcast, and father suggested that, as this was a famous trout region, we might do well to spend the morning in fishing. This plan pleased all but Miss Prillwitz, who whispered to father that she had particular reasons for reaching a telegraph station as soon as possible, and we accordingly directed our course at a rattling pace toward the shire town of Greenfield. On the way Miss Prillwitz confided to us her suspicions; and in order that the reader may understand them, I must anticipate the events which are to be related in the next chapter, and explain that, after the explosion at Rickett's Court, Solomon Meyer and one of the anarchists had disappeared from New York, and Mr. Armstrong had offered a reward for their apprehension.

The anarchist was known to be a Russian,

and though Miss Prillwitz had never seen
Solomon Meyer, she felt sure, from Lovey
Trimble's description of him, that he had decided to avoid the ordinary routes of travel,
and to journey toward Canada on foot, dis-
guised as an itinerant showman. She had
more proofs of his identity than these suspicions. The men had conversed very freely
with each other in Russian, never dreaming that there was any one present who
could understand the language. The Russian had complained bitterly that this accident would delay their journey to Canada,
and the Jew had replied that it might be as
well to lie hidden until the search was over.

Arrived at Greenfield, Miss Prillwitz telegraphed to Mr. Armstrong, and in two hours
received the following reply: "Have the
local authorities arrest the parties and detain
them until I can reach Greenfield."

Accordingly Mr. Stillman and father,
with a sheriff and a constable, drove back
toward Mount Toby in a sort of picnic
wagon. Father advised us to await him at
Deerfield, one of the most interesting
villages in the Connecticut Valley — both
from its intrinsic beauty and its historic
associations. We engaged lodgings at the

small hotel, where we found but one other traveler, a dejected book - agent. It was nearly dinner-time. and the landlord looked rather alarmed by the unexpected arrival of so many hungry-looking guests, but he soon set before us a capital dinner of broiled chicken, and after a little rest we took a stroll through the beautiful old town. We were informed that the Memorial Hall. a museum of antique furniture. books, costumes, and other curiosities. was well worth visiting; and so, indeed, we found it. One object which greatly interested me was an old spinnet, with a quaint collection of music, both sacred and secular. Here was a great bass-viol which formerely groaned out an accompaniment to the male voices of the choir as they took their part in such strange, metrical arrangements as

> " Come, my beloved, haste away,
> Cut short the hours of thy delay;
> Fly like a youthful hart or roe,
> Over the hills where spices grow."

The Library. too, a collection of " the (literary) remains " of many celebrated doctors of divinity, was a fascinating room, and one in which we would have enjoyed prowling

for a long time. Hawthorne has given such
an admirable description, in his " Old
Manse," of just such a library, that I cannot
forbear quoting it here.

" The old books would (for the most
part) have been worth nothing at an auction.
They possessed an interest quite apart from
their literary value ; many of them had been
transmitted down through a series of conse-
crated hands from the days of the mighty
Puritan divines. A few of the books were
Latin folios written by Catholic authors ;
others demolished papistry as with a sledge-
hammer, in plain English. A dissertation
on the book of Job, which only Job himself
could have had the patience to read, filled
at least a score of small, thick-set quartos,
at the rate of two or three volumes to a
chapter. Then there was a vast folio " Body
of Divinity." Volumes of this form dated
back two hundred years and more, and were
generally bound in black leather, exhibiting
precisely such an appearance as we should
attribute to books of enchantment. Others
equally antique were of a size proper to be
carried in the large waistcoat pockets of old
times: diminutive, but as black as their
bulkier brethren. These little old volumes

impressed me as if they had been intended for very large ones, but had been, unfortunately, blighted at an early stage of their growth. Then there were old newspapers, and still older almanacs, which reproduced the epochs when they had issued from the press with a distinctness that was altogether unaccountable. It was as if I had found bits of magic looking-glass among the books, with the images of a vanished century in them."

We lingered long in the Library, and in the Indian Room, where stands an old door gashed by the tomahawks of the Indians who, with a company of French, in 1704, surprised Deerfield, massacred a great part of the inhabitants, and carried a hundred and twelve as prisoners to Canada. Yellow and crumbling letters, uncertainly spelled and quaintly phrased, hung around the room, telling how perilous such a driving-tour as we had just taken would have been in those pioneer days. One, dated 1756 and written to Captain John Burt in the Crown Point Army, read as follows:

"Dear Husband.

"It is a Crasie time in this place. There is but little Traviling by

the Massachusetts Fort which makes it more
difficult to send letters. Capt. Chapin and
Chidester and his Son were killed and scalpt
by the Enemy near the new foort at Hoo-
sack."

Sarah Williams, of Roxbury, in 1714
announces to her friends at Deerfield the
expected return of many of their friends
who had been carried off in different raids—
" We have had news that Unkel is Coming
with one hundred and fifty Captives."
The number dwindled, and many who
were carried away on that dreary march
through the winter snow never returned, but
among the relics preserved in the archives of
Memorial Hall is a pathetic little red shoe
which walked all the way from Hatfield to
Canada and back, on the foot of little Sally
Colman. It is hardly more than a tiny sole,
with a rag of the scarlet upper clinging to it
but it tells the story of the cruel march, and
the heroic efforts of the noble men who
effected the rescue of their friends, better
than many a page of print.
We were so much interested in Memorial
Hall that it was long past supper-time before
we thought of leaving. The book-agent advised us to visit the old burying-ground, and,

after supper, offered to show us the way.
We found it grass-grown and neglected ; in
some portions, a thicket of climbing vines
and tangling briers. Indeed, the entire God's
acre was so given over to nature that the
birds built undismayed, while the squirrel
frisked impudently on the headstones, and
the woodchuck burrowed beside the tombs.
It had not been used for many years ; a
newer cemetery raised its white monuments
on the hillside, while here lichens nearly filled the carving, and the stones leaned at
tipsy angles, proving that grief for any
buried here had been long assuaged, that the
very mourners had passed away, and it was
doubtful whether a single aged man still
lingered in the town of whom it could be
said that

> " These mossy marbles rest
> On the lips which he has pressed
> In their bloom.
> And the names he loved to hear
> Have been carved for many a year
> On the tomb."

As Miss Sartoris remarked, the place did
not suggest sadness, but gentle retrospection,
while curiosity provoked the fancy to fill out
the histories so provokingly suggested in the

inscriptions. Here was buried Mrs. Williams, whom her epitaph declares to be "the virtuous and desirable consort of Mr. John Williams," and Mr. Mehuman Hinsdale, who was "twice captivated by the barbarous salvages."

The book-agent read us another epitaph, copied in Vernon, Vt., which suggested a three-volume novel in the history which it gave of early Indian times. Our imaginations sank exhausted as we attempted to follow the heroine through all her matrimonial complications, I give it as it was dictated to me:

MRS. JEMIMA TUTE,

SUCCESSIVELY RELICT OF MESSRS. WILLIAM PHIPS,

CALEB HOWE, AND AMOS TUTE.

THE TWO FIRST WERE KILLED BY THE INDIANS,

PHIPS, JULY 5, 1743; HOWE, JUNE 27, 1755.

WHEN HOWE WAS KILLED, SHE AND HER CHILDREN, THEN SEVEN IN NUMBER, WERE CARRIED INTO CAPTIVITY. THE OLDEST DAUGHTER WENT TO FRANCE, AND WAS MARRIED TO A FRENCH GENTLEMAN. THE YOUNGEST WAS TORN FROM HER BREAST, AND PERISHED WITH HUNGER. BY THE AID OF SOME BENEVOLENT GENTLEMEN, AND HER OWN PERSONAL HEROISM, SHE RECOVERED THE REST. SHE DIED MARCH 7, 1805, HAVING PASSED THROUGH MORE VICISSITUDES AND ENDURED MORE HARDSHIPS THAN ANY OF HER CONTEMPORARIES.

> " ' No more can savage foe annoy,
>   Nor aught her widespread fame destroy.' "

It was dark when we wandered back to the hotel, past the old manse built for the Reverend John Williams by his parishioners after his return from captivity. We were told that some one residing in the house of late had occasion to move a tall piece of furniture in one of the chambers, and discovered a door. Opening this, a secret staircase was found leading from the cellar to the attic. No one living had known of its existence, and many were the wild guesses made as to its object.

When we returned to the hotel we found that father and Mr. Stillman had not yet arrived. Miss Sartoris seemed very anxious, and feared that there might have been trouble in arresting the tramps. Winnie cheered us by suggesting the trout fishing, which Mr. Stillman had reluctantly abandoned when we left Mt. Toby. It would be a good night for fishing, the landlord said; perhaps they had remained for it, since the distance to Toby was too long to be comfortably made three times in one day. After breakfast the next morning, as our travelers were still absent, Miss Sartoris and I unpacked our sketch-boxes and began to make a study of the street from the north end, just at the point where the French and Indians, "swarming over the palisades on the drifted snow, surprised and sacked the sleeping town."

Miss Prillwitz and Winnie, with their botanists' cans, followed a little brook that ran at the back of the hotel, and came back laden with blue German forget-me-nots. Father and Mr. Stillman arrived just before dinner, Mr. Stillman carrying in one hand a string of beautiful speckled trout, and in the other something which looked like a buffalo-robe. He looked very triumphant and happy, while father followed, carrying in a rather sheepish manner—what but the old soldering furnace! We greeted them with so much laughter and so many questions that it was some time before they could give an account of their adventures.

Arrived at the Mount Toby railroad station, they had found it deserted. The men having evidently decided that it was not safe to await the recovery of the bear, had accordingly killed it, and secreted it in a cave at the foot of the mountain. The sheriff knew of this cave, and in examining it in search of the men, found the carcass of the bear.

"And so," exclaimed Mr. Stillman, exhibiting the skin, "I secured my rug, after all, but we concluded that the meat looked rather tough, and we would not take it. I shall express this skin straight to a taxidermist that I know, and have it handsomely mounted."

"But the men!" I asked; "you don't mean to tell me that they escaped?"

"No," replied father; "but if you can't keep quiet I shall not be able to tell you how they were caught. It was this very ill-luck-bringing soldering outfit that did it. When we found that they had left, I suspected that they had taken the morning train for Canada at the Montague station, for no trains stopped at Toby; and in case they had done that, there was hardly a chance of our reaching the station and ascertaining the fact in time to telegraph and effect their arrest before they could leave the country. We had driven from Greenfield pretty rapidly, and our horses were tired; then we took a wrong turning, and got off into Leverett, or some other unhappy wilderness; but after a while we found a farmer who provided us with fresh beasts, and we reached the Montague station toward evening. It was shut up, and the station-master had gone home, but

after another half-hour we found him. Yes,
our men had bought tickets for Montreal
that morning. Then you should have seen
our hurry to telegraph; but the station-
master advised us to keep cool, and wait a
little. 'They bought their tickets,' he said,
'but they didn't go there.' So that was a
feint, I thought, to throw us off the track.
But no; on their way from Toby they had
decided that they would have a cup of coffee,
and they had sat down behind a barn to
make it on my soldering furnace, and as
they were doubtless as tired of carrying the
old thing as I was, they left it there. The
wind blew the coals into the hay, and in a
few minutes the barn was on fire. Someone
had seen them leave the yard, and before
the train came along for which they were
waiting, they were arrested as incendiaries,
and taken to the Greenfield jail. As this
was precisely where the sheriff wished to
take them, there was nothing for him to do
but to return and notify the authorities that
the men would be wanted soon on more seri-
ous charges. And as the station-master informed us that there was some good trout-
fishing near by, we decided to spend the night
in Montague. So we let the sheriff and con-

stable drive back to Greenfield without us, and telegraphed Mr. Armstrong that his birds were caught."

"If they only turn out to be his birds!" said Winnie.

"I haf no doubtfuls of zat," said Miss Prillwitz.

"But why did you bring back that wretched little furnace and iron?" I asked.

"Why, the curious part of it is that the farmer who drove us over this morning had found them in the ruins of his barn, and he brought them along, thinking that we might like them to help in identifying the rascals. I couldn't refuse his kindness, but I certainly shall not carry them away from this place. I don't believe in such nonsense, but the gypsy's prediction has come true so far, and they brought bad fortune to the gentlemen to whom I presented them."

Mr. Armstrong, who had been telegraphed for, arrived with a police officer that night; and Miss Prillwitz, father, and Mr. Stillman were absent all the next morning making depositions to aid in the identification of the prisoners.

It was finally decided to remove them to New York to await trial on Mr. Armstrong's

charges. We set out that afternoon for Ashfield, our route leading us over beautiful hills,
and affording us views of rare loveliness.
Ashfield is a village loved by literary men as
Deerfield is by artists. Deerfield nestles in a
valley, while Ashfield lies on the breezy hill-
top; George William Curtis is the centre of
the coterie of rare minds who make Ashfield
their summer home. Mr. Curtis gives a lecture here once a year for the benefit of the
Sanderson Academy. At this time every manner of vehicle brings the country-people over
the winding roads, which converge in Ashfield like the spokes of a wheel in their hub.
We were not fortunate enough to light on
this red-letter day, and we accordingly rested
over night at the long low inn, and started
early the next morning for uncle's home in
Hawley. The distance was short, as the crow
flies, but it seemed to be all up-hill. The last
mile was through one of those gorges so common in this region, where the fissure between
the hills is so narrow that the sun only looks in
for two or three hours. Slowly climbing the
long, green-vaulted stairway, the dusky tap-
estry was at length looped back for us, and
the road, emerging from the wooded ravine,
gleamed yellow-white between the grassy

mounds. Crowning one of these knolls stood a long, white farm-house, spreading out wing after wing in hospitable effort to shelter the entire hill-top. Beside the road stood a post with a letter-box affixed, for the reception of the mail left by the daily stage. We passed a huddle of old barns and out-buildings, among which I recognized a carpenter's shop, a carriage-shed, a sugar-house in convenient proximity to a grove of maples, a dairy through which ran the brook, keeping cool and solid the eighty pounds of butter which my cousins made each week, a cider-mill, and behind it an orchard of russet apple-trees, and a long row of bee-hives fronting the flower-garden.

Uncle expected us, and it was delightful to see the meeting between the two brothers, who had not seen each other in twelve years. There were plenty of airy bedrooms, hung with pure white dimity, and after our gypsy life it seemed very pleasant to find once more the comforts of a home. We spent several days at the Maples, attending service in the dear old-fashioned church with its high, square pews.

Aunt Prue had all of our travel-soiled clothing neatly washed, and refilled the emptied hampers and lunch-baskets with abundant supplies from the products of the farm and her own good cookery.

Uncle was a large, easy man, who dearly loved to tell a story to match his own ample proportions, only the twinkle in his eye redeeming him from the charge of deception. Aunt Prue's rigid conscience revolted at uncle's romances. "Asahel Smith!" she would exclaim, "how can you lie like that; and you a church-member?"

"Now, Prudence," Uncle Asahel would reply, " the catechism says a lie is a story told with intention to deceive, and when I told these girls that I drove the oxen home with the last load of hay so fast that I got it into the barn before a drop of water fell, while it was raining so hard behind me that Watch, who was following the wagon, actually *swam* all the way up from the medder—when I told 'em that, I cal'late I didn't deceive 'em; I was only cultivating their imaginations."

Aunt Prue groaned in spirit, and began to sing, in a high, cracked voice.

> " False are the men of high degree,
>   The baser sort are vanity;
>   Weighed in the balance, both appear
>   Light as a puff of empty air."

While at The Maples we made an excursion to Cummington, formerly Bryant's home. We sat in the library, shut in by a thick grove, where he composed his translations of the Odyssey and Iliad, and we played with a little pet dog of which he had been very fond. Not far from the estate is a fine library, Bryant's gift to the little town. " Bryant's River " is a brawling little stream which flows through a very picturesque region. We amused ourselves by fancying that we recognized spots described in several of his poems.

There was a grand old oak upon the place which might have inspired his lines—

> " This mighty oak—
> By whose immovable stem I stand, and seem
> Almost annihilated—not a prince
> In all that proud Old World beyond the deep
> E'er wore his crown as loftily as he
> Wears the green coronal of leaves with which
> Thy hand has graced him."

The scenery about Cummington and Hawley tempted us to a frequent use of our sketching-materials. Mr. Stillman, too, found several birds new to him, and took some beautiful landscape photographs. Miss Sartoris gave him new ideas about choosing views where mountain and cloud, trees and reflections, composed well, and his photographs became much more artistic. He began to talk about the importance of placing his darkest dark here, and his highest light there, of balancing a steeple in this part of his picture by a human interest in the foreground, of massing his shadows, of angular composition, of tone and harmony, and the rest of the cant of the studio. Nor was it all cant; Miss Sartoris had taught him to see more in nature than he had ever seen before, and while his ambition had hitherto been to secure sharp photographs of instantaneous effects— mere feats of mechanical skill—his aim was now to produce pictures satisfying to highly cultivated tastes. He acknowledged that all this was due to Miss Sartoris, who had opened a new world to him, though it seemed to me that he really owed quite as much to Miss Prillwitz, but for whose influence he would never have taken up photography. I was a little jealous for our princess, and felt that, though Miss Sartoris was young and fair, and Miss Prillwitz old and wrinkled, this was no reason why honor should not be rendered where honor was due.

There was a pond with a bit of swamp

land on uncle's farm, which he considered
the blot on the place, but which Miss Sartoris
declared was a real treasure-trove for a picture. One end was covered with lily-pads,
and great waxy pond-lilies were opening
their alabaster lamps here and there on the
surface, while the yellow cow-lilies dotted
the other end with their butter-pats. Cat-tails
and rushes grew in the shallower portions,
and here was to be found the rare moccasin-
flower, a pink and white orchid of exquisite
shape. Miss Sartoris painted a beautiful
picture here. She said it reminded her of
the pond which Ruskin describes with an
artist's insight and enthusiasm.

" A great painter sees beneath and behind
the brown surface what will take him a day's
work to follow ; and he follows it, cost what
it will. He sees it is not the dull, dirty,
blank thing which he supposes it to be ; it
has a heart as well as ourselves, and in the
bottom of that there are the boughs of the
tall trees and their quivering leaves, and all
the hazy passages of sunshine, the blades of
the shaking grass, with all manner of hues of
variable, pleasant light out of the sky ; and
the bottom seen in the clear little bits at the
edge, and the stones of it, and all the sky.

For the ugly gutter that stagnates over the drain-bars in the heart of the foul city is not altogether base. It is at your will that you see in that despised stream either the refuse of the street or the image of the sky ; **so** it is with many other things which we unkindly despise."

We all regretted when our short visit at The Maples came to an end, but Miss Prillwitz felt that she must be hastening back to the Home, and we had already transgressed the bounds which we had set to our outing. We decided to vary our journey by returning through Berkshire. We drove, the first day, to Pittsfield, a flourishing little city, and now for the first time we felt ourselves out of place in the peddler's carts. Nowhere else had we attracted any special attention. It was a common thing for tin-peddlers to take their feminine relatives with them on their jaunts, and as we dressed very plainly, and conducted ourselves with gravity, no one gave us a second look.

At Pittsfield, however, we came in contact once more with "society," and the loungers on the hotel veranda gave us a broadside of astonished looks as we alighted. " It is very disagreeable to be stared at in

this way," Winnie remarked to Miss Prillwitz as we entered.

"My tear," replied the good lady, "it takes
four eyes to make a stare." *

Winnie colored deeply, for she knew that if
she had been less self-conscious she would
not have felt the curious and impertinent
gaze. We left Pittsfield so early the next
morning that none of the hotel loungers were
on the piazza to comment on our appearance.

We drove, that day, over the lovely Lenox
hills, once covered by stony pastures, dotted
here and there by lonely farm-houses, but
now a succession of beautiful parks and
aristocratic villas and mansions. Mr. Stillman had his camera out, and photographed
a number of the handsome residences as we
passed, and one of the gay little village-carts
driven by a young woman dressed in the
height of fashion, and presided over by a
footman in livery.

"That does not seem to me a sensible way
of going into the country," said Winnie.
"I don't believe she has half the fun that we
have in this old caravan."

---

* A remark once made by Professor Maria Mitchell to
a student of Vassar College who had made a similar com-
plaint.

"Perhaps not," I replied, "but I presume that Adelaide and Milly are driving about in much the same style; and we know that better-hearted girls never lived."

We picnicked near "Stockbridge Bowl," a lovely lake, blue as Geneva and encircled by beautiful hills. As father brought out the lunch-hamper I noticed a queer expression on his face. "What do you suppose I have found stowed away in the back part of the cart?" he asked.

"Not the soldering furnace?" we all replied, in unison.

He smiled grimly, and, instead of replying, placed it before us. "That Deerfield landlord must have packed it up without your knowledge," said Miss Sartoris. "Its reappearance is becoming really amusing; let us make one grand final effort to get rid of it by sinking it in the middle of the lake."

"Will you do it?"

"Certainly."

Miss Sartoris took the furnace and ran down to the lake, whence she presently returned empty-handed.

"Did you drown the creature?"

"Not exactly, but I gave an ancient fisherman whom I found there a quarter to commit the crime for me." I told him that it was something which we were tired of, and never wished to see again, and he promised me, in rather a mixed manner, that 'human hand should never find hide nor hair of it, nor human eye set foot on it again.'"

A general laugh followed this announcement. How should we know that the man's suspicions were excited by Miss Sartoris's anxiety to get rid of the object, and that instead of sinking it in the middle of "the Bowl" he wrapped it carefully in brown paper, and labeling it "To be kept till called for," hid it under the bank! "Somebody will come for that object," he said to himself; "shouldn't wonder if it was wanted at court as circumstantial evidence of somethin' or 'nother."

Another event occurred while we were resting at "the Bowl." Miss Sartoris remarked that a view which she had obtained as she returned from the lake was the most enchanting that she had seen on the trip. "How I wish that I had time to sketch it!" she said.

"I will photograph it for you," Mr. Stillman exclaimed, with alacrity, "if you will kindly show me just where you would like to have the view taken."

They walked back together, a turn in the road hiding them from our view. We waited for them a long time, and at length father became impatient and drove on, leaving me to hold Mr. Stillman's horses. When they came back there was an expression on their faces which told everything. I should have known it even if Mr. Stillman had been able to keep the words back, but he was too happy to be silent. "You were lamenting, this morning," he said to me as he took the reins, "that we had only two more days to journey together."

" That is all," I replied, " unless Miss Sartoris and you have decided to make a longer trip."

" Yes," he replied, " you have guessed it exactly : Miss Sartoris has just consented to journey on through life with me."

I was surprised, and yet, when I came to think of it, I saw that I ought to have suspected it from the time they first met; and, all things considered, they were admirably suited to each other. So I could only rejoice in their happiness, though I wondered, a little selfishly, what Madame's would be without Miss Sartoris, and whether I should ever have a teacher whom I should love as well.

When we caught up with the other cart father asked whether he got a successful negative.

"No," replied Mr. Stillman, "I didn't get a very decided negative, and I confess I didn't want one."

There was a look of blank astonishment on all their faces, and then a peal of laughter as his meaning dawned upon them. After the storm of congratulations and exclamations had ceased, Miss Sartoris suddenly exclaimed, "You left your detective camera!"

"That is so," Mr. Stillman replied, "Shall we drive back after it?"

"Not unless you want to catch that shower," father remarked, pointing to a threatening cloud.

"I'll get you ladies under shelter first, and then I really think I must look it up," said Mr. Stillman. But before we reached Stockbridge we met a coaching-party conducted by a nattily dressed young man of slender build, who managed his spirited four-in-hand with considerable skill, and who reined them in as we approached, exclaiming, "Stillman!

20

by all that's odd!" Mr. Stillman introduced the gentleman as a Mr. Van Silver, an old friend from the city, and mutual explanations followed. He was now on his way to Lenox, and agreed to stop at the spot which Mr. Stillman indicated, and if he could find the camera express it to Mr. Stillman at Scup Harbor.

Very little more of interest to the reader occurred until we reached home. We followed the Housatonic for the greater part of our way, and when we had nearly reached its mouth, drove across to New Haven, from which port, having completed our round-trip, we took the steamer for home. Father found a letter from Mr. Armstrong in relation to the thieves taken in Montague, who were proved to be the criminals of Rickett's Court, whose retribution shall be related in the next chapter. The little boys left in mother's care had conducted themselves in as exemplary a manner as could be expected, there having been no cases of really bad conduct, and only two slight accidents.

Miss Prillwitz took them under her wing and left with them for the Home, all looking happier, browner, and rounder for their stay in the country. Winnie regretted that our

scheme for filling the treasury of the Home
had not been a success, since the aggregate
of money made by peddling tinware and
rockets, and by taking tintypes, did not meet
the expenses of the trip. Mr. Stillman, however, insisted on presenting the institution
with a handsome check, "as an inadequate
thank-offering," so he said, for the great
blessing which had come to him in our
journeying "over the hills and far away."

Miss Sartoris left almost immediately for
her own home, and Mr. Stillman followed
her soon after. Two express packages came
to him before he left us. One was the bear-
skin, handsomely mounted, the other was
preceded by a note from his friend Mr.
Van Silver, which said that he had over-
taken a venerable fisherman walking off with
his camera, and that it required considerable
persuasion of a "sterling quality" to rescue
it from him. Mr. Stillman opened the package with grateful anticipation, and found—
the soldering furnace!

CHAPTER XV.

THE ESTATES DEL PARADISO.

"I have been here before,
  But when, or how, I cannot tell;
I know the grass beyond the door,
  The sweet, keen smell,
The sighing sound, the lights around the shore.

You have been mine before,
  How long ago I may not know;
But just when, at that swallow's soar,
  Your neck turned so,
Some veil did fall—I knew it all of yore."
—*Rossetti.*

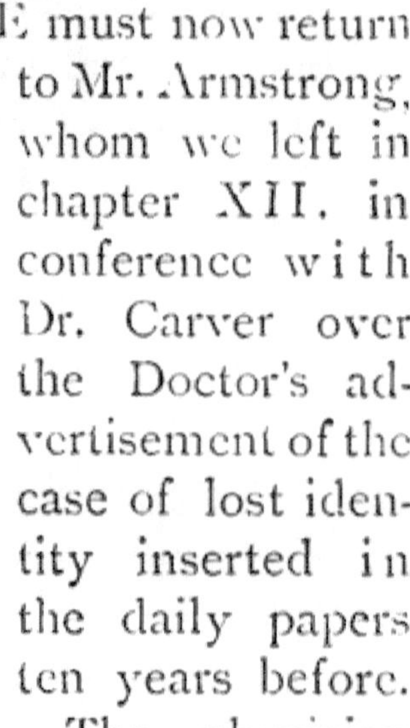

WE must now return to Mr. Armstrong, whom we left in chapter XII. in conference with Dr. Carver over the Doctor's advertisement of the case of lost identity inserted in the daily papers ten years before.

The physician listened gravely to Mr. Armstrong's account of the loss of his wife and infant son, the wild hopes which were now awakened, and to his request for the address of the lady referred to, and gave him a pitying glance as he replied:

"So many bereaved persons have come to me fancying that they recognized a loved one in that notice, only to be cruelly disappointed; and Mrs. Halsey has in the past been subjected to so many trying interviews of this description, that I hesitate to encourage your visiting her, unless you have positive proof of what you hope. A photograph would give this proof."

"And, unfortunately, I have none of Mrs. Armstrong."

"But I had one taken of Mrs. Halsey, which I have kept in the hope that it might be identified some day;" and the Doctor drew from his pocket-book a thumbed and discolored photograph, which he placed in Mr. Armstrong's hand.

The effect was unmistakable. The strong man rose to his feet, staggered, and fainted, for he had recognized his wife. The physician quickly restored him to consciousness, and after waiting until the effect of the shock had partially passed away, he said :

"I see that there is no danger of any mis-

take, and that I may direct you where to
find Mrs. Halsey—I beg pardon, Mrs. Armstrong. Her address, when I last saw her,
was No. 1 Rickett's Court."

"Rickett's Court!" exclaimed Mr. Armstrong, in horror.

"Yes, sir; it is not the best quarter of the
city, but many of the respectable poor live
there; and you must remember, sir, that
your wife must necessarily have had a hard
struggle to support herself and your little
son, alone and friendless, in this great city."

Mr. Armstrong groaned aloud. Rickett's
Court had not seemed so bad to him for
other men's children and wives, but that *his*
child, *his* wife, should live in such vile surroundings was horrible. He sprang to his
feet, seized his hat, and with a hasty "I will
see you again, Doctor," hurried in the same
direction which Stephen Trimble had taken
not a half-hour before. It was only a short
distance, but it seemed miles to him. Just
as he came in sight of the building every
window in its front was illuminated with a
sudden flash, and a heavy detonation shook
the earth. Then smoke poured from the
broken panes, and the air was filled with
flying splinters and débris, while shrieks

from within, and shouts of " Fire ! fire !" from without, added to the confusion.

The smoke cleared in a moment, and people were seen at the windows dropping down the fire-escape. Only a few minutes later a fire-engine came tearing around the corner, and the hoarse voice of a fireman was heard dominating the tumult and giving orders, but before this Alexander Armstrong, possessed of but one idea—that his wife and child were somewhere within—had rushed into the burning building. One glance showed him that this was hopeless. The staircase had been torn out by the explosion, and the flames were roaring up the space which it had occupied, as through a chimney. He was dragged back to the court by the fireman, who exclaimed, " Man alive ! can't you see that the staircase has gone, and that they are coming down the fire-escape ? There wouldn't have been the ghost of a chance for them but for that. Bless the man who had it put there !"

The words gave him a little heart, and he stood at the foot, helping the women and catching the children handed to him, hoping in vain to recognize his wife. They stopped coming. "Are all out ?" he shouted.

"There's some one in the fourth story," said
a woman, and before the fireman could lay
his hand on the fire-escape Mr. Armstrong
was half-way up. The façade still stood,
but the entire interior of the building was in
flames, and blinding smoke and scorching
sparks poured from the windows. At the
fourth story a man had staggered to the
window and lay with his arm outside, holding on to the sill. Mr. Armstrong uttered a
cry when he saw that it was a man, but, none
the less, he lifted him tenderly out, and into
the arms of the fireman following close behind
them. Then drawing his coat over his mouth
and nostrils, he entered the room. Another
man lay at a little distance, or a body that
had been a man, terribly torn and shattered
by the explosion. It was the anarchist who
had been the principal in the plot; the other
had escaped. Mr. Armstrong descended,
looking into every apartment as he came
down to be sure no living thing was left inside that furnace.

"You are a hero, sir! will you give me
your name? I represent ——" It was the
omnipresent reporter on hand for an item.
Mr. Armstrong turned from him, without reply, to the man whom he had rescued, Stephen

Trimble, who lay with a foot torn from
the ankle, and a broken arm. A hospital
surgeon knelt at his side bandaging deftly.
A policeman had sent the call when Mr.
Armstrong started up the fire-escape, and
the ambulance, a more conclusive " Evidence
of Christianity " than that dear old Dr. Hop-
kins or any other theologian ever wrote;
nobler exponent of civilization than the fire
department even, since that is the rich man's
provision for saving his own property, while
the ambulance is the rich man's provision
for saving the poor man's life—the ambulance, with surgeon on the back seat coolly
feeling for his instruments, and bare-headed
driver clanging the gong, and lashing his already galloping horses, had torn like mad
down Broadway. And as it came, aristocratic
carriages hurrying with ladies just a little late
for a grand dinner, and an expectant bride-
groom on his way to Grace Church, halted
and waited for it to pass ; express and telegraph agents, and rushing men of business,
gave it the right of way as it bounded on its
errand of mercy.

Alexander Armstrong spoke for a moment
with the surgeon, long enough to learn that
Stephen Trimble's injuries were probably not

mortal, and to urge every attention possible. Then he caught sight of Solomon Meyer bowing and cringing at a little distance, and he sprang upon him like a panther on his prey. Solomon, greatly surprised, could only imagine that the loss of the property had driven him insane, and gasped, " Ze insurance bolicy is all right," whereat the ex-landlord gave his agent such a shaking that his teeth rattled in his head, only pausing to inquire if he knew anything of a tenant by the name of Mrs. Halsey. Solomon Meyer assured him that Mrs. Halsey had long since quitted the building, but this only partially reassured him, for he placed very little reliance on the man's word. His wife, almost found, was lost to him again. He could not believe that she perished in the burning building ; still, there was this horrible possibility.

There was no one to tell him that she had just gone to Narragansett Pier at his daughter's bidding, and was occupying the very cottage where so many of her happier years were passed ; and he threw himself more unreservedly into his business projects, not, however, forgetting the poor inventor at the hospital, whom he visited frequently, and cared for as tenderly as though he had been his brother. After the excitement of the fire was over, he remembered that the law had an account to settle with Solomon Meyer, but he was not then to be found. His guilty conscience had taken the alarm, and the subtle magnetism which draws bad people together had caused him to form a partnership with the anarchist who had escaped the explosion, and but for Miss Prillwitz's timely recognition they would have fled to Canada. Mr. Armstrong found them, as we know, in the Greenfield jail, and had no difficulty in identifying them, and in having them brought to justice

As the time approached for the trial of Solomon Meyer and the Russian anarchist, Mr. Armstrong was troubled with the fear that Stephen Trimble might not be able to testify in court. He visited him frequently at the hospital, and whenever he approached the subject of his dealings with the anarchists he became excited and confused.

His little son, Lovey Dimple, was seated beside him during one of Mr. Armstrong's calls. He was allowed to visit his father, and waited upon him day by day, some-times telling him of the pleasant times he had had at the seashore, and at others watch-

ing him quietly. His presence seemed to do
his father good; and on this visit Mr. Armstrong was able to obtain much more information from Stephen Trimble than upon any
previous occasion.

"You are quite sure," Mr. Armstrong
asked, "that you never saw this check, which
someone has cashed at the bank, and which is
indorsed with your name?"

"Never, never!" replied the wounded
man.

"I see it, though," Lovey Dimple spoke up,
promptly. "Jim had come down to the
court to see me, and I wanted to show him
the machine in the Rooshans' room, and we
follered him in there. Mr. Meyer dropped a
piece of paper which looked like that, and
Jim picked it up. He could tell you what
was written on it."

"I must have Jim as a link in our chain of
testimony," Mr. Armstrong replied. "Is he
at the Home of the Elder Brother?"

"No, sir; Jim used to be there, but he had
the luck to be adopted. He went away just
for to be a tiger for some swells, and they
liked him so much they permoted him. He's
Jim Roservelt now."

So this was the lad of whom Adelaide had

spoken to him. Mr. Armstrong wrote to his friend Mr. Roseveldt, requesting that Jim should be sent to the city. His testimony at the trial was so clear and concise, and his entire appearance so manly, that Mr. Armstrong was greatly drawn to him.

" If my own boy had lived," he said to Mr. Roseveldt, who had come to the city with Jim, " he would have been about the age of this little fellow. I am about to make a western trip of six or seven weeks, and would like to take him with me. Should the liking which I have taken to him grow upon acquaintance, I beg of you to relinquish him to me ; I need him, for I am a stricken man, and you are a fortunate one, or I would not ask it."

Mr. Roseveldt replied that, though he was fond of Jim, he would willingly give him up to Mr. Armstrong for adoption after his return from the West, provided the boy's mother would consent to the transfer. Singularly enough, the name of that mother was not mentioned, and Mr. Armstrong took Jim with him to Colorado, little dreaming that the boy was his own son.

He had said that he needed Jim ; and he needed him in more ways than he knew. He

had grown world-soiled, as well as world-
weary, and the companionship of a soul
white and young was destined to exert upon
him a purifying as well as rejuvenating
influence. Before the grand mountain scenery Jim's fresh enthusiasm stimulated Mr.
Armstrong's sated admiration, and the child's
naive ideas of right and wrong were a rebuke
to the man's sophistries. They journeyed
together through the wild and beautiful
cañons of the Rocky Mountains, and the boy
was deeply impressed by the stupendous
cliffs rising on each side—walls that were
sometimes two thousand feet in height, and
so close together that the narrow river, which
had cut its way down from the surface, sometimes filled the entire space at the bottom of
the gorge. But even here the ingenuity of
man had surmounted the barriers of nature,
and the observation-car on which they rode
dashed along upon a shelf cut in the solid
rock, with a sheer wall on one hand, and a
dizzy precipice on the other. Such a cañon
was the Royal Gorge of the Arkansas; in
one portion an iron bridge hangs suspended
from strong supports fixed in the solid walls,
and the train glides along it, swaying as in
a hammock, over the brawling river.

The climax of their tour was reached in the Black Cañon. The scenes here are awful, even in broad daylight, for the sombre crags tower to the height of several thousand feet. Our travelers passed through the chasm at night. Far overhead the stars were shining in the little rift of sky, which was all that they could see between the walls; and in the mysterious half-lights of the illumined portions, and the utter blackness of the shadows, the grotesque shapes of the crags took on strange forms and awful suggestions. At times it seemed as if the train was about to dash itself against a wall of solid masonry, which opened, as though thrown back by genii, as they approached. At one point, catching the moonlight, a silvery cascade swept over the rocks like a bow of crystal; and at another, a mighty monument of rosy stone, the Curricanti Needle, towered far above the cliffs, like the sky-piercing spire of some grand cathedral.

"The people who live here must be very good," Jim gasped, as they emerged from the valley of enchantment, "one is so much nearer to God out here!"

"Nobody lives in the cañon now," Mr. Armstrong replied; "Indians lived here not very long ago. They used to hold their councils on that shelf of rock where the pines grow, the last accessible spot on the Curricanti pinnacle, but the settlers in the neighborhood did not have your idea about their being such very good men, and as the cañon was the best pathway through the mountains for the railroad, they were driven out."

"I am sorry for the Indians," Jim said, simply. "If I had owned that cañon I wouldn't have liked to have given it up, would you?"

Mr. Amstrong evaded the question. "You will not have so much pity for them when you know them better," he replied. "They are a low lot, and if they do not know enough to improve the advantages which they possess, it is only fair that they should be appropriated by those who will make a better use of them."

Jim did not quite understand what Mr. Armstrong meant by appropriating the Indians' advantages, but he was to learn more in relation to that word before the journey was over. Returning to Denver, Mr. Armstrong took the boy with him on a tour through some of the pueblos of New

Mexico. The word "pueblo" signifies town, and the Pueblo Indians are those who build houses instead of tents and wigwams, and live from generation to generation in towns and cities, instead of wandering about the plains and mountains like the other tribes. There are twenty-six of these communities in New Mexico, and some of the cities were old when the Pilgrims landed at Plymouth.

When New Mexico was ceded to the United States by Mexico, the right of the Pueblo Indians to their towns and to certain tracts of land surrounding them was confirmed by treaty, so that these Indians are better off in many ways than any others. Mr. Armstrong had a special reason for visiting the Pueblos. He had purchased several large herds of cattle, and wished to rent land of the Indians for pasturage. A man by the name of Sanchez, who traded among the Pueblos, could speak the language, and had gained the confidence of the Indians, happened to be on the train, and recognizing Mr. Armstrong as a wealthy capitalist, who had large interests in cattle, as well as in railroads, at once guessed pretty nearly the nature of his errand in the Indian country.

He introduced himself, and, learning that

Mr. Armstrong intended to visit the pueblo of Taos, to witness the celebration of the Festival of San Geronimo, offered his services as interpreter and courier. These Mr. Armstrong was very glad to accept, for he had heard of the man, and knew that he had considerable influence among the Indians. There was something repellent, however, in his insinuating, cringing manner which made one feel that here was a man who was not to be trusted. The party was increased by an army officer and a Catholic priest, who were also going to Taos to witness the festival. The pueblo lies at a distance of twenty miles from the railroad station, but an Indian was found waiting for Mr. Sanchez with a rough wagon, and that gentleman invited the others to ride with him. They crossed the Rio Grande River and drove along beside it in a northeasterly direction, through a not very interesting country. The coloring was all yellowish brown—the sandy earth, the crisp parched grass, the distant hills, even the water when taken from the turbid river, were all of a like monotonous tint. Now and then they met or passed an Indian, wrapped in a striped blanket and mounted on a small shaggy pony. Toward evening they came in sight of the pueblo. The first view was very picturesque. The houses of adobe, or sun-dried brick, were built in ranges one above the other, like a great stairway, the roof of the lower house serving as the door-yard for the one above. Ladders were placed against the walls, and up and down these, nearly naked Indian children scrambled like young monkeys. They parted their long elf-locks with their hands, and stared at the strangers with wild, black eyes. Mr. Sanchez conducted them to an unoccupied house, which he said would be at their service during the festival for quite a good sum. There was no hotel, and this seemed the best thing to be done. It had evidently been suddenly cleared for the unexpected guests, and some of the utensils and furniture remained. The priest pointed out with pleasure a gaudy print of the Virgin. There were strings of red peppers drying on the outer wall, and a great olla, or decorated water-pot, within, but there was no bedding or food. The gentlemen, however, had each brought with them army blankets, and Mr. Sanchez offered to act as their commissary and skirmish for provisions. He presently returned, followed by a woman carrying a bowl of stewed beef and onions, and a boy driving a donkey, whose panniers were filled with melons. This, with some coffee, which the officer made over a spirit-lamp, and some crackers contributed by Mr. Armstrong, constituted their supper, which hunger made palatable.

After this refreshment they mounted to their roof and watched the preparations for the festivities of the next day. Mr. Sanchez pointed out the entrance to the *estufa*, or underground council-chamber, into which the young men of the tribe were disappearing for the celebration of mysterious pagan rites.

"I thought the Pueblos were Roman Catholics," Mr. Armstrong remarked.

The Catholic priest shook his head sadly. "Our converts have always remained half pagan," he said; "the early missionaries were content to engraft as much Christianity as they could on the old customs, thinking that the better faith would gradually supplant the old, but the old rites and ceremonies have remained. Still we must hesitate to say that the Fathers did wrong, since it was the only way to win the savages to the holy faith."

The priest strolled away to visit the church and to find a Mexican brother who was to celebrate Mass on the next day. The church was a ruinous building which stood apart from the others. The army officer told of the siege which it sustained during the Mexican War, and pointed to the indentations made in its walls by cannon-balls.

The situation was such a strange one that Jim slept but little. All night long he could hear the dull beat of the tom-toms in the *estufa*, and as soon as the first streak of dawn illumined the sky the pueblo was awake and all excitement. Indians from neighboring towns poured in, some on foot, and others mounted on ponies or donkeys.

In the plaza stood a great pole resembling a flag-staff, but instead of a banner there dangled from the top a live sheep and a basket of bread and grain, with a garland of fruits and vegetables. The church bell was clanging for Mass, and Jim followed the others. An old Mexican priest was the celebrant, and a few young Indians in red cotton petticoats and coarse lace overskirts waited upon him awkwardly as altar-boys. When the Host was elevated, an Indian at the door beat the tom-tom, and four musket-shots were fired. The priest then marched down the centre of the church, followed by the altar-boys, one of whom bore a hideous painting, which Mr. Sanchez assured them was painted in Spain by the great Murillo, and might be had, through him, for a trifling sum. The congregation joined in the procession and followed to the race-track, where games, races, and dances were participated in by fifty young men of Taos against fifty from other pueblos. The sports were witnessed by fully two thousand spectators, who swarmed along the terraces, and formed a packed mass of men, women, children, horses, and donkeys around the race-track. There was a group of visitors standing near our travelers, who regarded the races with intense interest. It consisted of an old man dressed in white linen blouse and trousers, with a red handkerchief knotted about his gray locks, an obese and not over cleanly old lady in full Indian toggery, and a young girl in a pink calico dress, with a black shawl over her head and shoulders. They watched one of the runners with the most intense excitement, and when he came off victor in several of the contests, their enthusiasm knew no bounds. "That old man is the Governor of the pueblo of——," said Mr. Sanchez. "It is his son who has just stepped out to lead the corn-dance. The daughter, little Rosaria, is pretty, is she not?" He approached her as he spoke, with easy assurance, and taking her by the chin, made some remarks in the Pueblo language intended to be complimentary ; but the girl twisted herself from his grasp with hot indignation ; and Sanchez returned, grumbling that since she had been to the Ramona School at Santa Fé she was too much of a lady to speak to any-one. Jim was standing beside her; and sure, from her manner, that she understood English, he asked her to explain the corn-dance to him. She did so, very kindly, and the hunt-dance which followed, when the painted clowns brought out grotesque clay images, and after adoring them fired at them, and shattered them in fragments, the crowd scrambling for the pieces. The young man who had been pointed out as the Governor's son secured a piece, and brought it to the girl in triumph. "That is the ear of a wolf," she said. "It means that he will have success in the south ; we, who have been taught better, do not believe these old charms any more."

The last thing on the programme was the climbing of the pole for the sheep, which was finally won by a young brave of Taos.

There was racing on ponies afterward by young Indians and Mexicans, but this was informal, and not included in the rites of the day. The young girl looked at the races enviously. " My brother ought to win there," she said, " for we had the swiftest ponies of any of the Pueblos, and ought to have them, for our pasture lands are the best, but we have sold nearly all our live-stock, and the pastures are no longer of any use to us."

Mr. Armstrong overheard this remark, and asked Rosaria if her people would be willing to rent their lands. She conferred with her father in the Pueblo language, and Mr. Sanchez immediately joined in the conversation, talking volubly to the old man, and translating to Mr. Armstrong. " He says you are welcome to return to his pueblo with him," explained Mr. Sanchez, " and he will call a council of his townspeople to deliberate on your proposition."

There was more conversation, and it was decided to accept the Governor's invitation,

Mr. Armstrong engaging Mr. Sanchez to go with them and help him in the transaction. This seemed to him the only thing which he could do, since he did not understand the language, and the Governor seemed to place confidence in the trader. The party set out the next morning for San ——————, Mr. Armstrong and Jim in Mr. Sanchez's wagon, and the Governor and his children following on diminutive donkeys. Several days elapsed before the bargain could be made. The Indians were very suspicious of being entrapped into some fraud, and it needed all of Mr. Sanchez's eloquence to persuade them that the arrangement would be to their advantage. Mr. Armstrong had told Mr. Sanchez that he was willing to pay fifteen hundred dollars for the rental of the land for three years, and that he (Sanchez) might deduct his fee for services from this sum. " Then if I can persuade them to let you have the land for twelve hundred," asked Mr. Sanchez, " I may claim three hundred for my assistance in the matter ?"

" That is a pretty round fee," replied Mr. Armstrong, " but it does not matter to me who has the money. The land is worth fifteen hundred dollars to me, and if you can persuade the Indians to take less, so much the better for you."

Jim was much interested in the negotiations. He sat beside Mr. Armstrong in the council-chamber, trying to make out from the expressive gestures what it was that the Indians were saying, and sometimes it seemed to him that Mr. Sanchez did not translate correctly. At such times he went out to where Rosaria stood by the open door listening, with other children. She translated for him the treaty as Mr. Sanchez read it, and he was astonished to find that it offered the Indians only three hundred dollars as rent for their land, the wily Sanchez having reserved twelve hundred as his own share.

"But Mr. Armstrong is willing to pay your people fifteen hundred," Jim protested to Rosaria, and the girl slipped into the council-chamber just as the Governor was about to sign the paper, and snatched it from his hand.

"Is it true," she asked of Mr. Armstrong, "that you are willing to pay more for our land? Mr. Sanchez offers us but three hundred dollars!"

Mr. Armstrong, surprised at the man's

effrontery, acknowledged that he was ready to pay more, while Sanchez, furious at seeing his opportunity slipping from him, poured upon Rosaria all manner of abuse, and threatened Mr. Armstrong that unless he held to his bargain to allow him whatever margin he could make he would spoil the trade for him.

"Here's a pretty affair!" said Mr. Armstrong to Jim. "You had better have kept quiet and let the old swindler feather his nest. Now I fear that I shall not be able to make any bargain with the Indians."

"But it was not right, was it," asked Jim, "that the Indians should have so little and Mr. Sanchez so much?"

"The proportion does seem unfair," Mr. Armstrong admitted to Jim; but he added, to Sanchez, "I hold to my part of the bargain. I will give you whatever margin you can make between their demands and fifteen hundred dollars."

Sanchez attempted to regain his lost advantage, but all this time Rosaria had been talking excitedly, explaining to one after another of the Indians, now pointing to the figures in the treaty, now scornfully at Sanchez, arguing, entreating, scolding, and when the trader began his defense of her charges, laughing him to scorn. The Governor put an end to the altercation by tearing the treaty in pieces and ordering two stout Indians to lead Sanchez from the room. He then bade Rosaria tell Mr. Armstrong that fifteen hundred dollars was the very least that they were willing to take for their land.

Mr. Armstrong bowed, and replied that he would think over the matter. He expected to have an opportunity to discuss it with his agent, but when he left the council-chamber he saw his wagon on the road to Sante Fé, at a long distance from the pueblo, and was handed the label from a peach can, on the back of which was scribbled:

" That boy of yours is too smart to live; the plaguey Indians have given me an hour to leave their reservation. Manage your own concerns without the help of—

Sanchez."

The bargain was accordingly struck without the aid of a middle-man, and Mr. Armstrong was conceded the right to pasture his cattle for three years in consideration of the sum of five hundred dollars, to be paid in advance at the beginning of each season.

Mr. Armstrong was much amused. "It has turned out all right," he said to Jim, "but you must acknowledge that it was really none of your business, and I would advise you, in future, not to meddle in matters which do not concern you."

"I will try," Jim replied, much abashed. "I ought to have told you instead of Rosaria, and you would have fixed it all right," he added, cheerfully. "I ought to have known that you wouldn't have let the Indians be cheated."

Mr. Armstrong felt the reproach in the undeserved confidence. Here was a companion who was a sort of embodied conscience. It was not always profitable to have a conscience in business, and yet there was something satisfactory and refreshing in the way in which this affair had terminated. "They say 'honesty is the best policy,'" he said to himself ; "I wonder if this little fellow would not be a Mascot to bring me good luck. I have a notion to make him my partner in some of my risky ventures ; Providence seems to smile upon him and his principles ; perhaps if I make my good-fortune his as well, it will smile upon me." What he said to Jim was this : "You seem fond of a wild western life, Jim, and of the Indians. Our business among the Pueblos is ended. We are going back to Colorado. I have a notion to show you what the Colorado Indians are like. They are Utes, and they do not live in houses, like the Pueblos, but rove about in a perfectly savage manner; they are not peaceful and industrious, like the Pueblos, but lazy and ugly. I do not think that they are susceptible of civilization. I would as soon think of educating a coyote as a Ute.

"Now the Utes possess some of the best mining lands in Colorado, but will never develop them; so it seems to me better that they should be removed to the desert lands, which are worthless for purposes of civilization, and let the whites have their opportunity. I have my eye on a gulch which I discovered while hunting in the San Juan Mountains four years ago, and which I mean to pre-empt just as soon as we get the Utes to give up their present reservation and pack off to Utah. We shall go back that way, and I will show you the spot."

Jim opened his eyes very wide. He did not quite comprehend what Mr. Armstrong had said. Surely he could not mean to defraud the Indians in any way! He would doubtless pay them the worth of their mine, and if they liked the ready money better than the trouble of mining the silver for themselves it would be all fair.

At Antonito Mr. Armstrong left the railroad, provided himself with a span of horses, a wagon, camping outfit, and a brace of greyhounds, and struck out through the Ute reservation for the mountains. He told some gentleman whom he met at Antonito that he proposed to enjoy a little coursing for antelope; but there was a set of surveyors' instruments in the wagon, which proved that he intended to locate the mine which he had come across during his previous visit. His acquaintance attempted to discourage his making the trip alone, saying that the Utes had been restless of late, owing to a failure in receiving their supplies from Government, and it was hardly safe to approach their reservation.

"You need not be afraid of the Utes," another gentleman replied. "I knew their old chief, Ouray, and was entertained once in his house—a neater farm-house than many a white settler can show, and I was hospitably waited upon by his wife, Chipeta, who gave me peaches from their own orchard, and saleratus biscuit, and when I saw the familiar yellow streaks in them, and tasted the old chief's whisky, I had to confess that the Indian was capable of civilization."

Mr. Armstrong laughed, but the first speaker bade him be careful, for all the Utes were not like Ouray, who had so well earned his title of the White Man's Friend.

"Now," exclaimed Mr. Armstrong, after he had driven out of sight of the last human habitation—"now at last we can breathe! What do you think of it, Jim?"

"I didn't know the world was so big," the boy replied; "these must be the Estates del Paradiso which Miss Prillwitz talks about. Why, there's room for all New York to spread itself out, and every child to have a yard to play in. It seems a little bit lonely," he added, after a pause. "I should think you would have liked to have had some of those gentlemen go with you."

"Why, you see, Jim," Mr. Armstrong replied, "I am going to hunt up that silver mine, and I had a little rather not share the secret with any one but you. Besides, I like the loneliness. I grow very tired of people sometimes, Jim, and it seems good to get away from them. Don't you ever feel so?"

"Mother did," Jim said. "She likes helping at the Home very much, but she got a little tired just before the young ladies sent for her to go to the seashore, and she came across one verse in the Bible which sounded so beautiful. It was, 'Come ye yourselves apart into a desert place and rest awhile, for there were many coming and going, and they had no leisure so much as to eat.'"

"I didn't know they had such hurrying times down in Galilee," Mr. Armstrong replied, lightly. He was in good spirits, and they drove a long distance that day, camping at night by a small stream, in which he caught some fine trout. As Jim curled up close to him under the army blanket, Mr. Armstrong felt a slight tremor run through the boy's frame.

"What is the matter?" he asked. "Are you afraid? We are still miles away from the Indians."

"It isn't the Indians," Jim replied, "but it's all so still! I don't hear horse-cars, nor the Elevated, nor people passing, nor nothing. Down at the Pier it was something like this, but there was always the sea; and at the pueblo there were the dogs; while here it seems as if something had stopped."

"'All the roaring looms of time,'" Mr. Armstrong replied, quoting from Tennyson, "have stopped for a little while for us, my boy, and that's the beauty of it. But the old machines will have us in their grip again very soon."

The next day Mr. Armstrong enjoyed a rabbit hunt. Jim, though he took part in the sport, could hardly be said to enjoy it. "It seems such a pity to kill the pretty things!" he said. But this did not keep him from making a hearty meal of broiled rabbit, or from hoping that they might find antelope before the trip was over. The loneliness which he had felt the night before came on again toward evening, and Jim was not sorry, on their third day out, to see that they were approaching a new frame house.

"An old half-breed guide used to have a tepee here," said Mr. Armstrong; "I shall engage his services for our trip. He is a good cook, a good hunter, faithful to his employers, and he knows every rock and clump of sage-brush in all the region. His only fault is that he will get drunk. He was with me when I found the silver ore, and I need him to guide me to the spot again."

As they came nearer, Mr. Armstrong seemed greatly surprised to see a large field of waving corn in front of the house, while some cows were being driven toward an out-building by a young Indian in checked shirt and brown overalls.

"What can have come over old Charley!" exclaimed Mr. Armstrong. "When I was here before, nothing would induce him to degrade himself by farm labor. Some boomer must have established himself here. It's illegal, for the land still belongs to the Indians."

They drove up to the front door, and were met by the same young man whom they had seen driving the cows, but the overalls were replaced by a faded pair of army trousers, and a paper collar had been hastily added to the checked shirt. He bade them enter, in good English, and the interior of the house was clean and inviting. The walls were papered with newspapers, a bright patchwork quilt was spread upon the bed, and a pleasant-faced girl was frying ham and eggs over the stove; while there was a shelf of books over the table. An Indian woman

emerged from a shadowy corner and expressed a welcome by pantomine.

"Is not this Charley's wife?" Mr. Armstrong asked, and the woman smiled and
nodded her recognition.

"Where is your husband?" was the next
question. "Charley no good," was the wife's
frank reply; "gone hunting with white men."

This was a disappointment that Mr. Armstrong had not anticipated; he was not sure
that he could find his way to the silver mine
without Charley's help, but it was worth trying. The odor of the frying ham was appetizing, and the invitation to supper was
promptly accepted.

"Are you Charley's son?" Mr. Armstrong
asked of the young man, who presently
brought in a foaming pail of milk, and
assisted his mother and sister in waiting on
their guests.

"Yes, sir," was the prompt reply, "and my
name is Charley too—Charles Sumner."

Mr. Armstrong stared in astonishment.
"Where did you learn to speak English so
well?" he asked.

"At the Indian Industrial School at Carlisle, Pennsylvania."

"Then you are one of Captain Pratt's boys?"

"Yes, sir," and a smile lightened the somewhat stolid features. Mr. Armstrong did not believe in Eastern schools for Indians, and he asked, rather sarcastically, "And what did you learn when you were in the East—Latin and Theology?"

The boy shook his head. "I learned to work on the farm," he said, "and to read and write, and do a little arithmetic; and I learned some carpentry—enough to build this house, and make that table, and the cupboard and things."

"Very creditable, I am sure," Mr. Armstrong replied, half incredulously, "but how did you come into the fortune necessary to set you up in this flourishing style?"

"I helped build the new depot at S——, and they paid me off with the lumber that was left, and I built the house out of that. Then I had some money which I had put in the savings-bank from my earnings every vacation in the East, and I bought the cows with that; and then I made a churn, and we've been making butter the way I saw them do it in Pennsylvania, and I sell it for a good price at the Springs."

"Well, you have more stuff in you than I ever thought it possible for an Indian to have," Mr. Armstrong replied, fairly won, in spite of himself, to admiration. "I always supposed that those Carlisle students, as soon as they returned to old surroundings, went back to savagery."

"It is pretty hard for us," the boy replied. "Last year I planted about three times as much corn as you see here. I had taken a contract to supply the quartermaster at Fort ——, and I thought I should make a good deal of money ; but just as it was green, all of our relations came to see us. There were ten families. They camped there by the creek, and they stayed until they had eaten every roasting ear. They said they had come to celebrate my home-coming, and father made them welcome, and gave a dance, and killed one of our cows for them. They would have killed them all, but I drove them off into the mountains, and hid them. That is the reason I have planted so little corn here this season. I have another field over in a little valley in the mountains which I hope they will not find, and I drive the cattle up the cañon every morning, for they may be here any day."

"You poor fellow!" said Mr. Armstrong. "I have heard the proverb, 'Save us from

our friends !' but I never understood the full
force of it before."

After the hearty meal the little house was
put at the service of the travelers, the family camping outside, and, much to Mr. Armstrong's contentment, they passed a comfortable and restful night. The next morning Mr. Armstrong asked Charles Sumner if
he was familiar with the mountains, and
could guide him to a certain valley, which he
indicated as having a chimney-like forma-
tion at one end.

"Why, certainly," the young man replied ;
"don't you remember I was with father
when he took you hunting four years ago ?
He killed an eagle that had her nest on a
ledge high up on the chimney, and I climbed
up for the young ones."

" Ah yes, I remember now, but you were
such a little fellow then that I could not
realize the change."

" I grew more at Carlisle," said the young
man, significantly, than at any other time of
my life. We all grew at Carlisle."

"Then you will take us to the chimney,"
Mr. Armstrong asked, "and cook for us
while we are out ? What will you charge ?"

"I don't think I ought to ask you any-

thing, sir, for there is good pasturage there-
about, and I can drive my cows along, and
herd them there until after the visit of our
relatives. My sister is going to B—— with
all the green-corn that the ponies can carry,
so when they come they will find mother,
and very little else. The valley in which
my other corn is planted is in that direction,
and perhaps you will let me bring some of
it in your wagon when we come back?"

Charles Sumner rode cheerily beside them
on a diminutive pony, driving his cows and
the pack pony, and chatting freely of many
things. Sometimes Jim sprang from his
seat to make him change places and rest
awhile. The pony had a fascination for Jim,
and he speedily learned from Charles Sumner how to manage it, and to "round up"
the herd of cows and calves. The young
Indian taught him, also, how to make arrows,
and to shoot with them, to picket the
horses, and to use the lasso, to make camp
coffee, and to set up and take down the tepee,
or tent of buffalo hide, which the pack-pony
dragged between long poles.

"You would like to be a cow-boy,
wouldn't you, Jim?" Mr. Armstrong asked,
but Charles Sumner shook his head. "Cow-

boys are no good," he said, emphatically; "they shoot Indians as if they were wild beasts. Better stay in the East, where the white people are good. I wish I could, but the Government insists that as soon as we are educated we must go back to our reservations. I wish it would let us stay and earn our living in the East, where it is so much easier to stay civilized."

Jim, on the other hand, was delighted with everything he saw. "If all the boys in Rickett's Court could only come out here!" he exclaimed, "and ride, and herd cows, and hunt, and camp out, and all the Indian boys could only go East, and go to school, and work at trades—how nice it would be!"

Mr. Armstrong admitted that the change might be good for both, but while speaking they came in sight of the chimney-shaped pinnacle, and he hastily unpacked his theodolite and other instruments, and began to take angles, and to jot down memoranda.

"This is the first time that I have ever seen a surveyor on the Ute reservation," said Charles Sumner, "and I think that our troubles will be ended sometime by that little machine. Just as soon as the Government divides up our land and gives each Indian his own share, then each good Indian will cultivate his own farm, and will have some heart to work. How can he now, when the land belongs as much to every lazy Indian in the tribe as to himself? O sir, is it possible that the Government has sent you to begin this division?"

Mr. Armstrong confessed that his observations were made only for his own amusement. He was surprised to find that the young man had such advanced views on the "land in severalty" question, and he asked whether any of the other Indians of the tribe shared his opinions.

"There are a good many who have staked out farms and are cultivating them, just as I have," he replied, "but we know that we have no right to the land, and may be turned out any day, whenever bad white men persuade our chiefs to give up this reservation and move away to the bad lands in the West."

Mr. Armstrong winced a little under the earnest, questioning look with which Jim regarded him. To turn his train of thought he said, "There is the old eagle's nest on the ledge still, Charles Sumner. Can you climb up there to-day as nimbly as you did four years ago?"

For answer, the young man threw himself from his pony and began to ascend the cliff. It was very steep, but he chose his way cautiously, seizing each point of vantage in the way of a crevice or projection. He had almost reached the nest when he paused, looked away to the southward, and began rapidly to descend. "There is a band of Utes coming over the divide," he said; "I think it would be as well for us to go a little further up the valley." He hurriedly collected his herd, and drove them before him through a pass into a long, shady gorge. Mr. Armstrong followed with the team. "This is the place!" he exclaimed, excitedly, as they entered the ravine. "It was in this little cañon that I found the silver. A vein cropped right out to the surface, and I filled my pockets with the ore. I set up a buffalo skull to mark the spot. There it is—at the foot of that pine. It must have rolled down, for I placed it higher. Hold the reins, Jim, while I scramble up the bank and see if I see any signs of the vein." With the agility of a younger man, Mr. Armstrong climbed the steep bank, and came down with his hands filled with crumbled ore. "It is there, fast enough," he said, triumphantly; "if it were not on the Indian reservation I would be the owner of that mine now. They cannot hold the lands long, and when they are opened to settlement this cañon shall be ours, Jim. You say you would like to live a western life. If your mother, of whom you seem so fond, is of the same opinion, you shall pre-empt a claim here, and I will take one just beside you, and between us we will own the mine. You don't understand it, my boy; but I have taken a fancy to you, and I mean to make your fortune."

"And will this ravine be my very own?" Jim asked—"mother's and mine?"

"Yes, my boy; and I am curious to see what you will make of it, and what you will make of yourself while you are waiting to come into your possessions. I mean to put you in the way of getting a good practical education, which shall be of use to you out here."

"And can I learn surveying?"

"Yes; and mining engineering and assaying and mechanics, and all that."

"That is what Lovey Dimple would like to learn too. Can he come with me? He'd invent a machine right off to dig the silver just as easy."

"We will see, Jim. I would like to give him a good turn for his father's sake ; but don't take too many into our company, or we shall have to water the stock too freely."

They had nearly reached the head of the gorge, and they found that Charles Sumner had paused, and had corraled his cows in a little natural amphitheatre, where they were resting contentedly.

" I must watch them pretty sharply," the Indian explained, " for the corn I told you about is in the next valley, and if they should get into that, they would be as bad as our relations. Just walk to the top of the hill, Mr. Armstrong, and see what a nice field of it I have over there." Mr. Armstrong returned bringing an armful of fine roasting ears, but Charles Sumner thought it best not to build a fire until the party of Utes had passed, and they sat down to a cold supper of canned baked beans. After supper Jim had a long talk with Charles Sumner, and ascertained that the young man had fixed his heart upon making this particular section his home farm as soon as the reservation should be divided in severalty among the

Indians, which he hoped would happen before many years.

"Then," said Jim, "you think that the white people will never have a chance to come in here and take up land?"

"Do you think they ought to be allowed to do so, when the land is ours?" Charles Sumner asked.

"No, I don't," Jim replied, promptly. "I think it is really yours, and you ought to keep it; and I'll just tell you a secret about this cañon. It is worth a great deal more than you know. There is a silver mine in it, and I'll show you where, and you had just better go back East and study the best way to mine silver, and then when you get your claim you will know how to work it. I wish you would take me in as your partner, for Mr. Armstrong is going to have me taught all about mining. He thought he might pre-empt this mine for me, but, of course, when he sees that it really belongs to you, he will not want to, unless, perhaps, you would like to sell out your right in it."

Jim had spoken so rapidly that he did not notice that Mr. Armstrong had approached, and was listening with an astonished expression to what he was saying.

"Jim, are you crazy?" Mr. Armstrong exclaimed, as soon as he could recover himself. Don't you see that you are throwing away your chances?"

"Oh no," Jim replied, with a smile, "I hadn't any chance at all. You didn't know, but it all belongs to Charles Sumner."

Their conversation was interrupted by a whoop in the valley below. The band of Utes had discovered the traces of their last camp, and had followed their trail into the cañon.

"Drive over into the next ravine!" said Charles Sumner; "they will camp here when they find my cows. Wait for me just below the corn-field, and I will join you as soon as I can. They will not hurt you if they find you, but they will beg and steal everything."

Mr. Armstrong hurriedly followed Charles Sumner's advice, and was joined about midnight by the young Indian, who drove before him three cows, all he had been able to rescue from a herd of twelve.

The young man wiped his brow with a despairing gesture. "They were ugly," he said. "Some Durango cow-boys have been pasturing their cattle on the reservation, and

they insisted that my cows were a part of
the herd, and that the owners were somewhere near. If they had found you, they
might have treated you roughly. I think we
had better get away while they are feasting."

It occurred to Mr. Armstrong that it
looked very much as if Charles Sumner had
saved their lives at the sacrifice of his property, and a feeling of gratitude and liking
sprang up in his heart for the young man.

"I don't know what I shall do," the Indian
continued, dejectedly. "It doesn't seem to
be any use to try to be civilized in this
country."

"No, my poor fellow!" replied Mr Armstrong, "it really does not. In your place, I
think I should go back to the blanket and be
a savage with the rest. I will tell you what
to do: come East again with your mother
and sister. I will let you try farming on a
piece of land which I have taken a fancy to
in Massachusetts, where you will not have
these discouragements. When the land
question is settled, you and Jim shall come
back here and form a partnership. If it
is divided in severalty to the Utes, then I will
establish your right to the cañon, and you
shall take Jim in as your partner; and if it is

opened to the whites for settlement, he will take up the land and give you a share in it."

This proposition was accepted by Charles Sumner and his sister, the mother preferring to remain with her husband. After establishing the young Indians in Massachusetts, Mr. Armstrong brought Jim with him to Narragansett Pier.

A short space must now be given to Milly and Adelaide, who, though mingling in a very different class of society, had an experience that summer not unlike our own. Mrs. Roseveldt gave a lawn-party at the beginning of the season to organize a tennis club. Tennis was the rage that season. Many of the cottages had tennis courts, and the different players wished to plan for a grand tournament at the end of the season. A pretty uniform was designed of white flannel, the skirt embroidered with a deep Greek fret in gold thread, and laid in accordion pleats. A little jacket lined with gold-colored silk, and embroidered in the same pattern, was to be worn over the shirt waist, and a gold-colored sash ending in a tassel, with a white Tam o' Shanter, completed the costume. Milly had planned that

Mrs. Halsey should have the making of these costumes while at the Pier.

A fund was contributed with which to purchase a trophy for the prize player. It rose quickly to a hundred and fifty dollars, and a meeting was held to decide what the trophy should be. Most of the members thought that a gold pin in the shape of a racket, with a pearl ball, manufactured by Tiffany, would be the correct thing, and this idea would certainly have been adopted if Milly had not turned the current by a neat little speech.

"I am sure," she said, "that we do not want to vulgarize our club by making it professional, and a prize of any great money value would certainly do this. So I move that the prize be a simple wreath of laurel tied with a white ribbon, on which the date of the tournament and name of the club be printed." The members all agreed that this would be in better form, but asked what was to be done with the money already contributed. Then Milly rose to the occasion, and flung out the banner of the Home.

"It seems as if we had no right to be romping in this delicious fresh air while poor children are gasping in the vile smells of the city."

The Fresh-Air Fund and the Working Girls' Vacation Society were both popular charities, and were proposed by different members as proper recipients of our funds. Milly was ready to agree to this, but one young man, supposed until that day to be a mere gilded youth, without an idea above his neckties, suggested that it was always pleasanter to be the distributer of one's own benefits, and moved that the club get up a little Fresh-Air Fund of its own. " We might rent a cottage down here and send for a dozen or so young beggars, and take turns in caring for them."

A general laugh followed this remark. " What would you do, personally, Mr. Van Silver ? " asked one of the girls.

" I would put my coach and four-in-hand at the service of the enterprise," he said, " and make myself expressman and 'bus driver. I'd take the children out to drive every day, for one thing."

Everyone insisted that they would like to see him do it, but he persisted until they were convinced of his sincerity. Mr. Van Silver's patronage had given an aristocratic stamp to the enterprise, and some one now proposed that they rent a cottage for the children for the season.

Milly then explained that Adelaide had already fitted up her cottage for the purpose, and was expecting an invoice of children by the next day. Adelaide invited the party to visit the cottage that afternoon, and the entire club climbed to the top and interior of Mr. Van Silver's coach; Mr. Stacy Fitz-Simmons, the whilom drum-major of the Cadet band, blowing the coach horn for all he was worth.

They found a park overgrown into a forest, in the depth of which stood a pleasant cottage, with broad verandas, which once commanded a beautiful view of the glistening bay, with Newport in the distance.

"I intend to have some of these trees cut away, so as to leave a vista through to the water," Adelaide explained.

They entered the house, and found it renovated from the mold and decay with which ten years had encumbered it, sweet and fresh with new paint, and papering of pretty design. Light and graceful ratan furniture and chintz hangings added to the beauty of the room, simple straw mattings covered the floor. It was as lovely a home as heart could wish.

"I have done all I can afford," Adelaide said, simply, "and if the club would like to use this cottage for their city children it is at their service, but first Milly wants to entertain the younger children of the Home of the Elder Brother here for a couple of weeks."

"And we will each of us take his or her turn for a week," said Mr. Van Silver; and so the "Paradiso Seaside Home" was provided for.

Mrs. Halsey came with the children. From the moment that she left the station she seemed to be in a dream.

"It all looks so familiar!" she exclaimed; "I am sure I have been here before! There is something caressing in the feeling of the damp air, as though it kissed my cheek like an old friend. And the scent of the salt-water! I remember it so well; and shall we hear the surf? Oh, when was it, where was it, that I knew it all?"

When they drove into the grounds she shook her head. "No, it was not this place," she said, with a wistful look in her eyes; "there were no trees." But at the first glimpse of the house a trembling seized her, and she could hardly mount the steps.

Within doors a puzzled expression came into her face.

" It is familiar, yet unfamiliar," she said. " I cannot be sure. If I could only see some face that I had known before, then I could tell."

" Perhaps the face will come," Adelaide said; and it came.

A few weeks later Mr. Armstrong returned with Jim from the western trip, and came down to the Pier to make the visit which his daughter so greatly desired. Adelaide had driven to the station for them in Milly's pony carriage, Jim mounted to his old place on the rumble, Mr. Armstrong settled himself for the drive, and Adelaide took the reins.

" I am going to take you around by the cottage, papa," she said. " I want to show you what I have done there, and how happy the Home children are."

Mr. Armstrong drew himself up, as though wincing from some sudden pain. " I did not intend to go there again, daughter," he said ; " I shall miss a face at the window."

" I know, papa—the cameo; but she would have been glad to see the cottage used as it is."

They turned into the drive, and Mr. Armstrong nerved himself for the sight of his old home. Suddenly he cried out, and caught his daughter's arm. "Is it only memory, or have I lost my senses? The face is there!"

Adelaide laughed reassuringly. "I don't wonder that it gave you a turn, papa; it did me, too, when I saw the same sight in Miss Prillwitz's window last winter, but it is only dear Mrs. Halsey looking out for us."

"Then thank God!" exclaimed Mr. Armstrong, leaping from the vehicle and hurrying forward. "Do you not remember me? my own!—my wife!"

His wife remembered: the veil which had blinded her for years fell at the sight of her husband's face.

Happily the shock had not been as sudden as it seemed; during the time which she had spent in the cottage the conviction had grown upon her that this had been her home. She had asked Adelaide its history, and learning that it had been built for her mother, who had been drowned in the great steamboat disaster, a hope had sprung up in her heart, which she dared not express to any one, that she had found her own again.

Adelaide had said that she expected her father, and Mrs. Halsey waited only to see his face to be assured of the truth.

Adelaide's delight at finding that Mrs. Halsey was her lost mother, and Jim her brother, was genuine and intense. "I knew, all the time, that Jim was somebody's child," she exclaimed, incoherently. "It is all too good to be true! too good to be true!"

"Jim deserves a better father than he has found," said Mr. Armstrong, "and by God's grace he shall have a better.

"It is too bad to break up this nice little arrangement of a summer home for the poor children," he added, "and I will allow the cottage to be used for this purpose just so long as the tennis club desire to maintain it ; but I must have my wife. Please remember that we have been parted from each other a very long time. I am going West next week, and I must take her with me; and it will not do Adelaide any harm to have a glimpse of the great West before we send her to school in the fall. Jim has had as much of the West as he can stand at present, and we will leave him in the best school that we can find."

"But what shall we do for a housekeeper

for the cottage?" Adelaide asked, in dismay.

"Mrs. Trimble has just left the hospital, fully recovered, but I have no doubt she would prefer to run your little enterprise rather than to return to the store; and as I have deprived you of your housekeeper I don't mind paying Mrs. Trimble to supply her place for the remainder of the summer. It will do Mr. Trimble good, too, to complete his convalescence here, and perhaps in the winter they will accept the janitorship of your tenement."

"My tenement!" Adelaide replied, in surprise.

"Yes, I intend to give you the management of this property, which I have always considered your own. You have a matter of twenty thousand dollars insurance money, which, with the ten thousand which I have deposited to your name in the savings bank, you may use in erecting a model tenement on the site of the old Rickett's Court building. I think I shall have some more money for you to put into the enterprise if the patent works well. I shall give Mr. Trimble a share in the profits of that invention over and above the five thousand dollars already paid him, but I think that he would like one of your

suites of rooms in return for acting as janitor
and agent of the building, and it will not
interfere with his teaching mechanics to the
boys at the Home."

"If you please, papa," said Adelaide, " I
like the plan of engaging Mr. Trimble as
janitor, but I would rather be my own agent
and collect the rents myself; then I can see
just what improvements are needed, and be
sure that my tenants are all comfortable."

For the remainder of their stay in the
East the Armstrongs busied themselves
with architects' plans and specifications.
Adelaide enjoyed planning the bathrooms
and conveniences of different kinds. "And
the paving-stones must be taken up in the
court," she said, "and a nice grass-plot laid
out in their place, and we will have pretty
iron balconies before every window, and a
fire-escape."

"Yes, daughter," replied her father, "I will
make you a present of that, outside the
other matters—the very best kind of fire-
escape to be found in the city; and, while we
are about it, I will send one to the Home of
the Elder Brother."

Adelaide's interest in her tenement did
not wean her away from the Home, and

I have since observed that it is always those
who, seemingly, are already doing as much
as they can in the way of charity who are
always ready to lend a helping hand to other
enterprises, and that it is the earnest workers
of little means, as well as the wealthy philanthropists, who

> " To the ages
> Fair bequests, and costly, make."

The Armstrongs went West, and Adelaide
created an interest for the Home in her new
surroundings, while Milly kept up the enthusiasm of the tennis club at the Pier. That
club flourished in a manner unheard of, here-
tofore, in a place where everyone was so
busy doing nothing that even the exertion
of tennis had been voted a bore. It was not
tennis, however, that kept them together, or
gave the members their bright, jolly looks,
but the Paradiso Cottage.

> " For we may find a zest
> In any true employ
> Which, like a whetstone in the breast,
> Shall give an edge to joy."

But while we all worked in our different
ways, it was our corresponding secretary
who was the clasp to the necklace, or rather,

the central battery which sent currents of life pulsating through the connecting wires. The scapegrace who plotted and schemed mischief, she who had erstwhile reveled in the name of " the malicious, seditious, insubordinate, disreputable, skeptical Queen of the Hornets," had become a wise and enterprising central manager of a helpful charity.

The summer vacation is over, and we have all met again for another winter at Madame's; Amen Corner and Hornets all filled with a fine enthusiasm for our work, and a deep, true affection for one another.

The Home rests, we are told, on very slender foundations. There is no financier as a backer, no estate, no great endowment, nothing to ensure its existence from year to year but the hearts and hands of ten young girls. Nothing else? They forget that we have behind us and with us the Elder Brother, with all the estates del Paradiso.

> " By each saving word unspoken,
> By Thy will, yet poorly done,
> Hear us, hear us,
> Thou Almighty ! help us on."

THE END.

Crown 8vo, with Frontispiece, beautifully bound in extra cloth, 2s. 6d.,

Adèle's Love. The Story of a Faithful Little Heart. By MAUDE M. BUTLER.

'The book possesses an interest which will make it prove attractive.'—*Brechin Advertiser.*

'A pleasing little story.'—*Halifax Guardian.*

'The narrative is one of considerable and well-sustained interest. There is not a dull page in the book. On the contrary, there are signs of vigour and freshness, which shows the authoress to possess originality of resource and powers of description of the first order. We can heartily recommend the book to our readers, no less for its refreshing and healthy tone than for the evidence of literary ability it displays. By this work the author will considerably enhance the reputation she has already made in the literary world.'—*Walsall Advertiser.*

'A simple, artless, charming story, full of human interest.'—*Inverness Courier.*

'Is full of tender pathos and strong situations, and is told with a simplicity and naturalness that makes it very interesting to the reader.'—*People's Friend.*

'One of those excellent stories which, without any special plot, derive their interest chiefly from the manner in which they are told. A healthy and at the same time an interesting book; will make a very acceptable gift to young ladies, and will be interesting reading for all.'—*Society Herald.*

'A beautiful story delightfully told.—*N. E. Daily Gazette.*

'A book of more than ordinary interest.'—*Fireside News.*

'An exceedingly pretty tale.'—*Glasgow Herald.*

'The style is sweet, refined, and interesting.'—*Perthshire Advertiser.*

'We can warmly commend it.'—*Westmoreland Gazette.*

'A touching story.'—*Free Press.*

'Written with the great charm of simplicity; a strange beauty of affection breathes throughout the entire story.'—*Liverpool Post.*

'The style is good, and the plot is unfolded with genuine power.'—*British Weekly.*

'The tale of juvenile affection and maternal constancy told in the refined language of a cultured writer.'—*Evening Citizen.*

'A beautiful story.'—*Kilmarnock Standard.*

'The plot is an excellent piece of construction, and enchains the understanding, and as the story is delightfully unfolded, one is hardly able to rise till the end is reached.'—*Reformer.*

'Will be sure to be perused with interest.'—*Stirling Observer.*

'Extremely pathetic.'—*Academy.*

'Told with touching simplicity and pathos.'—*Northern Daily Telegraph.*

'A simple story, simply but touchingly told.'—*Northern Whig.*

'The narrative thrills one, it is so beautifully told, and is instinct both with impassioned and deep evangelical feeling.'—*Scottish S. S. Teachers' Magazine.*

'The story is pathetic and prettily told, and the interest is well sustained to the end.'—*Literary World.*

'Well worked out, and the character of the heroine is sweet and gentle.'—*Elgin Courant.*

'An interesting little story well told.'—*Leytonstone Express.*

'Decidedly original.'—*Nonconformist.*

'Well written and tastefully got up. People of all ages will read with delight and profit.'—*Presbyterian Messenger.*

Small crown 8vo, with Frontispiece, paper covers, 1s.; cloth, 1s. 6d.,

Love Conquers All. By A. C. HERTFORD.

'Unimpeachable in point of moral tone.'—*Glasgow Herald.*

'Pleasantly and simply written, may be heartily recommended.'—*Court Journal.*

'A pleasantly written tale.'—*Manchester Guardian.*

'Told with delightful freshness and natural feeling.'—*Montrose Standard.*

'A capitally told tale, in which there is graceful writing, and no little knowledge of human nature.'—*Haddington Courier.*

'A pretty story with a pretty moral.'—*Fife Herald.*

'Admirable in tone and clever in execution.'—*Walsall Observer.*

'A book of more than average ability.'—*Burnley Express.*

'A commendable story.'—*Fifeshire Journal.*

'Shows a very considerable insight into human nature. The story is a thoroughly good one, and may be read with profit as well as pleasure.'—*Leeds Times.*

'The tone is pure and the interest well sustained.'—*Methodist Recorder.*

'Will make an excellent gift-book.'—*Hawick Advertiser.*

'A finely written tale, the motive of which is well indicated by the title; characterized by elevation of tone and feeling.'—*People's Friend.*

'A very pleasant story, which cannot but commend itself to all classes of readers.'—*Kilmarnock Standard.*

'The salient points of character are hit off with a mingled pathos and humour which make delightful reading.'—*British Weekly.*

'One of the most enchanting books it has been our pleasure to read for a long time. There are delicate touches which indicate that the author is an artist of no mean order.'—*Hull Daily Mail.*

'Humour and pathos are admirably blended, and the book is one that will be sure to meet with the sympathy of a large number of readers.'—*Devon and Exeter Gazette.*

'A pretty love story prettily written.'—*Whitehall Review.*

'The book is bright and readable.'—*Kelso Chronicle.*

'A fresh little story.'—*Literary World.*

'Simple, natural, and well expressed.'—*Moray Express.*

'Will delight those who still find pleasure in a book where elevation of sentiment, purity of thought, and unaffected elegance of diction are the outstanding features. The fidelity of the sketch none who read it may gainsay.'—*Orkney Herald.*

Small crown 8vo, with numerous Illustrations, cloth extra, 1s. 6d.,

Johnnie; or, Only a Life. By ROBINA F. HARDY, Author of 'Jock Halliday,' etc.

'One of the happiest of Miss Hardy's efforts, overflowing with humour as well as pathos, and in every line a transcript from the life. One of its most notable features is the accuracy with which it catches the idiom of the Edinburgh poor.'—*Christian Leader.*

'We have seldom read a tale of deeper and more sustained interest.'—*Brechin Advertiser.*

'A story of much pathetic interest.'—*Manchester Courier.*

'A pathetic story.'—*Fife Herald.*

'Tone and treatment are excellent.'—*Westmoreland Gazette.*

'Extremely interesting.'—*Glasgow Herald.*

'Instinct with the fine feeling which runs like a golden thread through all Miss Hardy's works.'—*Free Press.*

'A healthy and wholesome book.'—*Fifeshire Journal.*

'A pleasingly conceived story.'—*Liverpool Post.*

'The work is one that will do Miss Hardy credit, and one that will afford as much pleasure to the reader as it certainly will do good for the district missionary work.'—*Haddington Advertiser.*

'Well told, and calculated to make the reader wiser and better; can be heartily recommended.'—*Dundee Courier.*

'Characterized by homeliness and pathos, and illustrates a phase of life in our social strata which is of increasing interest to Christian workers. The volume is nicely illustrated by views of the Canongate, etc., and presents externally a handsome appearance.'—*Aberdeen Journal.*

'The story is most touchingly told in capital Scotch.'—*Perthshire Advertiser.*

'Simply and sweetly told.'—*People's Friend.*

'Well written, and is permeated with the purest and kindliest of feelings.'—*Greenock Telegraph.*

'A well-written and pathetic little story.'—*Buxton Advertiser.*

'Deserves a hearty commendation.'—*Montrose Standard.*

'A tale at once captivating and realistic.'—*Stirling Observer.*

'A well told tale of Scotch life.'—*Somerset Standard.*

'A very touching story of patient endurance amid miserable surroundings, and will take rank among the very best works of the kind in our national literature.'—*Northern Ensign.*

'Should be interesting to all mission workers.'—*Scottish Congregational Magazine.*

'The book is one of great merit and of deep religious feeling.'—*Glasgow Herald.*

'A most affecting temperance story commending total abstinence.'—*League Journal.*

'Full of pathos.'—*Shields Gazette.*

'Suited in every way as a gift-book.'—*Fife Free Press.*

'No one can read the story without receiving impulses towards what is good, and especially towards kindness to the weak and the destitute and those who have few real friends.'—*Christian News.*

'A story that will enlist the sympathy of every one interested in the moral and social improvement of the poor.'—*Devon Gazette.*

'Miss Robina F. Hardy is an authoress by no means strange to the public, and her reputation will by no means suffer by the telling of this simple tale, the main characters of which are drawn from the humblest walk of life.'—*Moray Express.*

'A pleasantly told tale.'—*Manchester Congregational Monthly.*

'One of the most pathetic and sweetly told tales that have appeared for many a day.'—*Northern Whig.*

'There is much in the story of human nature.'—*Arbroath Guide.*

'Most touching and of deep pathos, besides being true to the life.'—*Ballymena Observer.*

'Miss Hardy writes much, but there is no appearance of haste or loss of freshness about this last book. It is well planned and well told.'—*Liverpool Mercury.*

'A beautiful simple story of sin, suffering, love, and abiding peace.'—*Arbroath Herald.*

'Distinctly better than anything else from the same pen.'—*Academy.*

'The interest of the tale is sustained throughout.'—*Pen and Pencil.*

'A well told tale of humble life.'—*Christian.*

'Reveals a power of vivid realistic portraiture which cannot fail to arouse the interest of the dullest reader; will be appreciated by all those whose tastes have not been depraved by unhealthy sensationalism; free from exaggerations of all kinds.'—*Freeman.*

New Edition, small crown 8vo, cloth gilt, with numerous Illustrations, price 2s.; in cheaper bindings, 1s. 6d. and 1s.,

Jock Halliday, A Grassmarket Hero; or, Sketches of Life and Character in an Old City Parish. By ROBINA F. HARDY, Author of ' Nannette's New Shoes,' etc.

'The narrative is swift and flowing, lit up with flashes of humour, and also with pathetic touches that are equally true.'—*Christian Leader.*

'Charmingly got up. . . . Sure to have an influence for good over the many readers which the book certainly deserves to have.'—*Daily Free Press.*

'A very sweet little story. . . . A simple idyl of everyday life, naturally and pathetically told.'—*Scotsman.*

'Fitted to do good service alike in connection with temperance and general mission-work.'—*British Messenger.*

'Pleasing and natural; . . . well rewards perusal.'—*Inverness Courier.*

'A delightful Edinburgh story.'—*Liverpool Mercury.*

'A good stock of healthy, mischief-making, but generous good-nature about the lad. . . . He is the very soul of tenderness to the little blind girl.'—*United Presbyterian Juvenile Missionary Magazine.*

'Full of lights and shadows, queer bits, laughter-forcing bits, moving bits. . . . Difficult to lay down.'—*S.S. Teachers' Magazine.*

'Written with much ability and feeling.'—*Christian World.*

'A fascinating story of humble life.'—*Dundee Advertiser.*

'A very effective story.'—*Haddington Courier.*

'Will assuredly take its place beside the productions of the author of "Rab and his Friends," and the tender and touching tales of Professor Wilson.'—*Brechin Advertiser.*

'A tender, spirited story of mission-work among the slums.'—*Sunday School Chronicle.*

'A capitally written sketch of Scottish city life among the humbler classes. —*Christian.*

'The story is an incident of city mission-work, and it is capitally told. It is a book which should find a place in every Sunday school or temperance library.'—*Southern Reporter.*

'The narrative, though plain and unadorned, will be found of great interest, especially on the part of those who appreciate Scottish life and character in its more homely phases.'—*Northern Whig.*

'A real story—one that interests and, in many of its pages, amuses, and therefore the moral is not obtruded on notice; but its moral is of the best. . . . We never saw a better of its kind.'—*Arbroath Guide.*

'Altogether, the book is one which excites the deepest interest, and conveys a moral in every chapter.'—*Derry Sentinel.*

'Have no hesitation in commending, not only to those who love a good and racily-told tale, but to those who are sometimes puzzled to know what sort of a gift-book to get for a young friend.'—*Newcastle Weekly Chronicle.*

'A good sketch of one of those sterling characters, who, in spite of their surroundings, develope into useful members of society, spreading wholesome influence around them in some of the least reputable quarters of our great cities.'—*Aberdeen Journal.*

'The pages are full of pen portraits, which must have been drawn from nature. Mission-work, as presented to us in this little volume, means very much more than a good story. The Christian heart, yearning over the fallen and lost, will find in it much to enjoy and much to learn. We could not conceive of any book more suitable for a prize, or better fitted to place temperance teaching in its proper niche. Among the illustrations are some choice bits of Edinburgh scenery.'—*Band of Hope Review.*

Extra crown 8vo, cloth extra, with Frontispiece by Robert M‘Gregor, R.S.A.,
price 5s.,

St. Veda's ; or, The Pearl of Orr's Haven.   By ANNIE S. SWAN.

'Unquestionably one of the most fascinating that she has yet produced. A delightful picture of life and character. Cannot fail to add another to the many literary laurels Miss Swan has already acquired for herself.'—*Haddington Courier.*

'**One of the most powerful of Annie Swan's works.**'—*Fifeshire Advertiser.*

'The power of the writer is clearly evidenced in the skill with which she composes new situations and new ideas. Undoubtedly, Miss Swan possesses considerable power in creating novel and dramatic situations, and, moreover, in representing them both vividly and powerfully. In all her works she appears to possess a skilful grasp and treatment of her subject, and the diction is remarkable alike for its power and grace. Her knowledge of people and things must be both large and comprehensive. Her sentences read both musically and sympathetically, and they serve to bring before the mind of the reader a living reality of the scenes and events which she attempts to portray.'—*Society Herald.*

'This is one of the most delightful books Annie Swan has produced.'—*East Fife Record.*

'A very well written and altogether charming story.'—*Whitehall Review.*

'Smoothly and naturally told, there is not a dull chapter from beginning to end.'—*Free Press.*

'Miss Swan has been fortunate in finding publishers of such enterprise and taste. The literary matter is well worthy of this beautiful garb, being admirable alike in the tone of its teaching and in the interest of the story which it tells.'—*Kilmarnock Standard.*

'A remarkably clever work. Without any undue straining after effect, the author tells her story in such an enticing and graphic style as never to allow the interest of the reader to flag.'—*Northern Whig.*

'A charming story of Scottish life and character, and of absorbing interest from first to last.'—*Liverpool Post.*

'The authoress will never want readers while she can give them such books as "St. Veda's."'—*Quiz.*

'A story by Annie S. Swan is always welcome. Her tales are all eminently readable ; they have that racy smack of the soil which distinguishes only a few of the best writers.'—*British Weekly.*

'One of the most romantic stories which Miss Swan has written, and we think, too, one of her best. She can always be pathetic, and sometimes strikes a note of great beauty and depth. The old skipper, in particular, is a study of a fine old fisherman that would do credit to any writer, and the two old ladies are nearly as good.'—*Spectator.*

Crown 8vo, cloth extra.   Illustrated.   Price 3s. 6d.,

Doris Cheyne, the Story of a Noble Life. By
Annie S. Swan, Author of ' Aldersyde,' etc.

'The tale is written with this gifted author's now well-known delicacy of characterization and power of pathos.   It has a sound morality lying unobtrusively beneath its interesting scheme of incidents.   It will make Miss Swan more popular among the wide circle of gentle readers to whom her stories have brought pleasure in healthy thoughts and sympathies.'—*Scotsman.*

'This is a pretty and most readable story, the scene of which is laid in the English Lake District.   It is told with the simplicity and clearness which characterize all the works from Miss Swan's pen.   No one can fail to be interested in the heroine, whose character is one of the sweetest and most unselfish ever depicted.'—*Society Herald.*

'When we get a volume of Annie S. Swan's into our hands we know pretty well what to expect.   Facile and graceful narrative, skilfully-drawn characters, and a tale teaching some high moral lesson which holds the reader from beginning to close.'—*Pen and Pencil.*

'A faithful and touching reproduction of human character as most of us have seen it, though the story itself is really thrilling in its details.   Nature and art have combined to produce a work which may well be placed in the hands of any young lady.'—*Oldham Chronicle.*

'Courage, self-denial, devotion are the virtues exhibited and held up for imitation.'—*Footsteps of Truth.*

'Miss Swan amply sustains her reputation in this latest product of her fertile pen.'—*Glasgow Herald.*

'The teacher of one of the largest Bible classes for young women in Glasgow has read more than one of Miss Swan's stories to the members of his class, with excellent results; and Mr. Spurgeon, who looks askance on the common run of novelists, has always a hearty word of commendation to bestow on the stories that proceed from the pen of the authoress of "Aldersyde."   In "Doris Cheyne" she teaches important spiritual and moral lessons in a strain so simple and persuasive, that the book is sure to become a popular favourite.'—*Daily Mail.*

'Quietly but charmingly written.'—*Methodist Times.*

'A story that one glides over with the keenest pleasure, and one's sympathies go with Doris, and the book is laid down with a sigh of regret that such a delightful companion as Doris should only live by the vivid genius of the gifted authoress.   Miss Swan's stories are charming.'—*Reformer.*

'We particularly recommend to young women, as well as to other classes of readers, the delightful story by Annie S. Swan, entitled "Doris Cheyne."'—*Literary World.*

'The most ambitious and the most successful book that Miss Swan has yet written.   Her characters are few in number, but they are all drawn with the utmost care.'—*The Academy.*

'A quiet gentle-flowing narrative of self-reliance and energy in the hour of need; but under its outward calm, there is a striking magnetic influence at work.'—*Educational News.*

'One of the very best books that have come from the pen of Annie S. Swan.'—*Helensburgh Times.*

Crown 8vo, cloth extra, with Illustrations, price 2s. 6d.,

Hazell & Sons, Brewers. By ANNIE S. SWAN.

'"Hazell & Sons" is a tale which we commend to the attention of all who are interested in the temperance movement. It is not a temperance story in the sense in which that term is usually understood, and yet it is calculated to do more good than a dozen of these thoroughgoing teetotal tales which bear on the face of them evidence that they have been, so to speak, written to order.'—*Barnsley Chronicle.*

'Really a capital story, and will keep the reader's interest from cover to cover.'—*Glasgow Herald.*

'The story is full of interest, and will no doubt find a ready sale amongst temperance reformers. Every Sunday School and Band of Hope should have it on its library shelves.'—*Shields Daily Gazette.*

'The book is full of good thoughts, and excellent moral teaching.'—*Dublin Evening Mall.*

'The climax is cleverly worked up, and the plot is developed with such skill as will secure the reader's attention throughout.'—*Somerset County Gazette.*

'Some critics have been bold enough to assert that in her later work she is but repeating herself, and has done nothing to compare with, or worthy the writer of "Aldersyde" or "Carlowrie." With this opinion we have no sympathy. She has contributed a wealth of healthful domestic fiction to current literature, and her writings are just of that character that is required to act against much of what is now put into the hands of general readers—works that may be powerful and striking, but works which altogether fail to rouse into action the best passions of the human breast. —*Huntly Express.*

'It is easy to see that Miss Annie S. Swan's new story, "Hazell & Sons, Brewers," has been written in the interests of temperance. But it is far above the ordinary temperance tale, if only in respect that the work is itself temperate in tone. It is a distinction among stories of the kind to be enjoyable without reference to their special purpose. The distinction can fairly be claimed for this fresh and charming story.'—*Scotsman.*

'Her style is graceful and easy, and there is a natural interest in her books from the opening to the close. The present story of "Hazell & Sons, Brewers," appears to be written for the purpose of enforcing a moral—that of temperance, and in this she succeeds well, for the reader is never conscious that the writer is moralizing, her dialogues and her monologues are so simple, graceful, and natural. The scene of the story is laid in and near Burnley, and although some of the place names are altered somewhat, a little conjecture may be indulged in as to the localities.'—*Barnley Gazette.*

'Messrs. Oliphant's series of 2s. 6d. books have acquired a very rapid and deserved popularity, and the latest of the issue cannot fail to enhance their reputation. The story has a connection with Lancashire which will make it all the more interesting to readers in these parts.'—*Oldham Chronicle.*

'It is one of those books that will be read with enjoyment, whether the reader agrees with the sentiment or not. As in most of the writings of ladies, it appeals more to the feelings than to the reason; at the same time there are no traces of milksoppiness.'—*Australian Trading World.*

'Those who admire pure, natural simplicity in narrative, with dignified and chaste writing, will not be disappointed in the perusal of this story. It is written in the authoress's best vein; and from first to last commands the attention and sympathy of the reader.'—*Leeds Times.*

'A well-written book, interesting and useful.'—*Warrington Guardian.*

'The tale is full of interesting situations, in which the peculiarities and intricacies of the God of Love play a prominent part, while the dangers of a slavish devotion to the God of Bacchus are forcibly shown up.'—*Whitby Times.*

'We should like our readers to take a special note of this work of Miss Swan. It is a temperance story somewhat out of the orthodox line, that will be sure to please the young, and will serve a useful purpose as well.'—*Teacher's Aid.*

'To the thousands of readers who peruse everything from the pen of this gifted authoress, the book will have as warm a welcome as anything that has gone before.'—*Pen and Pencil.*

'A temperance story for a socially higher class of readers than those for whom temperance literature is often prepared; written in the author's clear and attractive style.'—*S. S. Chronicle.*

'A story of real interest, full of quiet power and tenderness.'—*Christian Age.*

'Miss Swan writes earnestly and moderately, and brings her story to a bright conclusion.—*Literary World.*

Extra crown 8vo, cloth extra, with Frontispiece, price 5s.,

Sir John's Ward; or, The Heiress of Gladdiswoode. A Quiet Chronicle of Country Life. By JANE H. JAMIESON, Author of 'The Laird's Secret.'

'Instinct with the fascination of romance. Miss Jamieson has a rippling and attractive style, to which she adds a keen knowledge of homely Scottish life, and a poetic appreciation of the beauties of her native land.'—*Dundee Courier.*

'A wealth of descriptive power that makes up a very pleasant story.'—*Haddington Courier.*

'There are in the book many admirable delineations of types of womanhood, in the conception and treatment of which the author seems particularly to excel.'—*Scottish Leader.*

'A wholesome, breezy book, redolent of country life in the Scotch Lowlands.'—*Liverpool Post.*

'Enriches the great and ever-increasing store of Scottish fiction.'—*N. E. Daily Gazette.*

'Written with a simplicity and pathos altogether delightful, and the reader only regrets it is so short.'—*Liverpool Mercury.*

'Delightful and realistic glimpses of Scottish village life and country society.'—*Liverpool Courier.*

'"Sir John's Ward" introduces us to a number of pleasant people, with whom we soon get upon such good terms that when the final page is turned we part from them with regret.'—*Graphic.*

'Pure as the sparkling rill of water issuing from its rocky bed in the hillside—healthy as the breezes that blow over the mountain ranges of Caledonia—and bracing as the first clear frosts of the coming winter.'—*Leeds Times.*

'Charming pictures both of persons and places, the originals of some of which will not be difficult to recognise.'—*Northern Ensign.*

'One of the healthiest stories it has been our lot to read for many a long day.'—*St. Stephen's Review.*

'The county families, as represented by Sir John Maitland and his wife in Miss Jamieson's charming story, are fast dying out, and it is therefore all the greater luxury to find them reproduced in such a delightful manner.'—*Whitehall Review.*

'A most ably written, attractive story."—*Perthshire Courier.*

'An admirable story, well conceived in plot, and charmingly written.'—*Fife Herald.*

'Most pleasing and attractive story.'—*Northern Whig.*

'All the freshness and graphic power which distinguished the writer's first effort.'—*Academy.*

'Girls will delight in this story.'—*Literary World.*

'The Scotch colouring is charming.'—*British Weekly.*

Crown 8vo, cloth extra.   Illustrated.   Price 2s. 6d.,

In Glenoran.   By M. B. Fife.

'M. B. Fife, if we may venture to infer the writer's sex from certain features of the story, especially the allusions to female attire, is a notable addition to the long list of Scottish lady writers of fiction; and we shall be glad to meet her again.'—*Christian Leader.*

'Wholesome as well as pleasant, and deserves to be successful.'—*Scotsman.*

'A story of a brother's perfidy and eventual punishment, of a father's implacability, and woman's love, told in simple language.   The *locale* of the story is a secluded Scotch village, and many interesting traits of Scottish character are introduced with very good effect.'—*Sheffield Daily Telegraph.*

'The delineations of Highland scenery are particularly good, and a few clever illustrations enhance the picturesque value of the brightly-written and swift-flowing story.'—*Daily Mail.*

'Some of the characters are well drawn, and the illustrations, quaint sketches of rural scenery, deserve favourable notice.'—*Society Herald.*

'A story of promise, and is excellent as the maiden production of a young writer.'—*People's Friend.*

'Pictures the life of a small Scotch village with a skill that brings its outward scenery and its human interests very vividly before the reader.'—*Literary World.*

'This is a delightful story of rural life in a Scottish glen, told with much naturalness of feeling and knowledge of human nature, alike in its weaker and nobler aspects.'—*League Journal.*

'A work of fiction, healthy, natural, and engaging, without the faults of profundity or sensationalism.'—*Kilmarnock Standard.*

'The story is one which will fix itself on the memory, not only on account of its deeply interesting incidents, but because the writer exhibits a fine discrimination of what is best and worst in human nature.   The style is pure, fresh, and easy.'—*Reformer.*

'This is a homely story of the "Annie S. Swan" type, but only, to our minds, very much superior.'—*Fifeshire Journal.*

'A pretty tale of Scottish village life.'—*Athenæum.*

'This is really a most charmingly written story of crofter life in the north of Scotland, and will well repay perusal.'—*Ballymena Observer.*

'This is a capital story, well conceived in plot, and carefully carried out in detail.   The incidents are such as occur in everyday life, and this really forms one of the charms of the volume.   The actors are all well known to us—we have seen them often, and can match each of the *dramatis personæ* as they appear on the scene with people we have met in actual everyday life.'—*Leeds Times.*

'A story full of pathos.   It is an account of the love affairs of a young Scot, and does not seem to pretend to give anything more than a simple and natural description of his and his sweetheart's lives.   The tale is rendered very attractive by its unpretentiousness.'—*Dublin Evening Mail.*

'It is impossible to follow without the keenest interest the wooing of Allan Campbell and Mary Macnab; or to forbear a feeling of pity for the bright-eyed but unfortunate Phemie, who deserved a better fate than that which the author has accorded her.'—*Haddington Courier.*

'Miss Fife has a quick eye for what is essential whenever she attempts to render local colour; and her affection for the place and people whom she describes is unmistakeably of the heart, and not merely of the pen.'—*The Academy.*

Extra crown 8vo, cloth extra, with Six Original Illustrations, 5s.,

Briar and Palm: A Study of Circumstance and Influence. By ANNIE S. SWAN, Author of 'Aldersyde,' 'Carlowrie,' 'Gates of Eden,' etc. etc.

'Is as charming a tale as this talented writer has produced. It paints with quiet force and occasional touches of fine pathos, the career of a young doctor, Denis Holgate, a character in whom the author arouses a deep interest by the skill with which she has traced his growth through work and suffering to gentleness and nobility of nature.'—*Scotsman.*

'Furnishes another proof that the author of "Aldersyde" and "Carlowrie" is as much at home among English folk, both of the Southern Counties and of Lancashire, as she is among the people of Scotland.'—*Liverpool Mercury.*

'Some of the chapters indicate a larger outlook on life, and also a more intense dramatic energy.'—*Daily Mail.*

'We find Miss Swan quite as much at home in the Metropolis, and among the people of the Lancashire seaboard, as in her native Lothians. . . . She has evidently been working hard, and enlarging her knowledge of the treasures of literature, as well as of places and people.'—*Greenock Telegraph.*

'Take it all in all, the authoress shows a wonderful versatility and perfection in the art of telling a story pleasantly and well.'—*Pen and Pencil.*

'A lovely tale, honestly worth its weight in gold.'—*Sheffield Independent.*

'The book is instinct with that fine feeling and tender idealism which gives Miss Swan's work the stamp of uniqueness.'—*Evening News.*

'Miss Swan's versatility is truly wonderful, and in no previous instance has it been more powerfully exhibited than in this highly interesting and dramatic story.'—*Kilmarnock Standard.*

'In "Briar and Palm" Miss Swan is at her best, and the characters are so well drawn that they absolutely stand out from the page like living and breathing realities. Taken as a whole, this is the best effort of the talented authoress.'—*Leeds Times.*

'The whole conception is quite novel, yet vigorously worked out, and with a success that justifies the effort at showing how the influence of genuine Christian love and sympathy can soften and ultimately conquer, in a naturally noble woman, the harsher teachings of poverty.'—*Haddington Courier.*

'Need we say that the tale has a high moral purpose, and that it is told with a charm of style which rivets attention from the first page to the last.'—*Northern Ensign.*

'Another good story from this prolific pen, depicting the life of Denis Holgate, a young doctor. She paints some fine characters in the course of the book, notably little Daisy Frew and her good father the curate of the little sea-village, Crosshaven.'—*British Weekly.*

'A story that only Miss Swan could write, and it will be read with deep interest and sincere pleasure by her wide circle of admirers.'—*Dundee Advertiser.*

'A new departure for one who has won her laurels in depicting Scottish rural life. The work will in no way detract from the splendid reputation the author has won.'—*Helensburgh Times.*

'A powerful and well-written story, engaging the attention from its opening sentence till its close.'—*Dumfries Courier.*

'Told with all Miss Swan's dramatic and descriptive power, full of good thoughts and healthful suggestions.'—*Arbroath Herald.*

'The work gives manifest token of the growth of the young authoress alike in its analysis of character, dramatic energy, and deftness of literary touch.'—*Christian Leader.*

'This is one of the brightest and most interesting stories that we have come across for a considerable time.'—*Society Journal.*

REAL DETECTIVE STORIES.

New Edition, crown 8vo, paper boards, 2s.; cloth, 2s. 6d.,

CLUES: Leaves from a Chief Constable's Note-Book. By WILLIAM HENDERSON, Chief Constable of Edinburgh, and formerly of Leeds, Manchester, and Glasgow.

'No book sells better than the volume of short stories, or the collection of essays and descriptive papers, and yet for years past publishers have refused to let us have them, and have dosed us with three volumes of twaddle or unreadable polemical novels. It is a satisfaction to find the providers of literary food are beginning to see the error of their ways, and to be convinced that the British public must, before anything else, be amused. They will get plenty of amusement out of Mr. William Henderson's "Clues," which consists of nine stories derived from a Chief Constable's note-book. The author ought to know something of his subject, seeing he is now Chief Constable of Edinburgh, that he occupied a similar post at Leeds, and was formerly Chief Inspector of the Detective Department at Manchester and Glasgow. Each story is, in the main, a reproduction of facts, and they have that reality and interest which facts alone can give. The Chief Constable of Edinburgh has arrested our attention; we are unable to move on, for we have found listening to his entertaining recitals anything but hard labour.'—*Punch.*

'The straightforward simplicity of his narratives is no less attractive than their subject-matter.'—*Academy.*

'Mr. Henderson has a graphic skill in description, and an artistic faculty for leading up to the *dénouement* which renders his record of diamond-cut-diamond dealings with light-fingered gentry irresistibly fetching.'—*Whitehall Review.*

'Each story is related in a simple, straightforward fashion that makes it much more impressive than the most ingenious fabrication of the fictionist.'—*Christian Leader.*

'In his clever management of many famous cases, Captain Henderson won a reputation as a detective which secured him rapid promotion, and at the same time furnished the remarkable experiences now effectively related for the entertainment of the public.'—*Nottingham Express.*

'All the stories are so attractive in their style, which is eminently free from exaggeration or egotism, and so full of interest, not only of an exciting kind, but as regards the motives and modes of operation of the criminal classes, that not one of the stories will be left unread.'—*Liverpool Post.*

'Mr. Henderson was formerly Chief Inspector of the Detective Department in Manchester, and his book is certain to receive a warm welcome from old friends in this city and neighbourhood.'—*Manchester Examiner.*

'The inherent interest of the subjects and the freshness of the style will doubtless recommend the work to a large circle of readers.'—*Scotsman.*

'These episodes from Captain Henderson's note-book will be read with unflagging interest.'—*Glasgow Herald.*

'The groundwork of the exciting volume is, in fact, all true, and if, as is unquestionably the case, the chapters are exciting reading, they are also wholesome, for they go to show at a period of distrust how patiently and cleverly the detective work of our great cities is carried on. . . . He has tracked silk-stealers, lain for hours at a time amongst cellar cobwebs for the confusion of "wine samplers," and caught red-handed a wonderfully miscellaneous assortment of clever and unscrupulous scoundrels whose misdeeds and tricks he here lays bare.'—*Daily Telegraph.*

'I think the stories are excellent.'—HENRY IRVING.

'The stories are most interesting, and have given me much pleasure; they are very suitable to me, having played "The Artful Dodger" so often.'—J. L. TOOLE.

'A most interesting book. Your facts are as engrossing as many of the fictions of detective life.'—WILSON BARRETT.

BY ANNIE S. SWAN.

In extra crown 8vo, cloth, price 5s.,

The Gates of Eden: A Story of Endeavour.
New Edition. With Portrait of the Author by FAED.

'The subject of Miss Swan's "Gates of Eden" is one which demands, and receives from her hand, a skilful treatment. John Bethune rears his motherless boys in accordance with a preconceived plan. The elder is to be a minister, the younger is to follow the plough. Circumstances seem to favour his scheme; for the future minister has, it appears, the advantage in appearance, in manners, and in ability. But the real truth is different. The depth of character and the best mental gifts really belong to the latter. How the young man, conscious of his power, yet stedfastly walks along the appointed path till he is free to choose, and how, once free, he enters on his own way and overcomes all its difficulties, is very well told in these pages. We have not often seen a better portraiture than is that of the two brothers. Miss Swan is too skilful to make the weaker of the two a mere foil to the stronger. He, too, with all his faults, has virtues of his own, and the reader is glad to see them reaching their true development before the story is finished. The episode of the recovery of Willie Lorraine, a repentant prodigal, is full of pathos; as is also the love-story of Mary Campbell. The "Gates of Eden" is a worthy successor to the author's "Aldersyde."'—*Spectator.*

'A distinct success. . . . We follow the career of twin brothers through the book—Sandy and Jamie Bethune. Sandy, apparently getting all the brains, is sent to St. Andrews to study, and his conceits and fine talk on his visits home are humorously described. Then we see him transformed into the Rev. Alexander Bethune of Lochbroom. Jamie seems fit only for the harrows and the loom at first, but Aunt Susan always sees deeper than this, and we read with interest the story of his endeavour to rise to higher things. His character is well drawn, the earnest, noble soul following God's leading.'—*British Weekly.*

'The "Gates of Eden" is, like most of its predecessors, a homely tale of Scottish life and manners. The homely dialect is given with admirable fidelity, and there is much truthful delineation of character.'—*Scotsman.*

'The underlying conception—that of a contrast between two brothers, the one brilliant, clever, and superficial, but needing stern discipline before the real strength of his nature can be evoked; the other modest, unselfish, but earnest and indomitable—is strongly grasped from the first, and is wrought out with such power and consistency as to hold the reader's attention by a kind of spell. The book is one which everybody can read with pleasure, and from which many will profit.'—*Scottish Leader.*

'One of the most dramatically rendered scenes of the book is that in which the death of old Peter Bethune is described. If the author had never written anything else, this part of the story would justify her claim to the place in the front rank of our most gifted literary artists.'—*Northern Ensign*

'A happy note is struck at the very outset of the "Gates of Eden," and the quality of the good beginning is maintained throughout. . . . The best of all the stories that we have yet received from the pen of its accomplished authoress.'—*Kilmarnock Standard.*

'Remarkably beautiful, noble in spirit, rich in pathos, strong in the triumph of an earnest purposeful life.'—*Daily Mail.*

Now ready, crown 8vo, New Edition, price 3s. 6d.; or in plainer binding, without Illustrations, cloth, 2s. 6d.; paper boards, 2s.,

Bits from Blinkbonny; or, Bell o' the Manse. A Tale of Scottish Village Life between 1841 and 1851. By JOHN STRATHESK. With Six Original Illustrations.

'The daily life in a thoroughly Scotch rural village is described in the most lifelike manner, and one feels a personal certainty of being able to recognise any of the people described if one met them. The homely but pretty illustrations place the country scenery before our actual vision.'—*Athenæum.*

'Altogether, "Bell" is an exquisitely careful and finished study. The book abounds in quaint touches of Scottish humour, delightful specimens of our vernacular language, incidents and anecdotes grave and gay.'—*Scotsman.*

'The effect is really delightful, and the blending of quiet humour and natural pathos in the volume makes it a positive refreshment to the spirit. . . . The account of Bell's courtship with the shamefaced bachelor, David Tait of Blackbrae, is delicious.'—*Glasgow Daily Mail.*

'If there are not so many characters introduced as in some of Sir Walter Scott's works, the characters have an individuality as pronounced as any of his, and the lights and shades of character are finished off with an equal degree of care and truthfulness.'—*Huntly Express.*

'Bell is the heroine of the book, and a well-drawn character she is, with her quaint ways, her happy expedients, her clever but never shrewish tongue, her simple yet strong fidelity to the family she served, and her wise, droll, and pithy sayings. Dan Corbett, the one-eyed smuggler, poacher, molecatcher, and a dozen other things, ranks next to Bell as a finished portraiture.'—*Chambers's Journal.*

'Piquant and charming in its very simplicity. Enlivened in almost every page by bits of genuine Scottish humour.'—*Ayr Advertiser.*

'The chapter treating of "Wee Nellie" comes closer home in its power of stirring the heart than anything we have seen since the appearance of Dr. John Brown's "Rab and his Friends." The illustrations are true works of art.'—*Brechin Advertiser.*

'A story of homely Scotch life, pleasant and amusing. The dialect is well managed and faithful without being overdone.'—*The Graphic.*

'Scattered throughout the volume are several graphic sketches of village characters, including Gavin Sinclair, the beadle and gravedigger, an old worthy descended from John Brown of Priesthill, the covenanting martyr, Dan Corbett, the village poacher, etc.'—*Edinburgh Courant.*

'Pictures penned. . . . "Bell" is simply delightful. We defy any one to read it without a sense of real enjoyment.'—*The Literary World.*

'We have never seen Scottish village life better described.'—*Montrose Review.*

'A finely told story, which, for interest, excels not a few of our novels. A splendid study.'—*Hawick Advertiser.*

'The author describes the village life of Scotland with the fidelity and grace of Wilkie. We should have enjoyed hearing Burns read them to Tam o' Shanter over the last gill.'—*Sheffield Independent.*

New and Revised Edition, crown 8vo, cloth extra, gilt edges, price 3s. 6d. ;
or in plainer binding, 2s. 6d.,

Gertrude Ellerslie: A Story of Two Years.

By Mrs. MELDRUM.

' Will be read with keen pleasure on account of its being so true to life.'—
Christian Union.

' A well-sustained story, abounding in varied interest, and full of clear
character sketching; . . . fascinating book.'—*Christian Leader.*

' The book is one of unflagging interest, variety of scene, and numerous
characters.'—*Christian World.*

' A handsome volume externally, and within most gracious. So long as
we must have fiction, we hope women like Mrs. Meldrum will employ their
pure hands and loving hearts therein. Personal interest is here illustrated
by a charming story.'—*Sword and Trowel.*

' The story is simple, natural, realistic. The tone is thoroughly healthy,
and shuns all that is maudlin or silly. The lessons taught are unexception-
able, and those who relish a good story well told, would be delighted with
the book.'—*Canada Presbyterian.*

' There are persons who, in their superior kind of way, dismiss a novel as
intolerable which breathes a religious spirit, and pointedly inculcates the
lessons of evangelical faith and life. It is probably useless to restate the
arguments by which a defence may be sustained of such works of fiction, but
we would ask those who hold the unfriendly attitude we have indicated, to
read with impartial mind the story before us. We shall be greatly surprised
if the generous impulses and the high-toned spirit of the tale do not impress
its readers, who cannot, at all events, fail to be profoundly interested and
stirred by its pictures of varied life. The family portraiture of the various
groups is vivid and striking. . . . The character of Gertrude is very powerfully drawn. . . . The grouping is very artistic, and the details disclose an
amount of careful observation and discriminating judgment which find
expression at once simple and forcible in this most attractive story.'—*Daily
Review.*

' Ought to find favour with a large circle of readers. It introduces us to a
very large circle of characters, some of which are sketched with remarkable
vividness. The tale, as such, is extremely entertaining, so that the interest
never flags.'—*Christian Monthly.*

' The story has strong merits. The authoress is a woman of cultivated
intellect, and endowed with strong sympathies for the poor. The plot of the
novel is not a very intricate one, it possesses, however, a healthy tone. Some
of the characters are exceedingly well drawn.'—*Richmond and Ripon
Chronicle.*

' This is a story which will be welcomed by many, though it is written
chiefly for thoughtful girls. The characters are drawn from the homes of
our own day. We have met them, known them, and lived among them; but
they are on this account none the less interesting—perhaps we like them the
better that the scenes through which they move are familiar, and the life
they live so like our own. The book, like all Mrs. Meldrum's books, has
been written with an aim kept steadily in view—that of showing that one
may possess all the world can give, but only divine love and fulness can
satisfy a human heart. . . . The book will help and cheer weary folk; it will
guide seeking ones, and counsel those who fear to ask for advice. And yet
there is nothing dull, nothing wearisome in it. The motive and execution
are both admirable.'—*The Outlook.*

Crown 8vo, Illustrated, price 3s. 6d.; plainer binding, 2s. 6d.; paper boards, 2s.,

At Any Cost. By Edward Garrett.

'There is a peculiar originality and force in everything that proceeds from the pen of this gifted writer; but in the present work she reaches an unusually high standard of excellence. . . . Edward Garrett is a great preacher, with more sound doctrine in her novelettes than is to be found in a good many sermons of the regulation pattern.'—*Greenock Telegraph.*

'The book contains a sketch of the career of two young lads from Shetland, who are both launched on the world of London to make their way as best they can. The one sets out with the fixed determination of "getting on," and lets no scruples of conscience or family affection stand in the way of this determination. The other, while also bent on succeeding in life, never loses sight of the obligations he owes to others, and keeps his heart pure, and his hands clean amid the manifold temptations of London life. . . . The whole book is one we would like to see in the hands of every boy and girl setting out in life, for there is much useful advice pleasantly and plainly given, and the lesson of the book is so plainly brought out that he who runs may read.' —*Aberdeen Journal.*

'Mr. Garrett is known as a writer with a good moral purpose in anything he undertakes, and the lesson inculcated in "At Any Cost" is a very necessary one in this age, when men are hasting to be rich by means not altogether scrupulous. The author traces the career of two youths who come from the far north to push their fortunes in London, and without bringing all kinds of misfortunes upon the head of the selfish one, he leaves his reader in no doubt as to which is the nobler life—that which places honour first, or that which worships wealth. The story is calculated to do good to the youth of both sexes.'—*Academy.*

'The tale is well told—the pathetic scenes being particularly well described—and cannot fail to exercise an ennobling influence on the mind.'—*Perthshire Constitutional.*

'From first to last the story is one of unusual interest, while its morally bracing tone is everything we could desire.'—*Liverpool Mercury.*

'Well written and extremely interesting, and is, in fact, a good illustration of the text, "Ye cannot serve God and mammon."'—*Nonconformist.*

'The story is altogether a very satisfactory one, and the characters are well drawn. The sincere religious tone which pervades it is of the sensible and practical sort, which does not degenerate into mere sentimentalism. The book belongs to a healthy class of fiction.'—*Scotsman.*

'Its literary merits are decidedly above the average, the characters being vividly defined and brightly portrayed. Nor is it without a welcome vein of sharp and humorous satire.'—*Graphic.*

'Shetland and London! very different places, and considerably far apart; but of course there are many Shetlanders in the great city, whether or not there be any Londoners in our Ultima Thule. These are the poles that are brought together in this attractive book. . . . The whole story is well worth reading, as it is written not only persuasively, so as to draw the ingenuous reader on and on, but also powerfully.'—*S. S. S. Teacher.*

'The treatment of the old bookseller, with his scepticism and pessimism, born of disappointment and the ill-doing of others, is excellent. "At Any Cost" is a good story in more ways than one.'—*Spectator.*

'A story of undoubted power, and fitted to give the young reader a true impulse toward a pure and noble life.'—*British Messenger.*

'This handsomely bound and beautifully illustrated volume will add to Mr. Garrett's already high reputation as a writer of fiction, which many will consider sufficient commendation of a first-rate story.'—*Brechin Advertiser.*

Crown 8vo, 2s. 6d., Illustrated; cheap edition, paper covers, 1s.;
cloth, 1s. 6d.,

By Still Waters: A Story for Quiet Hours. New and Cheaper Edition. By EDWARD GARRETT.

' We like this "Story for Quiet Hours" very much better than we have liked any of Mr. Garrett's recent tales; he has shaken himself free from the leaven of Puritanism, and is at his best—always pleasant and readable, sometimes giving utterance to a really fine and graceful thought, and showing plenty of dry humour.'—*The Graphic.*

' We have read many books by Edward Garrett, but none that has pleased us so well as this. It has more than pleased, it has charmed us. All through it runs a golden thread of spiritual wisdom that makes you linger as you read. The best character, drawn with great care, is Sarah Russell. We have all of us, we hope, met such good, kind, wise women, who seem to be sent into the world to put things straight and lift everybody to a higher plane of existence.'—*The Nonconformist.*

' It possesses merits of a very sterling order. The book is a good one in every sense of the word. The author sets a high aim before him, and he achieves it. In Tibbie there is a grim humour closely allied to pathos underlying her queer epigrammatic sayings.'—*Morning Post.*

' The beauty of the language and the profusion of fine thoughts scattered throughout, constitute its chief charm.'—*Dundee Advertiser.*

'The volume is interspersed with some shrewd sayings.'—*Daily News.*

' Mr. Garrett is a novelist whose books it is always a pleasure to meet. His stories are full of quiet, penetrating observation. Few novelists photograph characters so beautiful and subtle as Sarah Russell's and Tibbie's, or envelope their tale in a like bower of tender, thoughtful love.'—*Echo.*

' Is full of good sense.'—*Westminster Review.*

' A natural, well-written, and deeply interesting story.' — *Primitive Methodist World.*

'The story is well and racily told; it is lit up with occasional gleams of humour, and, withal, with a better light still. It is a wholesome and a helpful book.'—*Leeds Mercury.*

' A fine combination of masculine vigour, spiritual insight, and racy humour. . . . To quite an extraordinary extent the volume abounds in sayings that are notable, both for the striking originality of their substance and their pointed style of expression.'—*Christian Leader.*

' We have received nothing of late better entitled to attention. . . . It is the fruit of robust, fearless thinking, and is brimful of quaint humour.'—*Greenock Telegraph.*

' Very well told, with much power of thought and breadth of sympathy, which is very pleasing to meet.'—*Spectator.*

' The characters are finely drawn. . . . Worth a legion of its contemporaries.'—*Brechin Advertiser.*

' A book to be read slowly and read again.'—*British Messenger.*

'A religious book in a good sense, and by no means bad reading from a literary point of view.'—*Athenæum.*

'Perfection of literary form, and vigour of thought. . . . The exposure of smug Pharisaism is executed with trenchant force. Let us hope the book will have the effect of lessening the number of the Pharisees. We expect it will make some of them very angry.'—*Kilmarnock Standard.*

Now ready, uniform with ' BITS FROM BLINKBONNY.'

New Edition, in One Volume, cloth extra, with Six Original Illustrations,
price 3s. 6d.; or in plainer binding, without Illustrations, price 2s. 6d ;
paper boards, 2s.,

Aldersyde: A Border Story of Seventy Years
Ago. By ANNIE S. SWAN.

The Authoress has received the following Autograph Letter from Mr.
Gladstone:—

> '10 DOWNING STREET,
> WHITEHALL, *April* 16, 1883.

'DEAR MADAM,—I have now read the work which you did me the honour
to present to me with a very kind inscription, and I feel obliged to add a line
to my formal acknowledgment already sent. I think it beautiful as a work of
art, and it must be the fault of a reader if he does not profit by the perusal.
Miss Nesbit and Marget will, I hope, long hold their places among the truly
living sketches of Scottish character.—I remain, your very faithful and
obedient,   W. E. GLADSTONE.'

'Sir Walter Scott himself never delineated a character more true to life
than Janet Nesbit.'—*Stirling Observer.*

'Readers who can follow Scotch idioms easily will be moved by the narrative of Janet Nesbit's life. . . . Incidents common enough, but eloquent of
character and well told.'—*Athenæum.*

'Full of quiet power and pathos.'—*Academy.*

'She has brought us into the presence of a pure and noble nature, and has
reminded us that a life of sorrow and disappointments has its deep compensa-
tions, and its glorious meaning.'—*Literary World.*

'If there is anything more noteworthy than another in this cleverly constructed story, it is the vigorous raciness with which the vernacular is
employed.'—*Haddington Courier.*

'A tale of deep interest; it is a work of true genius.'—*United Presbyterian
Magazine.*

'Hurrah! our good Scotch stories, with their dear rough old vernacular,
are not going to die out just yet, or, if at all, they are going to die hard.'—*S.S.
Teachers' Magazine.*

'Beautifully conceived and exquisitely written.'—*Airdrie Advertiser.*

'One of the best Scotch tales that has appeared for many years. . . . A
wealth of local colouring and fineness of touch rarely to be met in these days
of painfully analytic writing.'—*Kilmarnock Herald.*

'A book we must read through at a sitting. It lays hold of our interest in
the first page, and sustains it to the end.'—*Daily Review.*

'Deserves to occupy a prominent and permanent place among Scottish works
of imagination. . . . Not a dull page in the book ; while not a paragraph will
be skipped lest some of the finer touches should be missed.'—*Kelso Chronicle.*

'We have not read a fresher, livelier, or more wholesomely stimulating story
for many a day.'—*Kilmarnock Standard.*

'As a type of the sound-hearted, high-spirited Scottish gentlewoman, who
can sustain her dignity on a poor pittance, and who is tender and true without
any pretence of high sentiment, Janet Nesbit is a fine portrait of a noble
woman.'—*N. B. Daily Mail.*

'The central figure in the narrative is Miss Janet Nesbit, of Aldersyde,
a young gentlewoman who is early called to a life of self-sacrifice. This she
humbly accepts, working out the problem with so much sincerity and faith-
fulness that the grey morning is followed by a bright day.'—*Christian Leader.*

Crown 4to, cloth extra, with 150 Illustrations, price 10s. 6d.,

Edinburgh, Past and Present.   By J. B. Gillies.

With Notes of the County, Historical, Descriptive, and Scientific. By Rev. JAMES S. MILL, FLORA MASSON, and Dr. GEIKIE.

'"Edinburgh, Past and Present," by J. B. Gillies, is a handsome book— a sweet, dainty, and most pleasure-giving memorial of Edinburgh. The letterpress is first-rate. Mr. Gillies is a skilled writer, and he knows Edinburgh History. In this volume, in a style at once simple and graphic, he links the past with the present; and without any parade of antiquarian lore, he tells all, or nearly all, that is worth repeating regarding the public and domestic history of the capital and its famous buildings and institutions.'— *The Daily Review.*

'Mr. J. B. Gillies, if we mistake not, is a writer who already has attained a large share of popularity by his descriptions of storied scenes in the Modern Athens. Under this impression we may, perhaps, congratulate the "Benjie" of old upon the handsome appearance of "Edinburgh, Past and Present." Throughout the two hundred and sixty pages will be found a large number of illustrations, very beautifully executed, and adding no inconsiderable interest to the spirited text.'—*The Publishers' Circular.*

'The book cannot be too highly praised.'—*The Inverness Courier.*

'Readable from end to end, and in many places extremely amusing.'— *St. James's Gazette.*

'The illustrations of the book are gems of the art. No pains have been spared to make the book complete. It is finely and spiritedly written; it is eloquently embellished. Every American visitor of "Old Edinboro" will surely want this charming work.'—*Round Lake Journal, U.S.A.*

'A better man than Mr. Gillies, the author of the letterpress, no one could desire as a guide through Old Edinburgh, for no man knows it better. Readers of the famous "Edinburgh Supplement" of the "Graphic" must know his handiwork. The illustrations are the very things one would wish for in such a book.'—*Aberdeen Journal.*

'This is a spendidly got up book, both internally and externally. Author and publishers, artist and engraver, printers and binder, have all combined to make the work worthy of the subject.'—*Kelso Mail.*

'The vignette illustrations interspersed among the letterpress are charming. As a drawing-room book it is highly attractive.'—*Spectator.*

'Everything in and about the Old Town of Edinburgh is interesting, and that interest is very much enhanced in the present work by the numerous and well-executed woodcuts which adorn its pages. The author has earned the thanks of his contemporaries by the able manner in which he has woven into his work the most salient points of Edinburgh history. Its style and typography are of that high order which we might expect from a firm of publishers of such repute.'—*Western Antiquary.*

'This is an elegantly got up and altogether very interesting volume; and numerous as are the books about Old and New Edinburgh, there is nothing in existence so well adapted to the requirements of the general reader. Mr. Gillies' coadjutors, who have supplied the Historical, Descriptive, and Scientific notes, have done their parts exceedingly well.'—*Aberdeen Free Press.*

'One of those books which should be popular among the crowds who annually flock to the Scottish metropolis. . . . A book which can be taken up at any time, and will seldom be laid down without having given the reader some pleasure and profit. What publishers could do to make the work attractive and successful has been done.'—*Glasgow Herald.*

New Edition, crown 8vo, price 3s. 6d.; or in plainer binding,
without Illustrations, 2s. 6d.; paper boards, 2s.,

Glenairlie; or, The Last of the Græmes. By
ROBINA F. HARDY, author of 'Jock Halliday,' etc. With Six
Original Illustrations by TOM SCOTT.

'The tale is one of life and character in a Highland glen; it has a rather
complicated but well-managed plot, contains some shrewd and effective
studies of different types of Scottish character, and is imbued with an
emphatic but truthful local colour. Written with considerable narrative
and descriptive power, and having an enjoyable flavour of humour, with
here and there a touch of real pathos, the book is a wholesome and readable
story.'—*Scotsman.*

'Brightly written, and does not flag. The author is well up in the
Scotch dialect, and gives some good portraits of Scotch character, which
tends mainly to crossgrainedness and perversity.'—*Literary World.*

'Done in Miss Hardy's happiest, freshest, and quaintest style, is a scene in
the Highland parish kirk of Glenairlie, on the harvest thanksgiving Sabbath.
Everything in this sketch is brought out with the hand of an artist,—old Dr.
Cargill, and his sermon on Ruth; the creaking pulpit stair, and the pagoda-
like sounding board, with a gilt pine-apple on the top; and the square family
pews, adorned with green baize and brass nails; and the old crones in front of
the pulpit in rusty black, and Bibles wrapped in clean white handkerchiefs, with
sprigs of thyme or southernwood; and "Betty" coming in late and bustling, and
provoking an angry scowl from the laird for letting the folding-leaf of the seat
fall with a crash; and the close of the service, when there was a stir in the
elders' pew, and each seized his wooden implement for the "lifting of the
offering." The whole is admirable.'—*Perthshire Constitutional.*

'Rich racy Scotch humour.'—*Presbyterian.*

'A book which contains such characters as Miss Leslie, Betty, and the
impracticable "oldest inhabitant"—a *persona muta* only—can need no recommendation.'—*Academy.*

'The story is full of dramatic interest. Its principal events are grouped
with all the power which the gifted authoress can command. There is a
fascination in the detail, and a richness in the language, savoured with not
a few natural pictures of Scottish life and character, which compel the
reader to peruse it page by page to the end.'—*Kilmarnock Herald.*

'There is a fine Scottish flavour in the book; and it is made more attractive
by a set of original etchings, which help the reader to realize more vividly
the scenes depicted with so much graphic power by the story-teller.'—
Christian Leader.

'The plot is an admirable conception, and the incident is powerfully presented, while the tone of the story is healthy, as the writing is vigorous.'—
Daily Review.

'Shows keen insight into the motives and humours of ordinary human
nature, distinct literary power to sketch those motives, and the true novelist's
tact, that can draw into a complete and beautiful whole the severed and
tangled skeins of character and purpose. It is the story of homely life in a
remote parish of Scotland.'—*Fifeshire Journal.*

'The incidents are woven into the literary web with consummate skill.'—
Border Advertiser.

'The sketches of character are exceedingly good, and there is a flavour of
quiet humour which is thoroughly enjoyable.'—*Glasgow Herald.*

'Martha and her faithful maid are very truthfully drawn.'—*Athenæum.*

www.ingramcontent.com/pod-product-compliance
Lightning Source LLC
Chambersburg PA
CBHW021548110726
47902CB00004B/1070